DATE DUE

FE 2 4 '97			
MR 1 3 97			
RENEW			
JY 7 '9			
JE 7 06			
JUL 0 2007			

DEMCO 38-296

WHEN I WAS

WHITE

By

J & J Foote

56 PALMS PUBLISHING COMPANY
PALM SPRINGS, CALIFORNIA 92263-031

WHEN I WAS WHITE. Copyright © 1989 by Jim E. and Johnnie M. Foote. Published by 56 Palms Publishing Company, P.O. Box 31, Palm Springs, California 92263-031.

INDIVIDUAL ORDERS

BookMasters, Inc.
638 Jefferson Street, P.O. Box 159
Ashland, Ohio 44805
1-800-247-6553
1-419-281-1802

BUSINESS ORDERS (Bookstores, Libraries, etc.)

56 Palms Publishing Company
P.O. Box 31
Palm Springs, CA 92263
1-619-321-0083

Book cover and book design by J&J Foote

First printing, 1991

Printed in the USA

ISBN 0-9628752-0-1

This book is dedicated to our children. Without their loyalty, decency, and support, we would not have gained the knowledge, experience and liberty to accomplish this task.

It is also dedicated to our family, friends, and to all women and men of the world who have struggled to survive both physically and emotionally against the traditional constraints and restraints within their culture.

PART I

MILWAUKEE

- *1* -

Breaking Water

At the age of fifteen, Lilly Pearl stood with Bea watching Joe and Joe Junior as they toiled in the heat of Milwaukee's sun. Bea was filled with anxiety. And Lilly Pearl was filled with new life--her unborn child.

Cool, damp clots of black dirt rolled rapidly down on their sneakers as Joe and Joe Junior dug deeper, trying to avoid severing the long, securely embedded roots of the sprawling lilac bush. The bush grew beside a shaky, rust-peeled cyclone fence in the far right corner of old man Jacobson's back yard.

3

"You want me to dig some, Joe?" Bea asked.

"No, woman! You just stay outta my way. I ain't never seen a woman yet could dig up nothin deeper than a tulip. Plus, I must'a taken leave of my senses to let you talk me into diggin up this damn tree. There's no end to these motherfuckin roots. I'll bet they grows right down to hell. I'll bet a week's pay Ol Satan's down there holdin em."

"That's not no tree, Joe. That's a lilac bush," Lilly Pearl informed him.

"What the hell difference do it make if it be a tree or a bush? That mean devil down yonder ain't lettin go nohow. I reckon I'm gonna have to chop these long ones off so we don't dig ourself right into hell."

"But Joe," Bea pleaded, "you know it ain't never gonna grow right if you cut them main roots. You said so yo self."

"Whatever I said, I take it all back, cause I'm tired of diggin to free some roots that ain't got no end. I ain't goin to hell today. That's where the end of these roots is."

"But Joe, I want it to grow right. I mean, I want it to live and bloom like it suppose to." Bea looked at the lilac bush sympathetically as Joe yanked sinfully at it. He seemed to be violating those nurturing roots that held desperately to some unseen rail within the unplumbed depths of the earth.

Lilly Pearl's eyes grew large as she held her full, round stomach. "Ooooweeee, Joe! Them roots sound funny when you be breakin em like you doin. They sound like they's cryin."

"It ain't gonna grow right," Bea said.

Apparently the twittering, bat-like sounds of the

breaking roots echoed images of a dead lilac bush next spring. Bea looked extremely sad, for she loved plants. She had spent many hours during the early evenings and on weekends looking for the ideal shrub to plant beneath the large, unadorned window of her living room.

"Joe, maybe we should'a bought a plant instead of diggin one up. Cause when yall git it dug up, it's got to be set out right away. That means some more diggin when we git home."

"I ain't settin this damn thing out this evenin. It's got to wait til tomorra. I'm tired. Plus, I ain't no motherfuckin bulldozer. You don't see no big ol blade growin outta my ass for gougin holes in the ground. Shit, I'm a man, and a man gits tired, specially when he's workin like a damn machine."

"Joe, you shouldn curse like that in front of Lilly Pearl an Junior. You know he picks up all yo bad habits. He's mannish enough as it is. And old man Jackbson's gonna hear you, too."

"To hell with that old bastard. He only gave you this old tree cause he wanted it outta his yard. He already done admitted it ain't bloomin pretty like it used to. So, he suckered you into takin it. Now, I'm the mule that's gotta dig it up and drag it outta here. If it was worth anything, he'd want some money for it. You know how them tight-assed Jews is."

"What's a Jew?" Lilly Pearl asked.

"Well, Mr. Stubblefield, tell Pearl what a Jew is," Bea said, teasingly. She and Lilly Pearl looked at Joe and waited for his answer. Joe Junior leaned on his shovel and waited too.

Perspiration seemed to run down Joe's face more rapidly. "Well, uh. You see. Uh, uh, a Jew is one of them whites who wears them little black round caps, bout the size of a flapjack. You see, they's too cheap to buy a whole hat. They's real tight bout money. You think Uncle Elton's tight. Well, a Jew man would make Uncle Elton look like Santa Claws at Christmas time. You see? That's why they calls em tight-assed Jews. Any man too tight to buy a whole hat is worse than Uncle Elton."

Lilly Pearl's face turned red with anger. "Don't be talkin bout my papa, Joe Stubblefield! You didn think he was tight when he paid yall's bus fare up here. I know you was in trouble when yall left Pearl City. Papa lent you money to git away from the law an ol man Pickins."

"We don't talk about that, Pearl," Bea said in a whisper. "That's somethin we don't never mention."

"Sorry, Bea. But Joe ought'n talk about my papa. He took papa's money and ain't never offered to give it back."

"I ain't took yo papa's money. He lent it to me, and I plans on givin it all back someday."

"Well, Mr. Stubblefield, Senior," Bea said. "You don't look like no Jew to me, but yo behind was too tight for you to buy me a nice evergreen to put in the yard. That's why you's diggin now cause you got a whole lotta Jew in you. Ain't you?"

"Hell! I tole you I ain't buyin nothin to put in old Grinker's yard. I ain't buyin nothin to fix up no yard that ain't ours. Grinker don't care bout nothin but the rent."

"But, Joe, you know how much I like a nice yard with flowers, pretty green grass and little trees."

"You ain't in Pearl City no mo, woman. I done told

you, this ain't no place to grow flowers and stuff like that. It's too cold up here for growin pretty things. You plant flowers, and as soon as they git to growin good, it gits cold an kills em. Milwaukee ain't like down home. Ain't nothin up here like down home, not a damn thing."

"I reckon it ain't, Joe, but that don't mean I shouldn try to make that ugly, bald-headed ol yard look better. I can't stand bein round things that don't grow."

Joe was quiet for a moment. "I guess it won't hurt nothin if you wanna waste yo time tryin to make flowers grow in soil that ain't fit for nothin but corn. You just can't face the fact that you ain't home no more."

Joe Junior looked up into his father's teeth-clenched face. "Daddy, is we ever going back home?"

"What you mean, back home, boy?"

"Is we going back down South to live with Big Mama and Papa?"

"You's already home, boy. This here is yo home-- Milwaukee. You don't know nothin bout down South. You was too young to remember."

"Yes I do, Daddy! I remember Big Mama an Papa, Uncle Elton an Ain't Neallie, Satie Mae an Antredious. And I remember. . . ."

"Well, sir! I reckon you do remember more'n I'm givin you credit for, Junior. You got a good mind for recollectin. You got a lotta yo ol daddy in ya, boy. Yep! You's my boy all right--don't never forget nothin. That's important."

Bea felt the warmth of Joe's fatherly pride. Then fear underlined her thoughts as she wondered just how much her son did remember about the South and the mystery that had surrounded their northward departure. She casually smashed a long, fat earthworm under the heel of her shoe. "Junior, you recall the night we left Pearl City?"

"Yep!"

Lilly Pearl snatched Joe Junior's cap off his head and held it out of his reach. "Boy, you don't have no brains in that water-head. You can't remember nothin past this mornin. You just tryin to fool somebody, tryin to make us think you so smart. Yo daddy's always braggin bout your brains. Ain't no brains in that fat head."

"You shut up, ol yellow Pearl! Gimme my cap!"

Bea slapped her son sharply across his mouth. "I done tole you bout callin Pearl yellow. She can't help what color she is. Tell Pearl you's sorry."

"Well, she is yellow, Momma." Joe Junior was at the point of tears.

"Tell her you's sorry, boy." Joe spoke in an authoritarian manner.

"You see, Joe? That's why you ought'a watch what you be sayin round this boy. Kids ain't nothin but ears and mouth."

Joe Junior's voice was low and insincere. "I'm sorry, ol ugly Pearl." Then he turned to his mother. "Momma, I do too, remember bout us comin up here. Papa made us lay down in his ol truck, and he covered us over with lots of stuff!"

"Not so loud, honey. We don't want Mr. Jacobson to hear," Bea whispered. She had hoped the last four years would have erased the unpleasant details of that night from their son's memory.

Joe stopped tugging at the lilac bush and spoke in a

frightened tone. "You ever tell anybody else what you just said, Junior?"

"Nope! I ain't told a soul, Daddy. Honest I ain't!"

Bea stepped close to Joe Junior and brushed the loose dirt off his T-shirt. "Junior, I done told you bout sayin yep an nope when you answer grown folks. You suppose to say yes mam and no mam when you's talkin to a lady. And when you be talkin to a man, you supposed to say yes sir and no sir."

"Don't none of my friends talk like that. How come I got to?"

Lilly Pearl felt hurt and focused her anger on Joe Junior. She was also jealous that he got all of the attention. "See, I told yall that ugly little nappy-headed boy ain't got nothin in that big, flat water-head. He can't even remember how to answer grown folks."

"I can if I want to! I got mo sense than you, girl."

"Here! Take yo greasy cap." Lilly Pearl dropped it in the hole where he stood.

Joe Junior threw loose soil at Lilly Pearl. "You's dumb, ol pregnant girl. I bet yo baby ain't got no daddy." And before anyone could respond to what he said, Joe Junior tugged at his father's shirt. "Daddy, didn you say her baby ain't got no daddy?" he asked. "Didn you say that, Daddy?"

"Shut up, boy." Feeling embarrassed, he continued tugging at the unyielding roots of the lilac bush. "Don't be repeatin ever thing you be hearin. Ever thing's got some kinda daddy--worms got a daddy, dogs got a daddy. . ."

"Yo daddy ought'a be shame of his self," Bea said. "Talking that kinda trash round you."

Lilly Pearl's face was flushed, and tears were welling in her eyes. She turned away, hoping that no one would notice her silent cry. Bea continued in her efforts to coach Joe Junior. "You ain't gonna grow up like them little hoodlums you be playin with. You gonna have the proper raisin!"

"Junior," Joe interrupted, "You listen to me, son. You ain't never suppose to tell nobody where we come from. The past is the past, and it ought'a be left in the past. Don't never look back. Cause if you do, you might turn into a pillow of salt, like ol man Lot's wife."

"Now you mind your daddy, honey." Bea lovingly stroked Joe Junior's back, "He's tellin you right. Ain't nobody else's business where we come from."

"I ain't told nobody bout it, Momma. It ain't nothing to tell. Is it? I mean, we ain't never done nothin wrong to nobody. Is we?"

"No, son." Joe cleared his throat and answered quickly. "We ain't never done nothin that we wasn pushed into."

With one desperate tug, Joe freed the lilac bush, but not without breaking several of its major roots. The roots disconnected with such abruptness that Joe tumbled backwards. The lilac bush appeared to be wrestling with Joe. The branches scratched his face, irritating him terribly and embarrassing him. Then the soil gave way beneath his feet and he slid deeper into the hole. The bush was on top of him--an act of rebellion. "This motherfuckin tree is gittin on my nerves. Dammit! Open that trunk, boy!"

Bea brushed the damp, black soil from Joe's clothing. "It ain't stickin, Joe. The dirt ain't stickin. You won't get the seat dirty. Maybe Mr. Jackson's got some ol newspaper."

"I don't want nothin from that old sucker. And I ain't lettin you beg that ol bastard for nothin else. Forgit it! Yall just get in the car!" Joe tossed his shovel into the trunk. "Put yo shovel on top of mine, Junior." They had dug around the lilac bush more than six hours. Joe wiped the perspiration from his forehead. "Get that clothesline outta the back seat. We'll have to tie this thing in the trunk."

They tugged at the full-branched bush, trying to avoid the claw-like stems and leaves that scratched their faces and arms. It was almost four o'clock in the afternoon. Joe and his son had become tired and hungry. Bea seemed worried only about the lilac bush. The three of them had become so engrossed in its removal that no one had noticed Lilly Pearl's red eyes. Still echoing in her ears were Joe Junior's words--"yo baby ain't got no daddy". His father had told him that. She hated both of them. And, at that point in her life, she hated all men.

Joe Junior waited until his mother and Lilly Pearl had gotten into the car. He closed the door. Then he looked up into his father's eyes, "Daddy, who's ol man Lot?"

"What?"

"Who's ol man Lot, whose wife looked back and turned into a pillow of salt?"

"Boy, you still thinkin bout that?"

"Ain't never heard bout nobody turnin into salt before."

"Ain't nothin unusual, Junior. Folks turn to salt all the time. It's just they don't be lookin like salt. I mean, you can't tell they's turned to salt by lookin at em."

"But, how did ol Lot know she was salt?"

"You see, son, Ol Lot's wife was the first woman God ever turned to a pillow of salt. So, God let her turn to real salt. He had to use her to teach all the other women in the world if they don't take heed to what they be told to do by man, they's headin for the big punishment--bein turned to a livin, human pillow of salt."

"But, Daddy, suppose a woman ain't got no man to be tellin her what to do?"

"She be damned by the time she's child-bearin age. She be sho to turn to a pillow of salt. Get in the car, Junior! I'll tell ya later how to pick out them women who's done turned to salt." Joe Junior climbed into the car, still pondering the question of Lot's wife. As Joe slid under the steering wheel, he wondered how he might explain this mystery to his son's satisfaction. Joe was the sun that warmed his son's curiosity about life and the mysterious world around him.

Lilly Pearl saw that Bea's greatest concern at the moment was for the future survival of the lilac bush that hung from the trunk of their car. "Joe, do you think our bush'll live with all them main roots cut off?"

"Ain't no reason why it won't. I done seen lots of things grow back with broke roots. Plants is special like that. You break em off, they just keep a'growin. It's people what can't grow once they's been uprooted."

Listening eagerly to Joe's every word, Joe Junior nudged his father on his shoulder. "Daddy, do people grow from roots? Is babies got roots inside they momma's belly?"

Joe gripped the steering wheel and drove carefully out of the alley. "Why you ask me a crazy question like that, boy? Where you ever git a crazy idea like that?"

"You just said people can't grow when they's uprooted. I ain't never seen nobody wit roots."

Lilly Pearl, who shared the back seat with Joe Junior, reached over and thumped his head. She and Bea laughed at his question. "You crazy boy. You ain't got no kinda sense. Is he, Bea?"

"Leave him alone, Pearl." Bea stopped laughing. "He just wants to know what his daddy meant."

"Well, he ought'a know babies ain't born with roots dingling from em."

"You better keep yo ol yellow hands to yo self, ugly white girl." Joe Junior rubbed the back of his head. "Daddy, ol peckerwood Pearl thumped my head."

"You shut up, watermelon-head. I ain't no cracker."

"Cut it out back there, you two," Joe demanded. "Pearl, keep yo hands to yo self. Junior, you cut out that kinda name callin."

"But you said she's a cracker, Daddy." Joe Junior touched his father's back. "Didn you say she looks like a cracker, Daddy? You said she's a red-neck peck-a-wood."

Joe, glancing at Bea, could see the look of disapproval on her face. "I don't recollect sayin no such thing, Junior."

"Don't you remember tellin Mr. Sykes, and Mr. . . ."

"Shut up, Junior! Right now! I told you, I don't recollect sayin no such thing. Now what was you sayin bout them roots?"

"Joe, you got to cut out that loose talkin round Junior. I done told you bout talkin that kinda trashy talk round him. You know he got ears like a elephant. He don't never forgit nothin."

"I don't wanna talk about that no mo, Bea. Plus, I don't recollect sayin it in the first place. Now, that's that."

Lilly Pearl became quiet again. The pain in her bosom had returned. Silently, she vowed that someday she would make Joe pay for degrading her.

"Daddy, do babies be growin roots while they be in they momma's belly? Do they got roots when they be born?"

"I reckon you could say they's got somethin like one main root when they be born. Cept it ain't called a root. They calls it a neighbor cord. They cuts it off when the baby come into the world."

"That's a navel cord, Joe," Bea said. "It be connected to the baby's navel when it's born."

"Why they cut it off, Momma?"

"The baby don't be needin it no more."

"How come they needs it before they git born?"

"It connects em to the momma so they can eat."

"Did I have one, Momma?"

"Yeah. You had one."

"Did I cry when they cut mine off? Do it hurt when they cut it off?"

"No. You didn't feel a thing."

Joe cleared his throat and explained, "You see, Junior, people's roots is in the land where they's born, and where they momma, papa, and grandfolks come from. You take a man from where his roots is, he's uprooted. He don't never be right inside for the rest of his natural born life. He be walkin round empty inside, cause he ain't got nowhere to draw his strength from."

"Is you empty inside, Daddy?"

"No! Not me. I'm gonna be strong anywhere I go.

That's the way it is wit me, son. I got to be strong for you and yo momma. You understand?"

"I think I do, Daddy."

"You don't understand nothin, little ol pumpkinhead," Lilly Pearl teased. She leaned over and thumped his head.

"Daddy, Pearl is doing it again!" he yelled, rubbing his head. "She thumped me again!"

Bea turned around, "Pearl," she spoke frowning. "How come you like to keep that boy acting-up? You two is bout to drive me outta my mind."

"That didn hurt Junior, Bea. Yall just got him spoiled. I didn hardly touch that little monkey's head."

"Just cut it out," Bea pleaded. "I can't understand why. . ."

"Oww!" Lilly Pearl grabbed her belly with both hands. "That hurt!"

"What, Pearl?" Bea's eyes were big with concern. "What's the matter with you, girl?"

Fear grasped Lilly Pearl's heart as the warm water gushed from her body.

- *2* -

Jimmy Lee's Birth

"Oh, God, please help me!" she groaned loudly. Another one had come. This time it was longer and harder. "I can't stand this pain!" Lilly Pearl cried. "Help me! Somebody please. . ."

"Now, now young lady, I haven't touched you yet. You're getting yourself all worked up. It really isn't that bad." He stood over her bed smiling down on her. "It won't hurt so much if you just relax."

I hate him for saying that, she thought. *How can I relax? I'm dying*! She closed her eyes and prayed. *The Lord is my*

17

shepherd; I shall not want. He maketh me to lie down. . .

"Turn over, Miss Ealy," he said. "Open your legs. Let's see what's happening here."

The doctor lubricated his finger and slid it carefully into her rectum. "Oh, yes. It's coming." He patted her thigh gently and disposed of the rubber glove.

"Can I have a drink of water?" Lily Pearl asked, half crying. Her lips were swollen and slightly cracked.

"Nothing by mouth," the doctor replied. Then she was alone in the small sterile room.

. . . in green pastures. . ., she continued. *. . . He leadeth me beside still waters. . .*

"Are you Lilly Pearl Ealy?" the social worker asked as she entered the room.

"Yes, Mam." She wiped her tears on the back of her hands. "I'm Pearl."

"My name is Joan Clarke. I've been assigned your case." She looked at Lilly Pearl with apparent empathy. "How old are you?" She fumbled through the papers she held. "Oh, I see. You're fifteen."

"Yes, Mam."

"Are your legal guardians here?"

"Mam?"

"Your parents?"

"No, Mam. They's in Pearl City."

"Who's your guardian in Milwaukee?"

"Bea, I reckon."

"Is she in the waiting room?"

"Bea's at home. She couldn't stay."

Lilly Pearl felt the pressure grow more intense, bringing the agonizing pain again. Blood trickled slowly from her as the fetus strained for birth. Her face grew flush as beads of perspiration crept down her temples and mingled with the tears. Her eyes were pressed tightly as she gripped the bed rails. White-knuckled, she raised herself to a sitting position and wailed, "It's coming! It's coming!"

Joan Clarke ran from the room to find a nurse. Then the pain subsided. Drained and exhausted from twelve hours of labor, Lilly Pearl slumped to the bed panting and praying. She cried softly while Joan wiped her face with a cool wet towel.

Fifteen minutes had passed. The doctor entered the room again. "Miss Ealy, let's see how much you've dialated. Excuse us a moment," he told Joan Clarke.

Jesus! He's gonna stick his finger up my behind again, she thought.

"You're coming along just fine," he said. "We'll take you to delivery soon."

Delivery! She wondered how the baby could come out without tearing her apart. Lilly Pearl put her hand down below to see how much she had opened. *My pussy ain't big enough for no baby*, she cried uncontrollably as Joan stroked her hair. "I'm scared, Miss Clarke. I ain't gonna live to see my baby!"

"Oh, you'll be just fine, dear." She rubbed her arm affectionally. "Women have babies every day."

"But I ain't no woman!"

"Trust me," Joan said. "I've seen lots of girls have babies."

"How's it gonna come out?" Lilly Pearl wanted to know. "I can't stretch that big."

"Don't you know anything at all about childbirth?" Joan asked.

"No, Mam. Ain't nobody never told me nothin."

"You poor dear," Jane said softly. "Childbirth is nothing to fear. Your body's been preparing for this since you first conceived."

"What do you mean?"

"Have you ever seen an animal give birth?"

"A dog."

"Did you see the puppies come out?"

"Well, uh. . ." Lilly Pearl's face turned red. "That ol dog had a hard time spittin em out."

"It does take effort on the mother's part," Joan told her. "But before labor started, your baby was stationed here on the pelvic floor." Joan ran her finger lightly across Lilly Pearl's lower abdomen. "Your body has become elastic and moveable. This allows you to open up. You're not so tight anymore," Joan said. "And Mother Nature made your baby's head compressible so that it traverses quite easily."

"Traverse?"

"Yes. It moves through the birth canal. Your baby's head has several thin bones connected by soft tissue. When it comes out, the bones overlap. They squeeze together, like this." She demonstrated with her hands. "You'll see. The little head looks like a soft egg coming out. Once it gets through, the tiny body's no problem." She fingered Lilly Pearl's copper curls. "Childbirth can be one of the most beautiful experiences of your entire life."

"Beautiful?" Lilly Pearl asked. "Ain't there another way to git it out?"

"Yes, by Caesarean section," Joan said. "But they don't

do a C if they don't have to. Just try to think of it the way you remember your first sexual encounter--the painful beauty."

"How can pain be beautiful?" Lilly Pearl wanted to know. "I ain't had it but once. Wasn nothing beautiful bout that."

"When a woman sacrifices her innocence for love and new life, it's symbolic of the ultimate gift--the Godly gift. Don't you see? It's all about love."

"But I don't love nobody. And ain't nobody lovin me, cept my momma an papa."

"What about your baby's father?"

"He don't love nobody, specially me. My baby, he ain't got no daddy."

"You say he as if you know it's a boy."

"It's got to be a boy. I ain't bringin no girl into a world like this."

"Why do you say that?" Joan wanted to know.

"Girls got too much pain waitin for em. Men takes what they want. No pain."

"That isn't necessarily so, dear."

"That's what my momma say. Women hurts for everybody's wrong, no matter who do the sin. Momma say a woman can't hide her sin. When she fall, she be like trash on the ground. Man crawl on his belly in snot. He still be a man."

Joan cringed. "You sound so very old, dear, as if you have no future."

"I reckon it ain't much I got to look to."

"But it doesn't have to be that way. Those sayings are like old wives tales. They'll keep you living in fear and despair."

"That's what I be feeling."

"This world doesn't belong to men only. A woman can make her way, too." Lilly Pearl observed the serious frown across Joan's brow. "You can't just sit and let things happen to you. You've got to grab life by the balls and demand success."

"By the balls?" She chuckled in surprise.

"Yes. Life's like a mean man who respects a woman only when she fights back, even though he's kicking her ass."

"That's funny, Miss Clarke," Lilly Pearl laughed. ". . .real funny when you say it like that."

"Life isn't funny, my dear. And success doesn't come on a silver platter."

"But I ain't got nobody to help me. I'm just a poor colored girl."

Joan cupped Lilly Pearl's face. "You're a very lucky girl. You're young, beautiful and you could pass for white."

"But I ain't gonna be able to do much with a baby to look after."

"If you feel that way, maybe you should consider adoption, for your sake and his."

"No! Not my baby!" She started to weep. "I feel like a heavy fog's all around me. . .can't see tomorrow. But, whatever the future holds, gonna find me with my baby. Long as I got him, I got my own."

Tears settled in Joan's eyes. She wiped Lilly Pearl's face again. "Tell me. How did this happen to you?"

"I done prayed to God to let me forget, cause it don't matter no more."

"Were you raped, Lilly Pearl?"

"Like I said, Miss Clarke, it's best I forget. God's done took his name from my mouth."

"Your parents. . . Do they know?"

"No, Mam. I told em it was Jimmy Lee Blood."

"Who is he?" Joan asked.

"He's the one I wish it was. He joined the Army. . . got killed in boot camp. Momma said it's best I come up here. . .save me the shame."

"The shame isn't yours if you were raped."

"Down where I come from it don't matter. Nobody knows cept God'n me and the one who done it. I didn't want trouble for my folks. So, nothin I could do cept wait to see what God wants done."

The lights in the corridor sped rapidly past as Lilly Pearl was rushed on a gurney to the delivery room. Doctor Davis slid casually into green sterile garments and rubber gloves. When she entered the room he smiled at her and winked. "Breathe through your mouth, young lady, like this." He opened his mouth and began panting. "We're going to make you a mother real soon."

"We're putting you on the delivery table, Lilly Pearl," one of the nurses said. "Just relax."

The fear that gripped her that moment was greater than ever before. *I need my momma!* she thought. "Somebody please call Bea!"

"No time for that, my dear," the doctor said. "You'll be just fine."

Oh, God! I'm scared!

"Put your foot in this stocking, Lilly Pearl," the nurse

said. ". . .now the other one."

Jesus, help me!

"Raise your legs a little higher," the nurse told her. "I have to put them in the stirrups. Now, slide down. We need your fanny at the end of the table."

"Careful. It's coming," the doctor cautioned. "Now, you can push, young lady. Give us a big push!"

"But I can't!" she cried. "It's hurtin too bad. I can't have no baby."

"Push, Miss Ealy!" the doctor said.

"It's too big!" Lilly Pearl told him.

"You're making it hard on yourself, young lady. Come on, give us a hearty push. It'll soon be over," the doctor said. "Take a deep breath, hold it, and give it all you've got!"

Lilly Pearl could feel the strain on her vagina as it stood agape. She took a deep breath, closed her eyes and pushed, as if to empty her soul.

His head was in the doctor's hand. Then she could feel his tiny body pass through. "It's a boy!" The doctor laughed, "You've got a son, my dear."

The nurses wiped and weighed her baby, wrapped him in a receiving blanket and laid him across her breasts. For the first time she experienced the magnetism that exists between mother and child.

"Are you going to keep your baby?" the nurse inquired.

"Yes, Mam. He's all I've got."

"What'll you name him, Miss Ealy?" the doctor asked.

"Jimmy Lee, I reckon." She touched his face with a finger and smiled. "I'll call him Jimmy Lee."

- *3* -

Sweet Nancy

"See you later," Sweet Nancy told Nikolakopulos, the felony judge. "Park one block over. I'll leave the back door unlocked."

"What's up?" he demanded to know.

"Niko, please. Just do what I say."

She cut him short and hung up the phone when they stopped out front. Then she opened the door and called to Lilly Pearl, "Let me see that little fellow! I heard he's a cute little stallion."

Bouncing with each energetic step, her long black curls

seemed alive. The glistening sun on Sweet Nancy's mahogany face accentuated her noble cheeks and revealed her longing eyes.

"I reckon she'll sell im some pussy by the time he's crawlin," Joe said.

"Shsss! You oughta be shame, Joe, talking like that," Bea whispered.

"Hell. She's runnin here now to look in his diaper, to see how big his dick is."

Bea placed her hand on his arm, in desperation, "Joe, please. Nancy'll hear you."

"So what if she do? She can't whip my ass. Ain't my fault she's a whore."

As Sweet Nancy approached the car, her breast stood full and upright, pointing like two voluptous arrows, in line with Joe's lustful eyes. She leaned forward against the car and looked in. His nostrils flared, involuntarily. Slowly and slyly he inhaled, holding her fragrance in his lungs. His penis stirred vigorously. To conceal his arousal from his wife, Joe dropped his hands from the steering wheel. Hot saliva flowed under his tongue. He could taste her.

Reaching for the baby, Sweet Nancy pleaded, "Let me hold him, Pearl. He's such a precious thing."

With evident pride, Lilly Pearl lifted her child towards Sweet Nancy's cradled arms. Tears wet her eyes as she cuddled him close and remembered her tragic loss.

"Come in for awhile, Pearl. I've something for you."

"She's got to git some rest," Joe said cruelly.

"I won't keep her long," Sweet Nancy said. "Come, Pearl."

"I done told you, she can't go!" he spoke forcefully.

"I will!" Lilly Pearl said, excitedly. "Bea, I'm going for a little while."

"I done said you can't go. And that's that!" Joe shouted.

"But, I'm going," she announced, defiantly.

"Over my dead body," he said.

"I ain't planning on waitin til you's dead, Joe. I'm going now!"

He looked at his wife. "You hear this little ungrateful hussy? I think it's bout time we send her home. Ain't nobody stayin under my roof that's runnin with a sportin woman."

"Let her go," Bea said to her husband, in a sympathetic tone. "You ain't got no rights to act this way. Nancy and Pearl ain't done you no wrong."

"She's doing me wrong by being here! You think I like livin next door to a-a. . ."

Sweet Nancy cleared her throat loudly to get Joe's attention. Their eyes met, and there was a sudden silence that only the two of them understood. The baby quivered in her arms. She nestled him closely and turned away. Lilly Pearl followed Sweet Nancy.

"I hope you know how much you've hurt Nancy," Bea said to Joe.

"I ain't hurt nobody."

"You hurt people with careless words, Joe. You only see Nancy's faults, but God ain't made you perfect. When I had pneumonia, Nancy took care of me and Junior while you worked. She cleaned, washed, and cooked every day. And none of these, so called, nice ladies ever lifted a finger to help."

"Woman!" Joe grabbed Bea's wrist, "You had that slut

in my house? I promised myself and God she'd never. . ."

With a jerk, Bea was free. "That's why I never told you," she said tearfully. "Nancy's had a hard life, but she's a good woman. She's my only friend."

Apparently, moved by the frustration and anger that Sweet Nancy's numerous rejections had caused him, Joe slapped Bea violently. He was thoroughly convinced that Sweet Nancy's loyalty to his wife was the reason why she had said no. Joe Junior watched from the house as his mother fell from the car and scrambled to her feet. When she entered the house, she tried to hide her tears and regain her composure. But the scream of Joe's tires as he sped away left her shakened.

"You okay, Momma?" Joe Junior asked.

"Yes," she assured him and faked a smile. "I'm fine, honey."

"Ain't worth a damn," he growled to himself, heading for the Nite Life Tavern. "Fucks anything that's got a dime," he declared self-rightously. "A two-legged bitch," he called Sweet Nancy, while in his mind he stripped her bare and felt her soft flesh against his. Obsessed with desire to have Sweet Nancy, Joe swore angrily, "I'll call that whore and give her a piece of my mind."

Sweet Nancy marvelled at the innocence of the infant she held while his blanket absorbed her tears. "He looks just like mine," she told Lilly Pearl. "My baby looked exactly like him."

"But I thought you had no kids," Lilly Pearl said.

"Oh, I don't. He died."

"I'm sorry Nancy. I didn't know."

"It's okay," Sweet Nancy said. "That was sixteen years ago. A whole lifetime's done passed."

"Why did he die? I mean, what killed him?"

"They said it was crib death. I reckon that's as good a guess as any. I figured him to be a real smart baby, not wanting to live in this here world. I was only seventeen, left with five kids to fend for."

"Five children?" Lilly Pearl was confused again.

"My three sisters and two brothers," Sweet Nancy explained. "You see my father, the dirty rat, ran away with a white woman when I was fourteen. Momma started drinking and hanging out at Curley's, up on Third Street. That was my father's old hangout. She thought she'd catch him and his whore up there. But his buddies said him and that Jezebel had moved to Canada. Momma really took it hard. All that worrying and heavy drinking kinda drove her crazy. She'd get so drunk, they'd call me to bring her home. After our phone was off, she had to make it home on her own. One December night, it was fifteen below. I found her in our yard, bout six feet from the back door. Her coat had been left at the tavern, and I never found her shoes. Poor Momma, she just couldn't live without that no good rotten excuse for a man."

Lilly Pearl's eyes were filled with tears. "Oh, Nancy, I feel so sorry for you."

"Don't be shedding no tears over what's done happened in my life, Pearl. My hide's plenty tough. I tried to keep the little ones from seeing Momma laying out there in that dirty snow. But when the police came, everything got outta hand. Folks had come from all over the neighborhood looking at her like she was something from outer space. I had covered her with a quilt before the police got here, but they pulled it off and left her exposed like she was nothing more than a common dog. I kept telling em to cover her, but they didn't pay me no mind. The cops kept asking, 'Where's your dad?' I kept telling em, 'He's gone.' Lucky for us, they didn't take it the way I meant it. They thought he just wasn't home, not that he had run off three years earlier. Nobody bothered us til our caseworker got the news that Momma had died. That old witch turned us over to Child Protective Services. Without some help, we would've been placed in foster homes, not living together."

Nancy's eyes were wet as she tried to comfort Lilly Pearl. "Don't cry, Pearl. That happened a long time ago."

"I know. But you was so young."

"Not as young as you. And you've got a new baby to care for."

"I'll make it like you did, Nancy," Lilly Pearl said.

"I know you'll make it, Pearl, but not like me. Get a college education so you'll have a decent life. When my father left Momma, she didn't know nothing but housework and cooking. She said she'd rather starve than work as a white woman's maid. She made me promise to take care of the others, in case of her death. So, I did. There was this old German lawyer she had told me to go see if we ever got in trouble. He used to do free legal work for poor people. Momma had used him to put a tracer on Papa. Lawyer Krause remembered me when I called. He told me to dress up real pretty and meet him downtown in front of the court house. We ended up in Judge Nicholas Nikolakopulos' chambers. He explained my problem to the judge. Nikolakopulos looked me over and said to Lawyer Krause, 'Go downstairs and have a coffee, Herman. And you, young lady,' pointing in the direction of the plush leather sofa, 'take a seat over there'. I was really scared when he stood up and walked towards me, taking his coat off. 'So, you want to be declared independent and become the legal guardian of your siblings?' I didn't know what that word *sibling* meant, but I figured it to mean my sisters and brothers. 'Yes, Sir,' I said. He unzipped his pants and loosed his shirt and tie. I started to tremble when he squeezed my breast rather hard. You see, I was a virgin when I entered his chambers. His voice was low and commanding. 'Don't be afraid,' he told me. 'Pull your panties off.' I wanted to run, but he had the power to keep my family together."

"'I'll fix it so you can stay on welfare and keep your sisters and brothers,' the judge promised. I held back the tears when he had me for his pleasure."

"Did he keep his promise?" Lilly Pearl asked.

"Yes. He looked after me and the kids until they grew up and left home. I think I really loved him when I carried his son."

"His son?"

"Well, he was here every night."

"Why didn't you marry him?"

"He was already married. Plus, marriage between a white judge and a colored welfare woman was out of the question. You should know that, Pearl."

"Didn't he love you?"

"Honey, love had nothing to do with it."

"What do you mean?" Lilly Pearl asked, wide-eyed.

"Pearl, in a place like Milwaukee, I could've been a judge too, and we still couldn't have married. Things like that just didn't happen here."

"That's why you never married?" Lilly Pearl asked.

"If I had married, he would've been colored. And that could never be. I'd never trust a colored man. I'll go to my grave hating all of em for the pain Papa brought on us. Everytime I speak to one, I think of how Papa caused Momma's death, and left me and the kids to suffer. I see Papa's face on every colored man that looks at me. I live the life of a whore, but I don't sell to niggers. I wouldn't go to bed with one for all the melons in Mississippi!"

"You ain't never gonna marry?"

"No. Never. Niko takes care of me. He don't let none of these nosy cops bother me bout my personal business. I've got lots of big-money customers downtown--lawyers, doctors, politicians, and a few businessmen. I'll retire when I'm forty and move to Sugar Hill."

Joe was still angry when he reached the tavern. The Nite Life was seldom crowded, but it had a stinch that was composed of stale whisky and cigar smoke, combined with sweaty factory workers and the odor of an old dead rat that nobody could find. Short Form Phil was on the telephone that Joe had wanted to use. And on one corner of the pool table sat Pap Smear Perkins waiting for Short Form to get back to their game.

"Look who's here," Pap Smear said when Joe entered the tavern. "Hey, Joe, where you been, man? You lookin for somebody?"

With Sweet Nancy uppermost in his mind, Joe didn't

answer. He headed for the telephone and stood face-to-face with Short Form. "When is you gittin off the goddam phone, motherfucker?" Joe asked.

Short Form Phil placed his hand over the receiver. The dim naked light bulb that hung over the pool table was just bright enough for Joe to see the romantic expression fade from Short Form's face.

"Asshole, can't you see I'm on the phone with my lady. Man, ain't you got no manners?"

"Well, excuse me, Mr. Short Form. But if you and your lady don't mind, I'd like to make a busines call, pussy face."

"Like I told you, shit brains, I'm on this damn phone."

"You gonna be on the fuckin floor if you keep that phone tied up."

Seeing that all attention was focused on him, Short Form said goodbye to his fiancee. Without a sign of appreciation, Joe grabbed the receiver and proceeded to make his call.

The tiny infant squirmed in Sweet Nancy's arms when the telephone rang. "Who could that be?" she muttered as she carefully placed little Jimmy Lee in his mother's lap. "Hello," she said rather abruptly. "Hello! Who is this?" She seemed angry and annoyed. "If you don't answer, I'm hanging up!"

"Oh, uh, it's me," the voice from the other end responded.

"Who the hell is *me*?" Her anger grew. "Identify yourself."

"Uh, it's me, Joe," he said. "I thought you'd catch my

voice. It ain't like you never heard it before."

"What do you want?" she asked.

"Can we talk? I mean, is you alone?"

"You know damn well I'm not alone."

"Is Pearl still there?"

Hoping the girl wouldn't guess it was Joe, Sweet Nancy restricted her answers to *yes* and *no*. "Yes," she told him.

"Can I see you later tonight so we can talk?"

Emphatically, she answered, "No!"

"I've got a hundred dollar bill in my pocket with your name on it," Joe bartered.

"Hell, no!" Sweet Nancy shouted and slammed the receiver down. She looked at Lilly Pearl and managed a smile.

All eyes in the tavern were on Joe. "This son-of-a-bitch is tryin to buy some pussy, yall." Pap Smear Perkins slapped Joe on the shoulder teasingly. "Hell, nigger, for a hundred dollars, I'd suck your dick and your daddy's too."

They all laughed.

"Go to hell, mother-fucker," Joe told him as he hung up the phone.

"Hey asshole," Short Form teased. "What do a hundred dollars worth of pussy look like?"

Joe walked towards the bar. "I don't have to buy no pussy, I got me a wife."

"We heard you beggin somebody for pussy, man," Short Form and Pap Smear agreed.

"Well, I ain't like you, Pap Smear," Joe said, "I don't eat pussy. You keep hair in your damn rotten teeth all the time."

"You's a lyin ass, Joe. Your damn mammy eat more pussy than I do."

Short Form Phil braced himself on the pool table while he laughed heartily at Joe and Pap Smear.

"I don't know why you laughin, Short Form," Joe said. "You's a grown man and ain't never worked long enough to file income taxes. You raggedy son-of-bitch."

"Do you want me to leave, Nancy?" Lilly Pearl asked. She sensed that the caller was Joe. Although, she had no plans to tell Bea.

"Oh, no. You can wait til my company comes."

"When you were on the phone, I heard somebody come in the back door and go upstairs."

"Don't worry, Pearl. It was only Niko."

Finally, Sweet Nancy pulled a roll of money from her bra. Lilly Pearl looked wide-eyed as she peeled off six fifty dollar bills and handed them to her.

"Wow! Nancy, I ain't never seen that much money in my whole life."

"Don't ever mention this to anyone, honey. Maybe Bea, but nobody else. I want you to buy the baby a layette. And buy yourself some school clothes."

"School clothes?"

"Pearl, you've got to go back to school. You gotta have some book learning to make it in this world with pride and respect. Your face'll open a lot of doors, but you'll need a real good job so you won't have to raise your son on welfare."

"But, Nancy, look at all this you've got. And you ain't got no book learnin. You got all this by yourself. Bea's got a husband, and she ain't got no long couch like this, no marble tables with glass tops. Look at this pretty white rug and that Cadillac out front. Plus, you's pretty and you wear furs and diamonds anytime you want to."

"You're a beautiful girl, Pearl. And you've got the color to pass. But pretty ain't enough. A dumb woman'll never make it in this world. All you see around me is stuff that don't tell what I truely feel inside." Sweet Nancy's voice trembled as she spoke. "If I had book learning, I'd live like a real lady. This here ain't happiness. Everything you see, I got between the sheets. Ain't no honor in that. Ain't no respect in that either. I learned a lot in bed with educated men. But they ain't gave me no diploma. When I smile at a man, it's for money. When I let a man touch me, it's for money."

"Please don't say bad things bout yourself, Nancy," Lilly Pearl cried.

"I'm just a fleeting moment in a man's life. He plays. He pays. Then he's gone. I'm always alone, even though I see lots of men. They ain't never honestly with me. I'm like a car they rent to drive someplace. They reach their destination, and that's all they want. I don't see em again til they need another ride. On special days, I sit alone and cry."

"What about your sisters and brothers?" Lilly Pearl wanted to know.

"They hate me because I am who I am."

"I'll be your friend, Nancy. And I'll go back to school," Lilly Pearl promised.

Waiting in Sweet Nancy's bedroom, Judge Nikolak-opulos deliberately dropped an ashtray to get her attention. Lilly Pearl looked in the direction of the back stairs.

"I think I'd better go, Nancy." She secured her baby's blanket.

"I'll see you tomorrow," Sweet Nancy told her. Then she kissed his tiny hand and smiled.

- *4* -

The Great Unwashed

"I done told yall for the last time, turn that damn light off," Joe called out from the bedroom. "I got to git me some sleep," he said. "Bea, bring your fat ass to bed, right now!"

Lilly Pearl looked at Bea sympathetically. "Don't you hate it when he talks under your clothes like that?"

"Naw. It don't bother me none. I done got used to it."

"I ain't never takin no mess offa no man," Lilly Pearl said. "I might not never get married."

"Woman, did you hear what I said?" he called again.

Bea didn't answer her husband.

"I wish he'd shut-up," Lilly Pearl complained. "We gotta finish this chapter tonight. Mr. Jansen always calls on them who ain't ready. Seems like that old man's got a crystal ball behind his desk, showin im all the people who ain't studied the lesson."

"Yeh," Bea chuckled. "They's the first one he points at. He get a real kick outta catchin folks off guard. But you's smart, Pearl. You know the right answer every time."

"I know the answers, but I don't like explaining in class," she said. "They look at me so funny,"

"You just feel like that cause you ain't used to bein in school with white folks."

"I reckon that's what it is. I was tellin Momma Neallie bout it when I called. She laughed. Momma said these white folks up North don't care who they be settin with. She said it just ain't no tellin what this here world is coming to with these northern whites runnin things."

"I suspect there's a lotta truth in that," Bea said. "They's a whole lot different from them whites down home. Aint Neallie knows them whites down South. They ain't lettin no coloreds in their schools less they's cleanin."

"You know, Bea, sometimes I wish I was in class with only colored folks. Them whites laugh at the way I talk."

"Who laughed at you, Pearl?"

"This white guy in our history class asked me why I talk like this."

"What the hell he mean?" Bea asked angrily.

"He asked me why I talk like colored folks from the South."

"What did you say?"

"I told im I am colored, from the South."

"Then what'd he say to that?"

"He didn't say nothin. But when the class was over, he handed me a note."

"What'd the note say?"

"It said, 'You can't help being a Negro, but you don't have to talk like one.'"

"Tell im to kiss a baboon's ass, honey! That cracker ain't got no business tellin you that. Pearl, ain't nothin wrong with the way you be talkin. White folks think they know everything. They wanna tell the whole world how to talk and what to say. They think ain't nobody got no brains cept them."

With veins of anger standing in his temples, Joe walked across the room where Lilly Pearl and Bea sat talking. "Do I have to make you go to bed every night?" Joe asked Bea. Then he turned the lamp off and pointed in the direction of their bedroom, as if Bea could see in the dark. "You got three seconds to get in bed," he told her. "And, Pearl, if you can't pay the light bill, stop stayin up all night lookin in them damn books."

"I ain't just lookin, Joe. I'm studyin'."

On her way to bed, Bea peeked in at Jimmy Lee. He had fallen asleep chewing his Teddy's ear.

"So, remember, ladies and gentlemen, the foundation of a capitalistic society is the ownership of property," Mr. Jansen said, as he paced back and forth in front of the class. "And, thank God, I might add, we're living in a country whereas a high level of motivation and education, coupled with job opportunities, allow us to excell far beyond the economic status of our parents."

Lilly Pearl prayed that Mr. Jansen would not call on her. Sitting behind her in class, Jacqueline whispered in her ear, "Are you going with us to the cafeteria, Lilly Pearl?"

"I ain't got lunch money today. Can you buy?"

Apparently irritated by the disturbance, Mr. Jansen stopped his lecture. "Ladies, is there something you'd like to share with us?" he asked.

Embarrassed, Jacqueline and Lilly Pearl apologized immediately. Everyone in the class laughed except Jacqueline, Lilly Pearl, and Mr. Jansen.

"Miss Ealy, perhaps you'd like to explain the advantages versus the disadvantages of living in a capitalistic society," Mr. Jansen said.

"Well, uh," she began, "anybody can own a business and property. And, uh. . . Would you please repeat the question, Sir?"

"People," Mr. Jansen said, "this is an adult class. I wish you'd conduct yourselves like adults. A great deal of self discipline is required to pass this course. Remember, ladies and gentlemen, as I have said many times before, in this world, nobody gets something for nothing. However, if somebody does get something for nothing, somebody definitely got nothing for something."

A guard from security entered the classroom. "Please excuse me, Mr. Jansen. There's a man in the office for Mrs. Stubblefield," he said.

Bea's heart palpitated excitedly. Joe had forbade her to attend school that day. Lilly Pearl saw the frightened look on her face. *I'd better go too*, she thought.

Fear permeated the room where the secretaries stared, grateful that Joe's anger had been brought under control. "How come you ain't at work?" Bea asked him. "Is something wrong?"

With his head held high and his chest inflated, Joe came close to striking his wife. "Is it too much to expect for a man to want his wife home like decent people?" he asked. "I told you last night to keep your ass home. I'm the head of the house. My word is law. You's disobeyin me woman! While I works to feed my family, you's loafin the streets."

"I ain't loafing, Joe," Bea said. "You know how I feel bout school."

"You done passed goin to school. You's too old for that."

Bea and Lilly Pearl stood there, extremely embarrassed. "I could learn a trade and get a job," Bea spoke in a very soft voice.

"A trade?" he scoffed. "I ain't havin my wife on no job."

"Hey, yall," Lilly Pearl said, "let's go. We can't settle it here."

Bea shrugged, "You's right, Pearl. Let's leave."

"You keep outta this, Miss White Lady!" Joe said to Lilly Pearl. "You's the cause of it all. Bea ain't thought nothin bout school til you filled her head with that shit. She was real happy acting like a wife oughta. Can't you see, Bea wasn cut out for no book learning? She's a plain woman. She likes plain things. I ain't lettin you ruin her life with all this school nonsense."

Class had dismissed. Jacqueline Hyde and Invidia Malice beckoned to Lilly Pearl from the hallway. But she stayed. "Let's go, Joe," Bea said.

"I'm going too," Lilly Pearl told Bea.

"You don't need to, Pearl. I'll be alright. Don't skip your classes on account of me."

"I didn't come for you nohow," Joe said to Lilly Pearl. "This ain't none of your damn business."

I won't fuss with this asshole here in the office, Lilly Pearl thought. Then she walked casually towards her new friends.

"What was that all about?" Jacqueline asked Lilly Pearl as the three of them stood in the lunch line.

"I'll tell you later," Lilly Pearl answered.

Invidia paid the cashier, and they headed for their favorite table in the corner of the cafeteria.

McCray and Kenny, their fellow classmen, sat waiting for them. "Where's Bea?" McCray asked the three. "Didn't I see her this morning?"

"Her old man took her home," Jacqueline explained.

"Was she sick?" Kenny asked.

"Mind your own business," Jacqueline said. "You men want to know everything."

"What in the world has happened? I asked a simple question, and you're all over me!"

"Ain't nothing wrong," Lilly Pearl told Kenny. "She had to go home with her husband."

Sensing that the cause of her departure was a delicate matter, McCray told Kenny to drop the subject.

"Why're you always on the defensive?" Kenny asked Jacqueline. "You hate men, don't you?"

"Please, you two, don't get started," Invidia pleaded. "Everyday we have to listen to your quarrels. You're worse than an old married couple. Why can't you get along?"

"I think they're screwing each other," McCray said.

Everyone at the table laughed except Jacqueline. "Jacqueline," Kenny teased, "you remind me of an old redneck sergeant I had. He ate nails for breakfast and niggers for supper."

"You mean the sixty-nine?" Invidia asked.

"Hell, no, Invidia. I'm not talking about sex," Kenny said. "This old sergeant was from Alabama, and he hated us colored soldiers with a passion. Of course, we hated him too. We all wanted to kill im but nobody had the nerve. I had my gun aimed at the back of his head one day on the rifle range, but my finger froze. God saved his ass that day."

"You're right, Kenny," Jacqueline agreed. "I do hate niggers, especially the big ape looking so-an-so's like you," she teased. "You think you're so much cause you got that damn Purple Heart for getting shot in the ass."

"What's the sixty-nine?" Lilly Pearl interrupted loudly.

"Shsss! Don't talk so loud," Invidia told her. "Pearl, you've got a lot to learn. The sixty-nine is when a man and a woman go down on each other at the same time."

"Oh! That's awful. Who'd ever do something like that?"

"I would," Kenny said to Lilly Pearl. "Wanna try it?"

"You're crazy, Kenny." She was red with embarrassment. "I wouldn do nothin like that."

"If you were a colored soldier in Alaska, you'd do anything for sex," Kenny told her. "Pussy was so damn high, you couldn't buy but one piece a month." McCray laughed heartily while the women listened in disgust. "They charged us more than the whites," Kenny said.

"Why?" Lilly Pearl asked.

"The white guys had told em we were freaks. I remember the first time we went to town. I followed a lady eight blocks, just to smell her perfume. I went into a department store and pretended I wanted to buy lingerie, just to touch some panties. In a bar one night, I offered a broad twenty-five dollars. She laughed at me and told everybody, 'Look at this cheap mother-fucker, trying to buy twenty-five dollars worth of pussy.' I felt like crawling in a rat hole. Some smart-ass told her to rub her finger in it, and run it under my nose."

"What did you do, man?" McCray asked.

"I got the hell outta there."

Everyone at the table laughed at Kenny. "You sure can lie," Jacqueline told him.

"I'm glad you're not white, Jacqueline," he said.

"Why?" she wanted to know.

"You'd burn us niggers at the stake," he told her.

"Just the poor ones like you," she admitted. "I hate poor people, especially poor coloreds. I get sick every morning I ride the bus through the ghetto. I hate having to look at all those dirty, snotty nose, nappy headed welfare kids going to school. I hate having to look at bare yards, broken whisky bottles on cracked sidewalks, trashy streets and bitches in heat, with males sniffing behind em. I hate to sit by smelly old ladies with head rags on and old winos that slept in the gutter all night."

"But they're our people," Lilly Pearl said.

"Not mine!" Jackqueline said. "They're not my people."

"Mine either," Invidia added. "I could never identify with people like that. They're no more than the trash that line the streets and never try to lift themselves. I wish I controlled welfare. They'd have to get jobs and work like me. Welfare's nothing but a poor man's gravy train that fosters apathy and laziness. People become conditioned to sit and wait for that monthly check. Their lives are centered around a once a month hand out. They're like country dogs waiting in the backyard for their master to chunk them a bone."

"Well, I don't agree," Lilly Pearl said.

"Girl, what do you know?" Jacqueline and Invidia spoke simultaneously.

"Some folks gotta have it to live," Lilly Pearl explained.

"Honey, I could've been on welfare if I hadn't gotten a job to support myself and Christy," Invidia said. "Of course, Billy does pay child support. But I could've sat on my ass too. I see myself above that."

"It's not just colored folks on welfare," McCray butted in.

"I know it, fool!" Invidia told him. "I'm talking bout colored folks now. Whites gotta deal with their own trash. It's our trash that makes us look bad. Everybody looks at our worse and thinks it's typical of the whole. There're enough whites doing well to make the rest look good. The poorest white bum on skid row, by just being white, can identify with the president."

"Well, I'm proud of my people," Lilly Pearl said.

"Child," Jacqueline placed her hand on Lilly Pearl's arm, "you don't know nothing yet. You're still wet behind the ears. I know you're on welfare, and so am I. But we're trying to develop ourselves. That means we're not welfare mentality."

Kenny laughed. "Miss Wyman," directing his comment towards Jacqueline," you're on welfare? How can you dress like that, my dear?"

"Like what,?" she asked.

"Like Jane Wyman. You think we haven't noticed?"

"Kiss my ass, Kenny," Jacqueline told him. "You don't know nothing but Army, pussy, and that damn VA check. When we graduate, you'll still be here talking about pussy. You think with your dick."

When they arrived home, Bea let the sitter go. Jimmy Lee lay asleep in his crib. Joe stood quietly with an apologetic expression on his face. "Let's lay down for a minute while the kid's still sleep," he said.

"At ten in the morning?" Bea asked with contempt.

"I know you's mad," he said. "But you'll get over it. Don't you see, honey, I need a wife that's home when I get here. I need a wife that's a good mother for my boy. You's a good woman. And I don't wanna lose you. But this here school business is gonna break us up. Look at how much trouble it's done caused already. We wasn fightin before this school mess started.

"A man needs a woman in his corner, not out yonder in some school house. You don't need no book learnin. I'm taking care of you and Junior. Ain't I?" Bea nodded her head yes and started to cry. He walked close to her and cupped her face. "See how unhappy school's done made you? You never cried before." Joe closed his arms around his wife and pulled her body against his. When he kissed her wet face, she trembled. He squeezed her closer until his penis pressed hard against her. She whimpered as he took her to bed and gently stripped her bare. He stood nude before her. Then she gave in to the ecstacy that engulfed her while he licked her slowly, methodically, from one side of her abdomen to the other. Lower and lower he went until his searching quivering tonque traveled lightly across the short stubby hair, then rapidly he manipulated the tip of her clitoris. Faster and more firmly he moved it. Her wild fingers were entangled in his coarse kinky hair. Uncontrollably, she cried and spoke unintelligibly to him. Suddenly, Joe's nostrils flared. He rose and covered Bea like a gigantic black stallion in heat. Joe was hard and rigid inside her. Rapidly, his strong muscular buttocks flexed and pushed him deeper and faster, faster and deeper. And finally, at the moment she reached her peak, simultaneously they experienced the infinite sensation of paradise.

Bea promised she'd never attend school again.

- *5* -

Reflections

"Why don't you give up, Miss Ealy," Abigail Schwartz said. "You're not college material. Why don't you do the sensible thing and learn a logical trade?"

Lilly Pearl was appalled at the thought of compromising her aspirations. "What kind of trade?" she asked.

"Power machines," the caseworker said. "You'd master that in six months."

As she flipped calmly through new applications on her desk, Abigail Schwartz seldom looked up at Lilly Pearl.

"I already know power machines," Lilly Pearl told her.

"Then, why aren't you working, Miss Ealy?" she asked, flipping another sheet.

"For thirty dollars a week? No way! I can't feed my child on that."

"Not to worry, Miss Ealy," she said. "We'd supplement you."

"Of course you would! You'd keep me on welfare and love it. I'm sick of you telling me how long I gotta wait for a winter coat or when my baby can have new shoes."

Lilly Pearl's future, to a great extent, was at the mercy of Abigail Schwartz. And they both knew it. Mrs. Schwartz had memorized all the rules designed to deny recipients. When she would run out of departmental rules, she'd conjure her own and enforce them with strict adherence. Her behavior implied that all welfare allowances came directly from her purse.

Abigail Schwartz bit her chapped lips and wore a frown across her brow. And with cold control, she said to Lilly Pearl, "College takes too long, Miss Ealy. Even if you were smart enough, an education costs too much."

"But not as much as ignorance." Lilly Pearl said. "I've nothing but time. I've nothing to do. And I ain't going nowhere."

Finally, she looked up at her and shrugged. "It's completely out of the question. You'd never make it in college."

"I can too! I'm smarter than you. You have no compassion. If they teach that in college, you must've been absent a lot."

"I'm not going to argue with you," Mrs. Schwartz said. "You have my final decision."

Lilly Pearl ran downstairs to the registration window. "My caseworker's name is Abigail Schwartz. I wanna see her supervisor."

"What do you want with Mrs. Schwartz's supervisor?" the receptionist asked.

"It's something personal," Lilly Pearl told her.

"I'm sorry. You'll need an appointment," she said, as she glanced through a list of names.

"How can I get one when I don't even know him?" Lilly Pearl asked.

"It's Mr. Dew. I've checked his calendar. You'll have to come in next Monday."

Lilly Pearl cried when she walked away from the window. *Oh, God, please help me.*

It was during the month of January, a very cold day in Milwaukee. Ugly dark clouds hang low, threatening a few more inches of snow. *I hope everybody will be there tonight,* she thought. *Oh, Lord, please let me keep in step with the others. I feel so sorry for poor Kenny. Maybe he'll graduate in May.*

When she got off the bus near her home, the sight of light gray smoke curling slowly out of the chimney made her suddenly feel warm and secure. The sidewalk was slippery here and there where neighbors had failed to put down salt. She could see Joe's car out front parked ahead of two Cadillacs. *Why didn't Nancy park in the garage, on a day like this?* she wondered. *Whose new Cadillac is that?* she asked herself. When Lilly Pearl had reached Sweet Nancy's house, she heard her open the door.

"Here, Pearl! Come here!" Sweet Nancy beckoned

anxiously. She held in her hand what Lilly Pearl thought was a graduation card. "You'll have to guess what this is, before I give it to you," Sweet Nancy said.

"Is it a card with money in it?" Lilly Pearl asked.

"Well, you're partially right."

"Oh, please, Nancy, give me a hint."

"It's something big," Sweet Nancy said. "You'll really love it, Pearl. She shook the envelope near Lilly Pearl's ear.

"It's keys!" Lilly Pearl snatched the bulging envelope and found three hundred dollars and two keys in it. "God bless you, Nancy! You're my very best friend," she said with a zealous embrace. "Now I can enroll in college this spring. To hell with Mrs. Schwartz."

"But you haven't guessed what the keys are for."

"Oh, yes. The keys."

"See those two Cadillacs parked out front? The burgundy's mine. The white one's yours."

The long white Cadillac that Lilly Pearl had often admired was now hers. She became ecstatic with joy, hugged Sweet Nancy and covered her face with kisses. "You're so good to me, Nancy. I'm gonna make you proud. You'll see."

"That's your graduation present," she said.

"But, I can't drive."

"You'll learn."

Lilly Pearl ran to the car and fumbled with the keys until she had opened the door. Proudly, she sat under the wheel, turning it as though she were driving. Then an alarming thought stopped her.

Sweet Nancy looked from the porch smiling. Through

Lilly Pearl, she could see herself get a second chance. But slowly and sadly Lilly Pearl climbed from the car. "What is it, Pearl?" Sweet Nancy wanted to know.

"Oh, Nancy!" she said. "I can't have a car on welfare."

"Them SOB's can't keep you from driving my car. Right?"

"I reckon," Lilly Pearl replied with hope.

"So, put your mind to rest," Sweet Nancy told her. "It'll be your car but in my name."

Lilly Pearl fell to her knees and kissed Sweet Nancy's hand. "Get up, Pearl!" she said. "Don't ever kneel to anyone, unless it's the Good Lord."

Joe, next door, had watched Lilly Pearl and Sweet Nancy from his livingroom window, but he said nothing when Lilly Pearl entered the house. She knew quite well that he had seen her and disapproved of Sweet Nancy's gift. But she had learned to avoid arguments with Joe. She said, "Hi, Joe," and went quickly to her room. *If I don't make him angry,* Lilly Pearl thought, *maybe he'll allow Bea to attend my graduation tonight.*

Lilly Pearl's birthday had passed two weeks earlier, and she had hoped to celebrate both events that evening.

Unknown to Lilly Pearl, Leslie Logan had planned a surprise party in her honor. Leslie had asked Jacqueline and Invidia to bring Lilly Pearl to the lounge after the commencement was over.

Two hours had passed since Lilly Pearl arrived home. She smiled warmly at Joe, hoping he'd be in a good mood. "Would you please bring Bea and Junior to my graduation tonight, Joe?" she asked. "Momma and Papa couldn't come to see me walk across the stage."

"If you wasn such a hot piss-ass, you woulda finished high school in Mississippi," he told her.

She tried to remain calm while she and Bea prayed he'd say yes. Joe had predicted Lilly Pearl's failure and she had proven him wrong.

"Like I told you before, them kinda things remind me of funerals," Joe said, "just a waste of time. That school mess ain't nothin but bull-shit--all them folks walkin round in long gowns lookin like damn fools." That was Joe's conclusive answer.

"I'll help you get dressed," Bea said to Lilly Pearl. "You best not be late."

Joe stayed near the window looking out at the darkness approach. Apparently, he felt defeated and had no friends to confide in. Joe was a loner and often said that any man who depends on another for friendship is weak. Although, he did remain on friendly terms with the group that stole from the packing house where he worked. Each new shift would throw meat out of the windows to their buddies. Thus, Joe's family was well fed.

Bea pulled a small handkerchief from her bra when she and Lilly Pearl were in the room alone. She placed it in Lilly Pearl's hand and whispered, "I was saving it to buy Joe a winter coat, but you deserve it more." Nervously, Lilly Pearl took the thirty-eight dollars and pushed it under the mattress. "Don't tell nobody I gave it to you," Bea said. They laughed and embraced. It was a joke on Joe. "I'm proud of you, Pearl," Bea whispered. "I knowed you could do it. Go all the way, honey. Deep down in my heart, I feel every step you's taking is a step for me too."

When her class marched in, Lilly Pearl's eyes surveyed the huge auditorium. *I wonder if Nancy got a seat up front?* she asked herself. *I hope she'll get a picture for Momma.* Suddenly, a blinding light caught her unexpectedly. *Oh, God, I wasn't ready!* she thought. *I'd better wear a smile the rest of the program, in case she shoots me again.*

Jacqueline and Invidia had found it difficult to keep the party a secret. Leslie Logan anxiously waited to toast them on their graduation. But, her most intense desire was to be near Lilly Pearl.

Logan's Lounge, like a middle class social center, was common ground for blacks and whites who fraternized every Friday night. It was Lilly Pearl and her friends' favorite bar. Being atypical of the community as a whole, it was frequented by doctors, lawyers, politicians, teachers, counselors, principals; people who owned businesses, and famous athletes. Late in the evening, popular classics would float softly from the juke-box while Polish women from southside Milwaukee huddled in dark corner-booths with black married men. And, during the football season, at nine o'clock sharp, Vince Lombardi's assistant would pass through to gather his boys for bedcheck.

The party at Logan's Lounge took place immediately after Lilly Pearl and her friends arrived. The mere idea of partying with Judge Nikolakopulos and other bigwigs had Lilly Pearl excited. She proudly thought of herself as a debutante who was gradually undergoing a social and intellectual metamorphosis. She had learned to correct her own grammatical errors and effectively articulate with a mild air of sophistication.

About one hour into the party, Leslie took Lilly Pearl's hand and led her to a round table by the jukebox. She pulled out a sturdy chair and held it. Lilly Pearl climbed onto the table. Leslie called for everybody's attention and introduced Lilly Pearl to the crowd. Jacqueline and Invidia felt a tinge of jealousy, but McCray whistled through his teeth and cheered like the other men. Kenny looked on with sad pride. They all sang *Happy Birthday* to her. "Let's drink to her graduation from high school tonight!" the judge called out. Sweet Nancy looked at him fondly as she sat with her hand on his knee. Lilly Pearl smiled with a strong sense of independence, knowing that tomorrow she would move into her own apartment. When the singing and toasting had ceased, Leslie helped Lilly Pearl off the table, held her close for a moment and kissed her on the mouth. The jovial crowd was too preoccupied to notice, but Invidia Malice and Jacqueline Hyde stared at Lilly Pearl with cold eyes. "You know," Invidia said, "I didn't come here to be ignored. I get so sick of the way everybody takes on over her. I should've gone to the Chatter Box Lounge with Leon. He was dying to be with me."

Invidia flaunted her hour-glass figure, her perfectly shaped legs, and her small narrow feet. But her black, ashy complexion, her broad flat nose, and her very thick, heavy lips were most unpopular within their particular peer group. Invidia often said, "Lilly Pearl thinks she's so special cause she's got thin lips and a pointed nose. There's nothing precious about that," she said. "It's a clear indication her mammy was a white man's slut."

"They act like she's the only graduate tonight," Jacqueline complained. "Just think, we're the reason she's here. She didn't know her ass from a hole in the ground two years ago."

McCray and Kenny were so happy for Lilly Pearl that they were blind to envy and jealousy. Invidia and Jacqueline insisted on leaving, but Kenny held strongly against it. "To hell with what you're saying," Kenny told them. "Pearl's my real good friend." But finally McCray gave in to the ladies' demands and agreed to take them home.

"Kenny, you're such an irresponsible shit-head," Jacqueline said, as they were leaving.

"Buenos noches, La Vaca," Kenny said to Jacqueline and blew a kiss her way.

What he had said sounded so romantic, she looked at him and smiled.

Jacqueline insisted on a night-cap after she and McCray had taken Invidia home. "I'm driving, you know," McCray told her. "It's slippery out here. I think we've had enough."

"So what if it's snowing? How many times do you graduate high school?" she asked. "Let's have a little one for the road, McCray."

"If you get drunk, I'm not carrying you. I hope you know that," he told her.

"I'm a lady. You won't have to. I never over indulge."

McCray looked especially appealing that night. Never before had he looked so inviting. His smooth full face dawned dimples when he smiled, and the tan clothing he wore accentuated his brown complexion. His shoulders were momentous, seemingly the proper place on which to rest her head. "What's that I smell?" Jacqueline asked. She sniffed at his neck.

"Old Spice," he told her. "Let's stop at that place up ahead."

"I can't stand that place. It's too low-class. You know I avoid joints where poor niggers hang out."

"Oh, excuse me, Miss Rich Lady. I forgot your exquisite taste."

"Cut it, McCray. You don't have to be rich to hate poor niggers. Everybody does."

"You really believe that, don't you, Jacqueline?"

"Can you truthfully say you don't?" she asked.

"I love everybody, my dear."

"Bull-shit! You're lying. Nobody loves everybody."

The snowflakes were mixed with sleet and made a tapping sound on the windshield. The streets were dangerously slippery in spots. The strong westerly wind sounded cold and angry as it rocked the car slightly from side to side. "We'll have a mess out here by morning," McCray said.

"Who cares? We don't have school."

"I care! I work nights. Remember?"

"There's a nice place in the next block, McCray!" Jacqueline pointed anxiously.

Two hours later she was saturated with alcohol. She clung to McCray's strong arm as they slipped and slid toward his car. "Please take me to bed," she begged him at her front door. "I'm too drunk to undress," she said with a slur. "But don't forget I'm a lady--pure as a virgin."

"Yes, of course you're a lady, Jacqueline. I'd better leave."

"No! Dammit, McCray, I said help me undress."

"You'll be angry tomorrow. Believe me."

"Aren't you my old school buddy--my friend?" she teased.

"Certainly, I am, my dear. But, your kids?"

"They're not coming down. They're asleep."

Slowly, McCray pulled his overcoat off, watching the stairs. He spread it on the floor and laid Jacqueline on it. She lay almost limp while he carefully undressed her. "You're such a gentleman, McCray. Please make love to me." She fumbled at his fly. "I need you tonight. We don't have to tell anyone."

His breathing became more intense and coarse. "Let me go, Jacqueline, you'll hate me tomorrow."

"No! No! You can't leave. If you're my friend, you'll help me. I need you inside me, please McCray."

He could feel the heat of her body as he undressed her. No longer could he think logically about morality and the children upstairs. More and more they became engrossed in hot passion. She put her arms and legs around his body, and he pressed firmly within her. As he rose and fell, she started to cry profusely, "This is a terrible sin, McCray. I am a virtuous woman," Jacqueline said. "Please forgive me and leave right now."

"But I don't understand. You said you wanted to."

"You took advantage of me," she said. "I'd never agree to unmarried sex."

His posture was lost because of her crying. And the event fell short of such promising glory. In the cold of the night, McCray left half-undressed. He cursed the day he had met Jacqueline. And as he walked to his car, he could still hear her crying, lying on the floor reciting Hail Marys.

She hated him for leaving her incomplete and hated herself for needing him.

After McCray had gone, Jacqueline stroked her body softly and touched her erected clitoris. Like many times before, the rapid manipulation of it brought her sexual excitement. As she neared her solo-climax, Jacqueline cried remorsefully.

At Logan's Lounge, Sweet Nancy told clean jokes while under the table, Nikolakopulos stroked her thighs. "Well, what's next in your life, young lady?" Nikolakopulos asked Lilly Pearl.

"Living on my own and going to college," Lilly Pearl answered proudly.

"When is all this taking place?" he asked.

"Moving tomorrow. Starting college on Monday," Lilly Pearl said.

"Need any help, let Uncle Niko know," the judge told her.

"None of your help, Niko," Sweet Nancy said with a roll of the eye. "You helped me. Remember?"

"Now what the hell is that suppose to mean?" He laughed at her defensively.

"She won't need your help, Niko." Sweet Nancy sipped her drink and pused his hand off her thigh. "You can ride home with me, Pearl," Sweet Nancy said. "Looks like your friends are gone."

How could they leave without a word? she wondered. Then Lilly Pearl stood and spoke above the noisy crowd. "Thanks everybody for coming to my party. Thank you, Leslie, for being so kind. I really had fun tonight."

- *6* -

Rude Awakening

Cockroaches, like countless dark spots moving about the room, made Lilly Pearl jumpy and unable to sleep. The cotton stuffed mattress that Bea had given her felt unyielding and lumpy on the hardwood floor. And the excitement of having her own apartment diminished as the first night ticked laggardly by.

Through the half-closed door, the kitchen light shone harshly across her face while little Jimmy Lee slept nestled beside her. He'd stir momentarily on each occasion that she'd brush a roach from their bed. But, never opening his eyes, he'd suck his thumb and fall asleep again.

Lilly Pearl had nodded and let down her guard when Jimmy Lee squirmed vigorously. It was a pregnant roach, heavy with eggs, that crawled across his ear. "Get off!" she said with a slap. "You damn bug! Get the hell outta here!" The child emitted a sleepy coarse cry. "Please hush, honey." She kissed his face affectionately. "I didn't mean to hurt my baby." Lilly Pearl squeezed him close until he felt secure again.

In an escape attempt, dragging the hard rectangular pouch, the crippled insect wobbled away. Splash! With her shoe, Lilly Pearl squashed the mother, sending the detached eggs spinning across the floor. Then she scooped the sac into her hand and carried it to the stove. "You won't be populating my house," she said angrily. And a surge of excitement stroked her breasts as she listened to the sizzling eggs. *I wonder if it's a sin to kill things like this?* she asked herself. *No. They don't have a soul. God never intended low life creatures to take over mankind.*

As she drifted helplessly to sleep, Lilly Pearl heard a mouse nearby. Determined, but quite fatigued, she vowed, *I'll kill them all tomorrow.*

The odorous brown liquid on her face awakened her. She shook her head trying to gain some sense of where she was and what was happening. Her child sat on the mattress beside her, looking up. "See, Mommy," he pointed at the paint splattered chandelier. "Rain, Mommy!"

"This smells like shit! What the hell. . .!" Lilly Pearl cleared her eyes and studied the ceiling. *It's dripping from around that light--coming from the attic apartment.* She sat there puzzled, trying to psych herself into going upstairs. *I've got to be strong--with no man. May as well get off on the right foot and face problems head-on.*

The leak had slowed to an occasional drip, but one corner of the mattress was soaked with a nauseous liquid. *Somebody's going to pay for this,* she thought. *I'll call the landlord. But that would take too long. I'll go myself.*

Lilly Pearl and her child had slept fully dressed. She washed her face, changed her blouse, and ascended the dim staircase. Jimmy Lee clung to her neck as he rested astride her hip. She tapped lightly. The door flung open, and before them stood Stag Wilson. Dressed only in boxer shorts, he puffed a short cigar and blew the smoke down on them. Stymied by his appearance, she thought, *He looks like a cyclopean mammoth.*

"Yeah," he said. What'd you want?"

"Uh, my name is Lilly Pearl Ealy." She cleared her throat nervously. "I-I just moved downstairs last night."

"So?"

"Uh, a few minutes ago some water came through my ceiling."

"What kinda water?" Stag asked.

"Well, uh. . . It smells like toilet water. Uh, water from your toilet stool."

"You mean it smelled like shit?"

"Yes. I guess you could say that."

Stag stepped back and called over his shoulder, "Hey, Bulah, that stool running over again?" He called a second time and got no answer. Tugging his filthy shorts from between his buttocks, Stag toddled to the bathroom door, reached in and flushed the stool. The thick brown contents of the bowl swirled slowly, rising higher and higher. He gazed down at it without expression as it spilled over. Then he returned to the door where Lilly Pearl stood. "Yeah. It was water offa shit."

"Could you please refrain from flushing until it's repaired?" Lilly Pearl asked.

"Could I re-what?"

"I was asking if you could stop flushing your stool until you fix it."

"I ain't fixing it. This ain't my house," Stag said. "Talk to the landlord. My family's gotta shit somewhere. I pays the rent to shit up here." Without giving her a chance to answer, he slammed the door.

One-eyed, fat bastard. I wish I was a man. I'd kick the gorilla's ass.

It was a crisp January morning in Milwaukee, much warmer than usual. The sun shone brightly through Lilly Pearl's front window. And the composit of sounds from outside aroused her curiosity. On a favorable day such as this, everyone came out to soak up the sun. Nice days in January were rare. But when the weather permitted, and the men were home from work, one could see how crowded the area really was. When Lilly Pearl looked out, the Saturday morning ritual had already begun. Old rusty pails of warm water set by each car. And from the pails, lazy white steam curled slowly upward, evaporating into the chilly air. Every man in the block who owned a car was washing it. The men used worn pieces of bed sheets, old bath towels, and torn-up undershirts. Young men with sunken red eyes and missing teeth, and old men with stooped shoulders, arthritic hands, and occasional missing fingers, treated their cars like prized thoroughbreds. Their shabby clothes smelled of rawhide, tainted meat, and stale blood from packing houses where they eeked out a living. They drank cheap whisky, beer, and wine, and dreamed of striking it rich at Arlington Park race track. Cigarettes hang from their lips while they told lies of sexual conquests that angered wives who eavesdropped through slightly raised windows. Benny Ransaw praised his huge penis and bragged of scoring ten women in one night. His sex-starved wife listened and ached because of his impotency.

The neighborhood kids stood begging their fathers for money to buy candy from Bond's grocery store, over on Center Street. A few teenage boys stood listening to dirty jokes and watching while the older men instructed them on how to drink whisky and how to handle women in bed. Some of the teenagers earned movie fare by running to Jones Tavern to replenish the whisky supply. And others earned money by hauling away the empty whisky bottles and beer cans that lined each side of the street.

The teenage girls worked inside much of the day, cooking, making beds, and doing the week's wash while most of the wives played bid-whist, drank cheap whisky, and gossiped.

Lilly Pearl felt trapped and helpless as she gazed out her window. She could see patches of sooty snow melting from the housetops, making puddles of mud in yards where children played. *So many people in one block. So many old Cadillacs and ragged kids.* She looked at her car and saw three young men sitting on the hood drinking wine. Suddenly Lilly Pearl hated the long white Cadillac that Sweet Nancy had so proudly given her. It was symbolic of a psychological bond, linking her to the particular mentality that pervaded her immediate environment. "Hey!" Lilly Pearl called down, "Would you please get off my car?" The three young men took a long casual swallow from the wine bottle and pretended not to hear. They emptied the bottle and smashed it on the sidewalk.

Feeling anger rise in her chest, Lilly Pearl stuck her head out the window and shouted loudly. "Would you please get the hell off my car?" *Stupid bastards.* All eyes turned her way, and the three looked up at her in a jeering manner.

"Is you talking to us, bitch?" Duley Jones called out. "We ain't hurtin this ragged mother-fucker," he said. "Who the hell is you?"

"I'm the owner of that car. And I want you off," Lilly Pearl told him.

"Maybe you ought'a bring your white nigger ass down here and make us git off," Duley said.

Enraged, Lilly Pearl slammed the window down. Her child looked at her with teary eyes. "You'll never grow up in this hell-hole, Jimmy Lee," she promised. "Mommy's gonna get us out of here as soon as I finish college." *Oh, God, can I wait that long? Now I understand why whites want to keep us in a corner to ourselves.*

Suddenly she hated being Black.

"Need any help, let Uncle Niko know," Judge Nikolakopulos had told her. *What could a Greek judge do in a Black ghetto?* she asked herself.

Lilly Pearl hated the oil stained streets, the cracked

sidewalks, the skimpy trees, bare yards, and the old deteriorated German shacks that dominated the area. She hated the harsh evidence of her impoverished existence. *Oh, God!* she prayed, *I don't want to hate my people. But I can't keep loving them if I have to live with them in hell.*

Lilly Pearl started to unpack and found that some of last night's roaches had taken shelter in the boxes. And the mouse that she had heard scratching last night had given birth in her clothes. The repulsive sight of the furless, trembling creatures made her vomit. Jimmy Lee looked up at her sympathetically. "You sick, Mommy?" he asked. Without answering him, she rushed to the bathroom and washed her face with cold water. Trying hard to regain her composure, she sat on the rust stained stool with her head resting against the face bowl. Suddenly, she was jolted by a crashing sound from outside. Lilly Pearl ran to the window, and on her hood was a large piece of lannon stone amid shattered glass from her windshield. From the downstairs hallway, there was a pounding that rattled the front door violently. Lilly Pearl rambled through a box and found a butcher knife. Then she crept down the stairs to see who was there.

"It's us, Pearl," Joe said. "Open the door."

Never before had Lilly Pearl been so happy to see Joe. She embraced Bea and Joe Junior. But she was cut short when Joe brushed past her and started up the stairs. *He's a cold asshole,* she thought . . .*afraid to show affection.*

"We came to help you unpack and put the bed up," Bea said. "How do you like having your own place?" she asked.

Lilly Pearl's eyes grew misty. "I'm not happy here at all," she said. "The rats. The roaches. The leaky stool. The evil people. . ."

"Remember, Pearl, you's on welfare. They don't give enough to live like decent people. Everyday of your life you's reminded how poor you is. But you's strong, Pearl. You's a college woman now. Think about that when you's feeling low."

"Who broke your windshield?" Joe asked when they got upstairs.

"Some teenager called Duley and his friends," Lilly Pearl told him.

"We'd better call the police," Joe said. Then he walked to a corner phone booth.

Two hours had passed when the squad car drove up and parked in the middle of the street. The people outside disappeared like the rats and roaches at daybreak.

The two policemen walked upon the porch and knocked with their nightsticks. "You got trouble, Miss?" one of the officers asked Lilly Pearl. She showed them what had happened.

"Where's your husband?" the other policeman wanted to know.

"I'm not married," she told him.

"Why are you living in this neighborhood? Didn't you know it was colored?" the first officer asked.

"Yes. I knew it was colored," she said. "I'm colored, too."

The two policemen turned red with embarrassment, then one of them took out a pad. "I'm Officer Fred

Porinsky and this is Officer Bill Flanders. What's your name, young lady?"

She told Porinsky her name. He wrote it down.

"Are you on welfare?" Porinsky asked.

Hesitantly, she answered, "Yes."

"How is it you own a Cadillac car?" Porinsky wanted to know.

"It's not really mine," Lilly Pearl explained. "It belongs to my friend, Nancy. She's letting me keep it for transportation to school."

"Get the title," Flanders told her. "We need to look at it."

There were coded folders at police headquarters on every Black who owned a Cadillac. So Flanders took the title to the patrol car and ran a check on it.

Lilly Pearl told Porinsky about the three boys who were on her car that morning. "Can you give me a description?" he asked as he chewed on his pen and gazed down the neck of her blouse. "Two were medium brown. And that Duley guy was light tan with processed hair and finger waves. He wore a hair net and a large medalion. I guess he's about six-four, and his friends were much shorter."

When Flanders had gotten the information from headquarters, he called his partner aside. "This car is owned by Judge Nikolakopulos' whore. He'll raise lots of hell if we mess with her. In fact, quite a few fat asses downtown will be pissed. Let's get the hell out of here."

"But we've got to check around. Suppose he learned we came out and didn't do anything? He probably bought this damn car."

Officers Flanders and Porinsky went from door to door.

Lilly Pearl watched form the porch as every head shook from side to side. "No. I ain't seen nothing."

"Let's get the hell out of here," Porinsky said. "We've done our job." They told Lilly Pearl to tell Sweet Nancy to contact her insurance company. "We'll keep an eye out for future problems," Porinsky said. "If you find out where Duley lives, give us a call. We want to talk to him."

Joe wanted to know why no one was arrested. "If you had been a white woman, somebody woulda went to jail. These damn crackers don't do nothin as long as it's niggers doing things to niggers. We need us some colored cops in this neighborhood. They is some tough, lowdown dirty assholes livin round here. And you ain't even got no phone to call for help."

"I can't have a phone in my name," Lilly Pearl said.

"Joe," Bea spoke in a pleading tone, "could she get a phone in your name?"

"Well," Joe was slow to answer. "Your papa did help us get outta Pearl City when I knocked the hell outta Ol Pickins. I reckon I could do that. But I ain't paying no phone bill." He seemed disinterested as Bea covered his face with kisses and praised him. Lilly Pearl jumped up and down with joy. "Oh, thank you, Joe! God bless you."

Bea helped Lilly Pearl to unpack boxes while Joe and Joe Junior put up her bed.

"What the hell is this stinky wet spot on your mattress?" Joe wanted to know.

"It's from the toilet upstairs," Lilly Pearl told him.

"You've gotta get the health department out here on Monday," Bea said. "That's a health hazard."

When they had finished with all but the box with the mice in it, Joe casually picked the tiny pink rodents up by their heads and flushed them down the stool.

Standing quietly near the door, indicating that he was ready to leave, Joe reached into his inside coat pocket and slowly withdrew a twenty-five automatic pistol. The room grew quiet as he spoke, holding the gun pointed toward the floor. "This here is my favorite little gun, Pearl. I decided you'll need it more than me. I drove through here last night, and from what I saw, you gonna need something to protect yourself, seeing as how you ain't got no man. I don't hold with no woman havin a gun cept when she ain't got no man to be protecting her. This here ain't no toy. So keep it outta Jimmy Lee's reach. And don't point it at nobody less you's intending to use it. It ain't for scaring folks. It's for keeping these bad ass niggers offa you and your son."

Joe's six-foot frame seemed taller than ever in Lilly Pearl's eyes. His huge nose and thick lips were beautiful as he stood there offering her protection. She carefully took the gun from his hand, looking at it as though it were her salvation. "Thank you, Joe," she whispered. *Oh, God, will I ever have to take a life with this,* she wondered.

Bea looked at her husband with admiration. Joe felt quite gallant as he walked towards the bed to get his hat. Suddenly the stifling brown liquid from Stag's upstairs toilet drained freely on his head.

- 7 -

Kenny's Last Ride

As he sat in the student cafeteria sipping a coffee, Kenny was filled with a deep anger and self-pity that was so all-consuming; it left no room for logical reasoning. He sat with slumped shoulders and a bruised, swollen face, vowing that he would kill his girlfriend, Tina. Then he'd take his own life. He knew not exactly how, or when, but it would be soon.

The cafeteria was crowded on the first day of the Spring semester, and Kenny had been teased all morning about his missing teeth and black eye. Tina never really loved him, but she tolerated his presence and lavish gifts.

When they arrived in the cafeteria, Jacqueline was her usual critical self, but Lilly Pearl and McCray struggled for the appropriate words to comfort Kenny and relieve his heavy-heartedness. "I know you're hurting mentally and physically, man," McCray told him, "But you shouldn't make plans while you're in this mood."

"I gave her all my money--treated her like a queen," Kenny said. "When I got home from work last night, my key didn't fit." He wiped the tears from his eyes on the back of his hands like a small child. Kenny had sat by the cottage door pleading to get in, but his patience grew frayed, and his passions flared when he heard a masculine voice inside. Crashing through the door, he met the granite fists of Big Seymour Sharp.

"Forget that bitch!" Jacqueline said in anger. "She's not worth killing. I never liked her anyway. She thinks her shit don't stink. I don't know what you see in her--she's not pretty. Take that damn make-up off, and that lousy wig, she'd look like Medusa." Lilly Pearl kicked Jacqueline under the table because of her insensitivity.

"That's a damn lie!" Kenny retorted. "Tina's a beautiful lady."

"Lady!" Jacqueline laughed scornfully. "She's a cheap whore--been whoring all her life. She had to get a hyster- ectomy by the time she was six." Kenny's scalp tingled with anger. Inflated veins rose in his temples and his heart was beating rapidly. With trembling fingers, he gripped his chest to avoid striking her.

"Kenny," Lilly Pearl stroked his arm sympathetically, "don't do anything while you're upset. There're lots of nice girls here on campus. Why don't you look around? Five years from now you'll laugh at this whole thing."

"I'm not interested in finding another woman. I can't imagine life without Tina. I'm ending it all. It hurts too much."

"But maybe God has someone who's better for you, Kenny. Taking your own life is the unforgivable sin."

"Sin?"

"Do you believe in God?" Lilly Pearl wanted to know.

"Not since Korea, I don't. I believe in me. That's all." Tears settled in his eyes again.

It was more than lost love that weighted heavily on Kenny's shoulders. He had failed to graduate from the Adult High School with his friends. Now they were taking college courses and he was repeating last semester's work. He usually passed most courses on the second try.

Kenny's friends all knew that sometimes his mind wouldn't click when he needed it the most. He had suffered shell shock in the war. And the excessive use of alcohol, when he was much younger, had left him with permanent brain damage. Kenny was a handsome fellow, tall and thick--a complexion like coffee with a touch of cream. But most times he was quite dull.

Moose Lowe, who took great pleasure in annoying Kenny, jolted him terribly with a rather hard slap on the back, after noticing his damaged face. "Hey, Ken! Looks like you've been in a hatchet fight," he said jokingly, "and everybody had one except you. Please don't tell me you ran into a door." He gave out with a hearty laugh. And before Kenny could respond, the fifth period bell rang. So, Moose swiftly departed, enjoying the psychological pain he had inflicted.

"Promise me, Kenny, you'll meet us here after sixth period," McCray pleaded. "We've got to talk this over before you do something tragic."

"But I can't," Kenny told him "I'm leaving for Madison right now. Mama's in critical condition."

McCray sensed that Kenny's tension was growing. He seemed to be reaching out for help--needing someone to talk him out of the destruction he'd planned.

"I'll ride there with you. Just be here," McCray ordered him. But he didn't promise to wait.

"We love you, Kenny," Lilly Pearl said, with a kiss on the forehead. "We'll see you later."

They had five minutes to reach their class. But before she left, Jacqueline reminded the heart-broken man that Tina was a no-good slut, not worth the worry.

At that same table, for the past two years, they had sat together during lunch. Sitting there alone, Kenny thought of the jokes they'd shared. The arguments between Jacqueline and McCray. The arrogance of Invidia. The naivety of Lilly Pearl when she first entered school: "What's a sixty-nine?" she had asked one day with loud, wide-eyed innocence. He chuckled to himself. "Shut-up, fool!" Jacqueline had whispered. "Someone might hear you." He remembered how embarrassed and repulsed Lilly Pearl had been when they explained what it was.

Kenny loved the uniqueness of the community college. One could advance from zero-level through an associate degree. It was a warm institution with supportive friends, like having one's own family. But soon Lilly Pearl, Jacqueline and McCray might be transferring to the University of Wisconsin.

Kenny knew that something was abnormal inside his head--something over which he had no control--something that snapped in Korea. But, more immediate than the scars of Korea, his ego was terribly bruised--more so than his face. His heart throbbed with pain and ached for Tina Marie.

By the end of the sixth period, Kenny had arrived at the University Hospital in Madison. When he stopped at the information desk for a visitor's pass, he was advised to see the nurse in ICU on the sixth floor. "I'm here to see Sarah Weatherspoon," he told the ICU nurse. "And who're you?" she wanted to know.

"Her son, Kenny," he said.

"I'm very sorry, Mr. Weatherspoon, your mother passed this afternoon at 2:10." He stared at her incredulously--a sudden sinking sensation in his stomach. "I'm here to see Sarah Weatherspoon," he repeated himself, as if she hadn't understood him at first. The nurse assured him, "Mrs. Weatherspoon passed away at 2:10 this afternoon, Sir. Your two sisters are expecting you. They're downstairs in the waiting room."

Kenny walked down the gloomy corridor towards the elevator, traumatized. There was no sound except for an occasional paging of a doctor. The elevator door rolled open with a soft screech; on the way down, he closed his eyes until it had stopped. In the lobby, the people he passed were blurs through his tears. He braced himself on his car as he opened the door and sat under the wheel, resting his head on it. The stiffling realization of his mother's death made it difficult to breathe. Trying to calm himself, he rolled down the window and fumbled in his coat pocket for a match to light a cigarette. His heart was aching, and waves of dizziness swept over him. He sat there fighting the pain. For a while, time had no meaning. Then slowly he became aware of the visitors passing his car staring at him. Fate, with its macabre sense of humor, had dealt him a traumatic hand.

In dazed fascination, the grieving young man watched the January sky explode into a spray of white confetti that instantly blanketed the area. The soft snow would soon turn the roads into sheets of slippery glass. He knew he must not stay there.

Headed for Highway 18, Kenny weaved his way out of the hospital parking lot. He looked over his shoulder at the cold imposing building, nestled on the lonely hill, over-looking Madison like a citadel of death.

Speeding towards Milwaukee, half blinded by tears, Kenny followed a long open-bed truck. The driver had noticed for quite a few miles how closely the little black Chevy had been trailing him--much too close for the road conditions. He turned on his signal long before reaching the Waukesha exit. But the distance between them grew shorter as Kenny's foot pressed harder on the accelerator. Staring into the darkness, between the blinking red lights on the rear of the truck, he became hypnotized. Within that dark frame, Kenny saw Tina Marie and his mother smiling and beckoning to him. He pressed his foot to the floor.

Lilly Pearl, Jacqueline, and McCray waited in the

student cafeteria past seventh period and finally concluded that Kenny had already left for Madison. "I'll catch him at work tonight," McCray said.

When Lilly Pearl arrived home, she apologized for being late. But Seallie was outraged. "I don't stay overtime," she warned her. "I ain't paid to stay til five," she slurred. "The ladies in the neighborhood said you ain't really going to school nohow. You's whoring all day-- dressing-up every morning, carrying them books to fool folks."

"I was at school today," Lilly Pearl said defensively. "But we were trying to help a friend who's headed for trouble."

"It ain't my problem," the baby sitter retorted with insensitivity. "I gets paid extra for stayin late. You wait til your caseworker hears about this."

The damn funky, fat bitch, Lilly Pearl thought. *All she did today was sit on her lumpy ass looking at soap operas and stinking-up my couch. She didn't even bathe Jimmy Lee and change his clothes.* "I'll pay you for the overtime when I get my welfare check. Okay?" Lillie Pearl promised Seallie. "But I want my child bathed and changed every- day. I laid his clothes out before I left this morning."

"He don't need changing everday," she spoke with indignation. "Who the hell you think he is? He ain't no white boy living in Whitefish Bay. I don't care how yellow he is, he still ain't white. And you best treat him like the nigger he is. He ain't none better than the other kids round here. I ain't your maid, Miss Lady. You an your high an mighty ideas don't move me."

Anger began to rise in Lilly Pearl. *Filthy Bitch!* "I'll bathe and change him myself," she told the sitter.

When Seallie got up to leave, Lilly Pearl noticed how she staggered towards the door. The sickening smell of her body and cheap whisky made Lilly Pearl fear for Jimmy Lee's safety.

The coroner had completed his examination. They had covered his body with a dark green canvas. "Kenny Weatherspoon's death," the reporter wrote, "was caused by decapitation when his car skidded underneath the bed of a truck, after it had slowed to make the Waukesha exit."

Kenny's two sisters, who were on their way back to Milwaukee from Madison, screamed hysterically when they identified their brother's detached head.

The aura of death surrounded the little weatherbeaten cottage that Kenny and Tina had shared. The bed on which they had made love many times now reeked of Seymour and Tina's sweat. Seymour, angered by her decision to remain with Kenny, cautioned her, "You won't be playin me for no fool, you whorish bitch! I ain't no damn retarded asshole like that supid mother-fucking Kenny!"

"But you've been spending his money, darling," Tina reminded him. "I give you everything he hands me," she said. "Who's gonna pay the rent if he moves out? You ain't got no job."

He looked at her with flared nostrils. "What about the bucks you make on your back?" he asked.

"It ain't enough," she tried to reason with him. "Remember how you love to gamble? Sweet Daddy, you've lost what I gave you last night."

"Then, bitch, that means you gotta sell more pussy," he told her.

Tina feared Seymour. He was an egotist and a sadist who had killed his wife two years earlier--charged only with manslaughter. After serving eighteen months in Waupon, the leniency of the parole board sent him home to sponge off his mother, who also feared him.

Seymour Sharp had a shaved head and a brown bulldog face. But his physique compensated for nature's cruel joke. In his bare feet he stood six-foot-six, with the chest and shoulders of a Green Bay Packer. "I ain't puttin Kenny out," Tina said with shaky bravery. "Please try to see things my way, Seymour."

Without another word, Seymour's fists crashed into her face repeatedly. The blows were totally unexpected, and the impact sent her crashing against the T.V., knocking it off the stand as she fell to the floor. She tried to get up, but when she was halfway off the floor, Seymour kicked her in the stomach with the tip of his boot. Tina fell writhing to the floor in agony. "You don't fuck over Big Seymour," he said.

Tina looked up through the blinding waves of pain at the giant monster that towered over her. She rose half-up and tried to speak, but his fist crashed into her mouth. Again, she was on the floor with four missing teeth. She whimpered like a tiny pup and trembled uncontrollably as he kicked her in the right temple.

Through a red blur, Seymour was barely discernible. Tina could hear his voice coming from some distant place through a muffled filter, fading in and out. Then she felt something sharp smash into her ribs, sending exquisite pain through every fiber of her being. She was not seeing reality clearly now. She felt another blow to her face and then slipped into unconsciousness. Seymour lifted her limp body and placed her on the bed. And, as he stood over her with the machete raised high, some remote part of Tina's mind watched with detached interest. The shimmering curved blade caressed her volupuous throat. At that moment, for Tina, all of the worry, the pain, and the frustration that had plagued her life became insignificant.

- *8* -

The Weeping Lady in Fine Array

Lilly Pearl was feeding Jimmy Lee and listening to the Channel 6 news when she heard of Kenny's death. She ran into the living room, and on the screen before her was a picture of Kenny in Army fatigues, wearing a wide familiar grin that showed his broken tooth. She stood frozen, in shock and disbelief. *Jesus Christ, he did it!* she thought. *He's gone, just like that! I never imagined he'd do it today.* Lilly Pearl rushed to the phone and tried to reach Jacqueline, and McCray; she got no answer. McCray was at Kenny's job looking for him.

The strength drained from Lilly Pearl's body. She crumbled to the floor. "Why didn't you wait, Kenny?" She pounded her fist on the floor. "You didn't have to die today."

For the first time, death had invaded Lilly Pearl's little world. A melancholy gloom hovered over her like a stubborn gray cloud. Suddenly she was affected by feelings of fear, insecurity, and uncertainty. And, as she sat there embracing her child, salty tears wet her face. Lilly Pearl considered her own life and how quickly it could end. She cried for Kenny. She cried for herself.

Early the following morning, Lilly Pearl, Jacqueline, and McCray met in the student cafeteria to discuss Kenny's death. "I don't believe it was an accident," McCray said. "My intuition told me to skip class and stay with him. But I thought he'd wait. It's my fault he's dead. He shouldn't have been alone."

"But, McCray. . ." Lilly Pearl said, "you couldn't have known he'd kill himself in a few hours. He planned to kill Tina first. Remember?"

"I wonder if that bitch knows he's dead?" Jacqueline interrupted. "We'll see that little whore fall off her pedestal now."

"Quiet!" Lilly Pearl whispered. Doctor Bill Washbourn was approaching their table. "I wanted to tell you how sorry I am about your friend's accident," he said. "Weatherspoon was a rather nice fellow."

"Thank you," they said. "Would you like to sit, Doctor Washbourn?" McCray stood.

"No. Keep your seat. I only have a moment. But I also

wanted to congratulate you three on the excellent work you've done over the past two years--making the honor roll every semester. It's quite gratifying to see young people so academically inclined. This is an exceptional institution, but you're limited here. In my opinion, you should be at the University. The ultimate here is only an associate degree."

"But we don't have the financial means," McCray said with an embarrassed expression.

"Being poor," Doctor Washbourn explained, "is the superlative qualification for acquiring student financial aid."

They were intrigued by his suggestion. Transferring to the University of Wisconsin-Milwaukee the following fall would be most prestigious. They'd be able to by-pass the associate and go for the baccalaureate degree.

Since the tragedy had taken their friend, they were psychologically ready to leave the community college. It would be a constant reminder of Kenny.

"Suppose a person is on welfare, Doctor Washbourn?" Lilly Pearl asked. Jacqueline listened attentively.

"This money," he said, "is designated for educational purposes only. I tell you, young ladies, you'd be so much more attractive with a formal education. And you, Mc-Cray," Doctor Washbourn said, "must consider how desperately a colored man needs a college education, if he is to become a productive member of society, especially in Milwaukee. These Germans might never love us, but they do respect an industrious colored person who rises above the stereotypes. With marketable skills, you'll have a bargaining advantage."

Doctor Washbourn had started to perspire and seemed

stirred by his own lecture. "Stop by my office tomorrow," he said, as he walked toward the faculty lounge.

They were headed for sociology class when Lilly Pearl suggested meeting at Leslie Logan's Lounge later that evening. "She's raising money for the funerals."

"Funerals?" Jacuqeline and McCray spoke simultaneously.

"I thought you knew. His mother died just before Kenny reached Madison," she told them. "They're having a double funeral."

"Well," Jacqueline said with a shrug, "like they always say, tragedy strikes in threes. I wonder what's next?"

"Has anyone heard from Tina?" McCray asked. "Does she know?"

"Bette and Estelle probably called her last night," Lilly Pearl surmised.

"I doubt it," Jacqueline said. "His sisters hate the ground Tina walks on. They blamed her for most of Kenny's problems. And I agree. She was his problem."

"Not really," McCray said. "Kenny had a multitude of problems. She was just one of them. But she could've made him feel more like a man."

Jacqueline looked at McCray with a roll of the eye. "Well, let's say she was a major difficulty in his life. He had adjusted to the rest."

"We'll meet at 6:30. Okay?" McCray looked at his watch. "I'll stop by Tina's on the way."

Seallie was pleased that Lilly Pearl had arrived home on time. She was also besotted beyond the ability to walk downstairs alone. Jimmy Lee was asleep on the floor, curled in a fetal position. His thumb was in his mouth and dried tears streaked his face. *I've got to get rid of her,* Lilly Pearl thought. *She can't take care of my baby drunk all day.*

Trying to help Seallie down the steep staircase proved to be an awesome task. Her five-two, barrel-sized body weaved back and forth on vein-streaked, stem-like legs. She bounced first against the wall and then off Lilly Pearl. "I can walk by myself," Seallie slurred. "I don't need your help--little yellow bitch. I ain't drunk."

I should turn this old bag loose, Lilly Pearl said to herself. *I should let her funky ass roll down these stairs.* "You can't make it by yourself, Seallie. And don't be calling me a bitch. If I were, I'd go back upstairs right now."

It was 4:45. There wouldn't be adequate time for Seallie to sober up. So, Lilly Pearl fed her child, bathed and dressed him, praying that Joe would allow Bea to keep him.

After Lilly Pearl had taken her child to Bea, she stopped at Bond's Grocery Store to cash in a case of soda bottles. For Kenny's funeral, she'd give all that she could raise.

It was dark when McCray stopped to see Tina. He rang the bell several times and finally noticed the door was slightly ajar. He tapped lightly and called to her; then he slid his hand along the wall and found the light switch. A sudden overpowering fright possessed him. Some distant, remote part of his mind was trying to conceptualize the horrific sight before his eyes. The only reality he perceived was panic. Tina's head was on the bloody bed between her thighs. Her dead eyes stared at him. The hammering deep inside his chest and the painful wrenching inside his bowels sent him tumbling backwards down the steep wooden steps, tearing his shirt and cutting his face as he fell. He ran for blocks, leaving his car behind, until finally, the sobering, wracking pain in his body flooded his memory with the total recollection of what he had seen. Nearby, he found a phone and called the police. When he returned to the scene, they were there. He identified himself--standing on the porch, a torn shirt, drenched in sweat, and bleeding from the face. Gradually he became conscious of the perspiration sting in the long shallow cut on his cheek. He touched it and was surprised to see blood on his hand. Lt. Frank Polubinsky, the older detective, was looking at his face. McCray wondered what he was thinking. The lieutenant automatically filed it away as an interesting piece of evidence. "You're the one who called?" he asked, noticing how uptight McCray appeared to be. Polubinsky pulled out a worn, cracked, leather wallet with an aged badge pinned onto it. "Lt. Frank Polubinsky, Fifth Precinct." He indicated his partner. "Detective Bob Schade. We're from the Homicide Division. May I see some identification?" McCray fumbled in his back pocket and presented his wallet. "Take your license out." Polubinsky studied the driver's license. "Richard," he asked, "is that your car there?" McCray shook his head, "Yes."

　　"Where were you coming from, walking?" Polubinsky wanted to know.

"The phone booth," McCray told him.

"Why didn't you call from the house phone?" Schade asked.

"I-I didn't think. I had to get away. I mean, I couldn't stay in there with her messed-up like that."

"You'll have to come downtown with us, Richard. We want to ask you a few questions," Lt. Polubinsky informed him.

McCray looked at the two officers, puzzled. He knew whatever they might think, he hadn't done anything wrong. So when they handcuffed him, McCray was completely acquiescent. Tears streamed down his face as they led him to the squad car. He knew that Kenny was incapable of committing such a brutal act.

McCray watched from the back seat of the squad car while Polubinsky and Schade talked with the coroner who had just arrived. When they finished their conversation, the coroner pushed his way through the onlookers and policemen who moved busily about the little weather-beaten cottage. McCray looked at his watch. It was 6:10. At that moment, McCray wished he had let someone else discover her body.

Downtown, he was taken to a very small stuffy room where Lt. Polubinsky removed the cuffs and offered him a cigarette. Schade left the room and returned with three black coffees.

"Richard, what the hell did you use on Tina?" Polubinsky asked McCray. It took a few seconds for his words to sink in. Then the muscles in McCray's body began twitching involuntarily. "Are you trying to say I did it?" McCray shouted in disbelief. He felt perspiration begin to bead on his forehead and spread under the armpit of his torn shirt. Polubinsky's eyes darted up and down, from McCray's face to his shirt. McCray became aware of how guilty he must appear to be. It was the strangest feeling he'd ever experienced.

"I didn't use anything. I didn't do it! Call my lawyer."

Polubinsky and Schade grinned. "If you're innocent," Schade said, "you don't need a mouthpiece."

"Tell me, Richard," Polubinsky demanded to know, "why does an innocent man flee the scene of a crime?"

"Flee? I don't like the way you put that," McCray said. "You're making it sound like I killed her and took off. It didn't happen like that."

"Okay, Richard," Polubinsky said, in a phony compromising tone. "Why don't you explain the torn shirt and bloody face. While you're at it, explain to me and my buddy why you flew like a bat outta hell when it happened."

"I wasn't there when it happened," McCray spoke defensively. "I've told you, it's quite simple. I panicked. I've never seen anything so catastrophic before. I completely lost my head."

"Catastropic? Ha!" Polubinsky raised his brow. "Such a man-sized word, Richard. Do you often lose your head when you're excited or angry?" McCray looked at them a moment. "You're denying me the rights to call my lawyer."

Polubinsky and Schade looked at each other and took a sip of coffee. They continued to interrogate McCray for three hours, leaping from one subject to another, exploring, taking his answers out of context, trying to catch him in a lie. When he thought they had finished, they'd switch to another subject.

"Where did you say you work?" Polubinsky asked for the sixth time.

"Pabst Brewery, third shift, janitor," McCray answered in a tired voice.

"So what do you do all day, pimp around?" Schade asked with a chuckle.

"I've told you several times, I'm a fulltime student at Milwaukee Institute of Technology."

"You were there yesterday and today?" Polubinsky asked.

"Yes. From third period through sixth--from 9:45 a.m. to 2:45 p.m. weekly--Monday through Friday," McCray repeated angrily.

"Were you there yesterday the whole day?" Polubinsky asked, repeating himself again. "Seems like she's been dead for hours and out of curiosity you returned to the scene, like murderers often do."

"Murderer?" McCray's nostrils flared. "I was in school all yesterday and today. Check attendance."

"What are you taking, auto mechanics?" Schade asked presumptuously.

"No. I'm in the associate degree program."

"You're not happy being a janitor, huh?" Schade asked. McCray refused an answer.

Someone tapped at the door. Polubinsky and Schade stepped out and talked for a brief moment. McCray drank the cold coffee that Schade had given him earlier. Then they returned.

"Where were you yesterday between 1:00 and 2:30?" Polubinsky asked as he lit another cigarette.

"I was in my fifth period class."

"Can you prove it?" Schade challenged him.

"My instructors," McCray answered. "They take attendance every day."

Polubinsky and Schade knew they'd have to charge McCray or release him. They had denied him the phone call he'd constantly demanded. Morris, the rookie at the door, had informed them that, according to the coroner's report, Tina had been murdered between 1:00 and 2:30 yesterday. But they vied for the necessary time to verify McCray's alibi.

It was like a wake. Leslie Logan's Lounge overflowed with inquisitive people from the black community, most of whom gave generously to pay for the funerals. As the crowd filled the bar, Runny knew exactly what drinks to mix for those individuals who had faithfully frequented the lounge. Lilly Pearl and Jacqueline had rushed for their favorite seats at the oval end of the long mahogany bar, where everything and everybody could be seen. Runny had given them a bottle of Schlitz beer, which they'd nursed for two hours, until Leslie had given them another one on the house. She often gave drinks to students, knowing they'd remain loyal once they were employed. And beautiful women at the bar always attracted men who had money. Leslie was an intelligent businesswoman, well respected in the black and white community.

After two hours had passed, Lilly Pearl and Jacqueline wondered why McCray hadn't arrived, nor had he called. It wasn't like McCray to be so late.

As each customer drank, Runny quickly refilled their

glasses. He was a whiz behind the bar, friendly and a show-off. He'd flip a bottle in the air, catch it behind his back and pour a perfect shot. He'd dip his finger into a shot of Hennessy, strike a match to it and light a lady's cigarette, while pouring a drink with his left hand. Runny was a handsome young man with a collegiate look. The ladies loved him almost as much as they did Leslie. He was an excellent drawing card.

The booze was flowing and everyone there had intellectualized the how and why of Kenny's accident. Lilly Pearl and Jacqueline never believed it was an inadvertent accident.

Leslie, like an exalted amazon, strolled through the bar carrying a large serving tray spread with money and personal checks. She counted the small change that Lilly Pearl and Jacqueline had dropped into the tray. After a while, she touched Lilly Pearl in the side and slid a fifty dollar bill into her purse when she felt no one would notice. "Buy yourself a nice dress for the funeral, Pearl," she whispered in her ear. Then she stroked her thigh with a gentle touch. Lilly Pearl looked at her, surprised, not knowing what to say or how to react. She quietly went to the ladies' room to see what Leslie had put into her purse. Leslie followed her. "You're going to the funeral, aren't you?" she asked. Lilly Pearl shook her head, "Yes. But I can't accept this. Leslie, I really appreciate your. . .your kindness. I couldn't repay you. I mean, not all at once."

"Don't worry your pretty head," Leslie stroked her hair with the back of her hand. "Who's asking for pay?" She kissed her on the lips. "Just take it and keep your mouth shut."

"But, I. . ." Leslie pulled her face to hers, licked her lips with her wet quivering tongue, and quickly returned to the bar.

Lilly Pearl stood frozen, confounded by Leslie's behavior. She wet toilet tissue with cold water and pressed it to her face. For the rest of the evening, Lilly Pearl avoided Leslie's burning eyes, feeling guilty, as if everyone knew what had transpired in the ladies' room. She felt extremely disconcerted and unable to tell Jacqueline.

Lilly Pearl noticed the time. She'd have to leave soon. Suddenly Jackqueline nudged her. "Look who's coming in the door," she said. "That asshole finally made it. And he's the big man who said we'd meet at 6:30."

McCray stopped at the table where Bette, Estelle, and Leslie were counting the contributions. He dropped twenty dollars on the tray and apologized for being late.

"What the hell happened to your face?" Leslie asked.

"I'll tell you about it later." McCray walked towards Lilly Pearl and Jacqueline. They eyed him with curiosity.

"Well, Mr. Big Stuff," Jacqueline said," you finally made it after keeping us waiting over four hours." She took a closer look at him. "What the shit's wrong with you? Your face an shirt--what happened?" Before he could answer, Lilly Pearl stood up. "Sit down, McCray. You look like you could stand a stiff drink. Were you in an accident?" she asked.

He took her seat, lit a cigarette, and ordered a double Jack Daniels. "I guess you could call it a crazy kind of accident, or an unfortunate coincidence."

McCray quietly explained the situation that had caused his injury and detained him. Lilly Pearl trembled uncontrollably and started to cry.

"Go to the toilet and calm yourself, girl," Jacqueline said. "It's just a simple case of poetic justice, in my opinion. The bitch got exactly what she deserved. Kenny said he'd kill the slut."

"But he couldn't have," McCray told her. "Kenny was on his way to Madison when she was murdered. It couldn't have been Kenny."

"Well, it must've been that guy Seymour, or one of her other tricks. All I got to say is good riddance."

McCray gulped down the double shot and looked at Jacqueline with wet eyes, remembering the night they'd almost made love. "Woman, you're so cold," he told her. "Go check on Lilly Pearl."

Leslie, Bette, and Estelle had finished counting the contents of the tray. Leslie gave the twelve-hundred dollars and sixty-five cents to Kenny's sisters, in a large Manilla envelope. They were leaving when Lilly Pearl and Jacqueline came out of the ladies' room. Lilly Pearl ran after them. When they were outside, she gave them a folded fifty follar bill. "This man came in the side door," she said. "He asked me to run this out to you."

"What man?" they wanted to know.

"Uh, a stranger. I never saw him before," she muddled the lie. "He-he handed it to me and left. . ."

At eight Wednesday morning, Lilly Pearl, Jacqueline, and McCray were waiting at Doctor Washbourn's office to apply for student financial aid and pick up a University of Wisconsin admissions applications. He never smiled, but he was quite pleased to see them. "This is probably the most intelligent decision of your lives," Doctor Washbourn told them.

"Do you think we can compete there?" McCray asked.

"Do you think you can't?" he answered.

Doctor Bill Washbourn was the only black counselor at the junior college. He wore a charcoal-gray, Persian lamb, small brimmed hat with a small pheasant feather tucked in the band. It gave his square ebony face an elongated appearance. Doctor Washbourn spoke with a heavy Bostonian accent that was sometimes incomprehensible because of the large, unlit pipe he habitually gripped between his teeth. He walked the hallways alone. He ate alone and spent much of the day in his office alone. At a time when integration had become a major political issue, he had been hired to integrate the certificated staff. And, although he had been hired to integrate, Doctor Washbourn was generally excluded from all intimate gatherings among faculty and staff.

I've got to look nice at Kenny's funeral tomorrow, Lilly Pearl thought. *I'll ask Sweet Nancy to lend me something to wear. I guess it should be something in black, or anything in a dark color.*

"No! No! Not black," Sweet Nancy told Lilly Pearl when she asked for advice. "That's for old folks. I've got the perfect outfit for you, Pearl." Sweet Nancy looked through her closet and chose a very conservative winter-white, tailored suit. She took a one-string pearl necklace from her jewelry case and scrambled until she found the matching diamond and pearl earrings. Lilly Pearl's eyes grew wide with excitement when she unzipped a heavy brown bag and pulled out an autumn haze mink stole. And from a shelf that was stacked with shoe boxes, Sweet Nancy handed her a pair of brown suede pumps; then she walked to a tall chest of drawers and found the matching purse. "Now you're ready for your friend's funeral. You'll be the finest lady there. I promise."

Lilly Pearl was breathless, trying to imagine herself in such fine array. "I'm scared to take these expensive things home tonight, Nancy. I'll dress here tomorrow. Okay?"

"Bring Jimmy Lee," Sweet Nancy told her. "I'd love to keep him. And guess what else I'm gonna do?"

"You've been so nice, Nancy. I can't imagine anything more."

"I'm gonna let you drive my new Cadillac."

Lilly Pearl embraced Sweet Nancy and kissed her face. Then suddenly she withdrew, remembering what Leslie had done. "How well do you know Leslie Logan, Nancy?"

"Well, I've heard she likes women. Has she been bothering you?"

"Not really. It's not worth talking about."

Sweet Nancy looked at Lilly Pearl with a smile of satisfaction and adoration while Lilly Pearl giggled and buried her face in the mink fur. "Oh, I almost forgot!" Sweet Nancy walked to the closet again, pulled out a hatbox and placed a white, wide-brimmed felt hat on Lilly Pearl's head. It had a mink band that matched the stole. "Look at me. Let's see how you look in it." Lilly Pearl put her hands on her hips and modeled for Sweet Nancy. "We'll do something with your hair tomorrow," she told her. "Oh, one more thing," she gave Lilly Pearl a pair of white, kidskin gloves. "Now, you'll be the bell of the ball!" Suddenly, Sweet Nancy remembered the occasion. "I'm very sorry, Pearl."

"Oh, that's okay, Nancy. I know you want what's good for me. You're my very best friend in the whole wide world. I wish we were kin."

"We are, Pearl. Let's just pretend you're my pretty little sister who's a smart college lady. I'd blow up the universe for you."

Two bronze caskets were placed end to end, across the front of Holy Temple Baptist Church, immediately in front of the first row of seats. On each casket was a large spray made of red and white carnations. And large elaborate arrangements of flowers and wreaths on wire stands were strategically placed on the floor, extending the full width of the church. A large burgundy velvet rope reserved four rows of seats up front for relatives. But Bette and Estelle ordered the ushers to escort Lilly Pearl, Jacqueline, Invidia, McCray, and Leslie up front. They felt honored.

Leslie stared angrily at Lilly Pearl with a sneaky side glance. She knew that the fifty dollar gift she'd given Lilly Pearl would hardly buy the gloves she wore.

"Will they open his casket?" McCray whispered in Estelle's ear. "Yes. You'd be surprised at the excellent job they did on him. He looks great."

Nearer My God to Thee was playing softly on the organ while the church filled beyond capacity. People stood in the vestibule, on the front steps, and spilled into the church yard. The ushers placed metal folding chairs in the aisles, but it made no significant difference in the number of people left standing. *Kenny never had lots of friends,* Lilly Pearl thought. *His death brought him more attention than life ever did. I guess certain things do bring us together,* Lilly Pearl concluded, *even if it's death. I do love my people.*

Lilly Pearl felt extremely nervous. She had never attended a funeral before. As she sat there listening to Reverend Quigley eulogizing Kenny and his mother, it was still inconceivable that her friend was really dead. *How ironic it is, he followed his mother and Tina in death,* she thought, *the two women he loved the most. His mother died of heart failure and he of a broken heart. Kenny lost his head over Tina; she lost her head too.* Tears rolled freely down her face as she tried to accept the reality of her friend's death and the permanent nature of it all. *We just die,* she thought. *They put us in a fancy box decorated with pretty flowers, packaged like some precious gift. They sing, talk, and look us over with inquisitive wet eyes, then discard us like refuge in the ground. And the beat goes on.*

When Reverend Quigley had finished, the organist played *Precious Lord,* in a solemn, mournful tone. Two funeral home attendants wearing navy blue suits and white gloves opened the caskets, with care and dignity. Kenny's sisters' soft weeping evolved into hysterical screams. First, the standing congregation was ushered past the caskets for final viewing. Relatives were last to see the bodies. Lilly Pearl stood staring down at Kenny. "Goodby my dear friend." She touched his hand. It was damp and cold. But he appeared to be smiling. "I hope you're happy now," she said. *Maybe he's smiling because he's got Tina all to himself.*

Jacqueline nudged Lilly Pearl. "Go back to your seat,

girl." Then Jacqueline looked at Kenny sympathetically and moved quickly past the coffin. Invidia held McCray's arm as they wept, saying farewell. She pulled McCray away when he placed his trembling hands on Kenny's broad chest. "I'm gonna miss you, man," he sobbed. "Please forgive me for not being there when you needed me. Kenny, please forgive me."

The ushers cleared the aisles and doors. The two men closed the caskets and beckoned for the twelve pall-bearers. Bette and Estelle's hysteria had become contagious. Everyone stopped and stood in place until the caskets were down the church steps. The four male ushers literally carried Bette and Estelle to the waiting white Cadillac limousine parked behind the second hearse.

The church was cleared. Lilly Pearl stood just outside the door. "You're looking quite elegant, my dear," someone whispered close behind her. "I guess I underestimated your wardrobe. Next time I'll know better." She recognized Leslie's voice, but she didn't respond.

"Are you going to the cemetary, Pearl?" Jacqueline called from the church yard.

"I can't. I couldn't stand to see him put in the ground. Did Kenny seem to be smiling, Jacqueline?"

"Well, it sort'a looked like a smile," Jacqueline said. "I tell you, if he were, he's glad to be rid of Jezebel and all the crap life threw him. Life treated him like Tina--a whoring bitch that had him by the balls. The more he squirmed, the tighter the squeeze. You gotta be strong, or just don't give a damn. He couldn't handle it, kid. Kenny wasn't strong and he cared too much."

As the funeral procession moved slowly away, Lilly

Pearl stood alone on the steps of the church thinking: *Oh, God, what is death? When life seeps from our body, is that the end of our total being? Is Kenny in some other dimension, seeing everything we've done today? I refuse to believe he just doesn't exist anymore. I can still hear his voice. I see his face and feel his presence. I can smell him.*

- *9* -

Staying Alive

The vigorous, cold wind off Lake Michigan swept a continuous flurry of tiny dry snowflakes across the University campus. Lilly Pearl leaned into the force of the wind with her books pressed close to her chest, in an attempt to block its fury. The thick, fur-lined mittens she wore made it difficult to adjust her long woolen scarf. Tears whipped from her eyes and crystalized on her cheeks like little round diamonds. And each time she'd breathe, the steam from her lungs frosted in her nose.

This is the coldest place in Milwaukee, she thought. *A*

person could freeze to death from the library to Mitchell Hall.

"Chills you to the bones. Doesn't it?"

The deep magnetic voice behind her made Lilly Pearl's heart flutter. She looked over her shoulder and there he was. *Ricardo!* she thought. Ricardo Lewis wore a broad friendly smile that embarrassed her momentarily, rendering her speechless.

Ricardo's face was a beautiful tan, with a perfectly sculptured profile and dark-brown eyes. His coarse black hair lay in deep waves that turned up into duck-like curls. He was tall, athletic and walked with the strength and grace of a huge lion. *If there's a kernel of truth in Greek legend, I'd bet my welfare check he's the reincarnation of Hercules,* she thought.

Lilly Pearl was both fascinated and captivated by Ricardo's quintessence and his affable manner. She could feel the burning power of his personality when he was near. It came in waves that penetrated her body like the balmy breeze of a tropic island. He had a classic Roman face that was the result of a mulatto mother and a Mexican father.

Becky Lewis and Jesus Morales were never married, but Jesus' chauvinistic influence was deeply intrenched within his son's mana.

"Are you ready for mid-term exams?" he asked.

"About as ready as I'll ever be," she said.

"Professor Fuchs lives and breathes *The Dynamics of Human Behavior.* And he thinks everybody else does. I really hate his class," Ricardo said, "but love being captured with you for fifty-five minutes."

She blushed. "The class is okay, but I hate the long walk to Mitchell Hall."

During the two years that Lilly Pearl had been at the University, she'd seldom dated. The traumatic experience with Trodder, early in her life, had planted a repulsion toward sexual intimacy until she'd met Ricardo. He'd stalked her cautiously and had studied her. The streetwise man sensed her fears.

As a second semester junior, Lilly Pearl had proven to be quite an asset to the thirty-three year old freshman. Ricardo was a handsome man, but a genius he was not. However, he was deceitfully clever. He'd sit near Lilly Pearl, who was so much in love, she'd make it easy for him to copy.

When Lilly Pearl entered the University, she had been forced to tell Seallie's caseworker why she had put Jimmy Lee in daycare, rather than leave him with Seallie. The welfare department had issued Seallie an ultimatum--enter DePaul, or no more general relief. Consequently, Lilly Pearl felt guilty and obligated to look after Seallie's needs. Since Seallie couldn't get alcohol, she needed plenty of Fig Newtons.

Every Wednesday and Sunday evening Lilly Pearl and Bea visited Seallie at DePaul Rehabilitation Hospital. This was the twelfth time in two years she had unwillingly committed herself, in order to qualify for welfare assistance.

After the nurse had issued a pass, Lilly Pearl and Bea walked down the long corridor to Seallie's room. Seallie snatched the two bags of Fig Newtons that Lilly Pearl had brought her and devoured one bag quickly, as if they'd been her first meal in days. With her mouth crammed, she persistently begged Lilly Pearl to bring her a drink on Sunday. "Everybody out here gets booze from the outside," she said. "Yesterday I seen this girl bring her boyfriend a half pint hidden in her bosom. But her old man don't share nothin."

"Seallie," Bea tried to reason with her, "you know we can't bring whisky in here. They search our purses and packages at the front desk."

"That damn nurse don't trust nobody," Seallie said, as she slammed the second pack of cookies to the floor. "She took my mouthwash, too. Everytime I brush, I gotta go to that damn bitch to gargle. She thinks I'll drink the shit! Would you believe the huzzy pours me one cap and watch me like a damn hawk til I finish gargling and spit it out?"

"Seallie, it's for your own good," Lilly Pearl told her. "They don't want you to have anything with alcohol in it." Lilly Pearl picked up the Fig Newtons. "I thought you'd be happy I brought two packs."

"You doing good at that University, Pearl?" Seallie asked.

"Just fine. I'm passing all my mid-term exams."

"How's my boy?" Seallie wanted to know.

"Jimmy Lee? He asks about you a lot, Seallie. He wanted to come with us this evening."

"Yeah. I know. They won't let im in. Hey! You could bring him Sunday. Maybe they'd let me walk down to the lobby."

"I'll ask the nurse when we leave. Okay?"

Joe had forbade Bea to visit Seallie, but she hated the idea of Lilly Pearl driving through the southside alone, especially at night. All sensible black people avoided the South Side, but that's where DePaul was located. Also, found on the South Side were the very, very poor Polish, Germans, Nazis, and the Klu Klux Klan. Strange accidents had happened to unwanted ethnic groups on the southside of Milwaukee. It was impermissible turf for Blacks and Jews specifically. The only neutral ground where all indigents met was the Milwaukee County Department of Welfare.

Joe had argued that no one would ever guess that Lilly Pearl wasn't white, but this thought brought no comfort to Bea. "Pearl would tell em she's colored if they'd ask," she said.

Joe laughed and puffed his cigarette. "When a nigger get scared, lies start flying. Them Nazis grab her ass, she'd try passing for the mayor's wife. Going over there's a waste of time anyhow," Joe said. "She'll be drunk the first day she's out."

"There's always hope," Bea told him.

"For Seallie it ain't. She's been drunk since she was crawlin. Her pappy raised her on Old Crow. The whole damn family's whisky-heads. That place ain't gonna change her. They don't work miracles. I know a plenty's been through there. Ain't seen em change nobody yet."

"They might help her this time," Bea said.

Joe laughed and smashed his cigarette. "Only if they sews her mouth shut."

The following Sunday, Lilly Pearl, Bea, Jimmy Lee and

Roosevelt went to DePaul. Lilly Pearl stood Jimmy Lee and Roosevelt under a large white birch on the side of the hospital near Seallie's window. She looked out and waved with teary eyes. "He's shootin straight up like a twig," she said. "I love that boy like he's my own," Seallie said. "Who's that little kid with him?"

"My brother, Roosevelt," Bea told her. "He's living with me now cause Momma's low sick."

"He looks young as Jimmy Lee from here," Seallie said.

Roosevelt was well behaved and intelligent, beyond his eleven years. The relatives called him *Change Baby*. He was conceived during Miss Claudia B.'s menopause.

"Where's your boy, Joe Junior?" Seallie asked Bea.

"He's with his daddy," she said.

"I reckon he don't want him over here visiting no old drunk like me. He don't like me, and I don't give a damn bout him neither."

"Don't talk like that, Seallie," Lilly Pearl pleaded. "You'll get yourself upset."

Lilly Pearl gave Seallie the brown bag. "I brought you some more Fig Newtons."

"Fig Newtons?" Seallie grabbed the bag and opened it hopefully. "Hell, girl, I told you to bring me a little nip!" She slammed the bag in Lilly Pearl's face and wept.

"I knew you'd get yourself upset," Lilly Pearl said.

"Upset? Me, upset? How else can I be? I did my best, taking care of your baby." She was pointing at Jimmy Lee. "I even stayed with him when you was late coming home, but what thanks do I get? You don't have enough God in your heart to bring a dying woman a little drink," Seallie said. "I need something to calm my nerves. I got a right to be upset!" Seallie smashed the cookies with her feet. "Just get the hell outta my room and don't come back til your heart's right. Stick these motherfuckin cookies up your ass! I'm a dying woman. I don't need cookies. I need a drink! You hear me?"

Bea tried to calm the hysterical woman while Lilly Pearl ran for help. The nurse came with a hypodermic in her hand, and they watched Seallie become lethargic as the tranquilizer took effect. "Rest is what she needs," the nurse told them. They put on their coats to leave and Seallie cried, "Don't leave me, Pearl." She whined like a very young child. "Can I please have my Fig Newtons?"

On Monday morning the mid-term scores had been posted, each listed by student I.D. numbers. Lilly Pearl had passed all exams with flying colors, excluding Professor Fuch's class. He had indicated an incomplete.

Frustrated and frightened, Lilly Pearl ran towards Professor Fuch's office. *Oh, God, did he see Ricardo copying my answers?* she wondered. *What else could it be? I finished the exam. I answered all questions. Maybe I forgot to put my name on it.*

When she reached his office, Professor Fuchs was looking at her exam with a perplexed expression on his face. "I know why you're here," he said. "I was expecting you. Please close the door and be seated, Miss Ealy."

Her eyes were wild and her heart beat rapidly. She rested her books on her lap and folded her hands across them in an attempt to conceal her anxiety. He held the paper firmly as if he expected her to snatch it and run. "How old are you, Miss Ealy. . .it is Miss Ealy, isn't it?"

"Yes. Miss. I'm twenty-one. . .almost twenty-two."

"And where were you born?"

"Pearl City. Pearl City, Mississippi," she said. *What the hell does this have to do with my exam?* she wondered.

He puffed on an unlit corncob pipe and leaned back in the old worn leather chair. "I see that you're a second semester junior."

"Yes, Sir. I've earned eighty-four credits."

"What's your major?" he asked.

"Elementary education," Lilly Pearl told him.

"How're you doing in your other courses this semester?" he wanted to know.

"Fine. Just fine. Good grades."

Professor Fuch's bag lunch was on his desk with a small polished apple beside it. He never carried the apple in the bag; it would look untidy and would mash his sandwich.

For lunch Professor Fuchs always brought a sandwich made of thinly sliced bologna on rye bread with mayonaise, cut on an angle, and wrapped methodically in waxed paper. He'd buy a small carton of milk from the machine in the faculty lounge and eat in his office with a *Do Not Disturb* sign hanging on the door.

Mrs. Fuch was much younger than her husband. They'd met when she was his student. For his fifty-first birthday, eight years ago, she'd brought him a very conservative toupee. It looked almost like his natural hair when he'd wear it pushed back off his forehead.

On Mondays and Wednesdays Professor Fuchs wore his brown suit. On Tuesdays and Thursdays he'd wear the tweed. And Friday would be either brown or tweed day. Some gossip on campus was that he economized so that he could afford to live on Lake Drive.

"What are your future plans, Miss Ealy?" Professor Fuchs asked.

"Elementary school teacher, I hope."

"Who's your academic counselor?"

"Oh, uh, Dean Stanley." *Why the hell doesn't he get to the point,* she wondered impatiently.

"May I ask, Miss Ealy, are you serious about this Ricardo Lewis?" He laid the exam on the old mahogany desk and looked at her seriously.

I knew it! Lilly Pearl thought. *He saw me show Ricardo my answers. Oh, God. I'm in trouble!* "We. . .we're good friends."

"I understand," he said. "Does your parents know you're involved with him?" he asked.

"I don't live with my parents. I live alone with my son."

"Oh, you have a child, Miss Ealy?"

"Yes," she answered nervously, "His name is Jimmy Lee."

"Nice southern name." He cleared his throat, picked up the exam and rolled it in his hands like a scroll. "Do you participate in extra-curricular activities or belong to any special interest groups, Miss Ealy?"

"No. None. I don't have the time," she told the professor.

Professor Fuchs stood up and walked slowly to the window, puffing on the unlit pipe, holding her exam rolled in his left hand, tapping the palm of his right hand with it. "Miss Ealy, I hope you won't be offended by what I'm about to say."

If he's trying to get around to something like sex, he can just forget it. I'm not screwing for a grade, she thought.

"I'm primarily concerned about your answer to the essay question, whereas I instructed the class to discuss the psychology of Negro behavior, as it relates to the destructive attitudes of inner-city dwellers," Professor Fuchs said. "I was definitely seeking objective views, Miss Ealy. However, it seems to me you're attempting to justify this type of behavior by analogously comparing the violent behavior of inner-city Negroes to that of Melville's young Billy Budd," he told her. "You stated that Billy Budd was provoked to strike out physically against evil and injustice, because of his inability to verbally articulate his grievances. You seem to believe that the illiterate coloreds also strike-out by destroying property, robbing, and stealing from others, because they cannot articulate their grievances. Miss Ealy, this is the most pronounced illustration of pappekak I've ever read.

"Melville's work reflected despair and contempt for human hypocrisy," Professor Fuchs said. "Billy Budd is symbolic of good over evil, even though he willingly died for destroying the life of an evil individual. This concept has no relationship to the subject at hand. Miss Ealy, I'm sure you're aware of that. It's most baffling that an intelligent white woman like yourself could shelter such radical views," Professor Fuchs said. He walked back to his seat and looked at her seriously. "I do admire empathy in a young lady's character," he said. "It's a rather tender feminine attribute. But it seems to me you've come dangerously close to identifying with Negroes," Professor Fuchs told her. He finally sat in his chair and leaned back. "I do admire the athletic prowess of some Negroes. But

God knows they're at a terrible disadvantage when it comes to critical thinking. Why else have I turned my head when you've shown your answers to Lewis?"

"I don't know, Sir," Lilly Pearl answered in a frightened voice.

"Well, Heaven forbid that a colored should be called upon to answer a question requiring inductive or deductive reasoning. I'm sure you're aware of that.

"You're a bright young lady, Miss Ealy," the professor said. "However, I cannot grade this paper until you rewrite the essay. Otherwise, it's an *A* paper." He threw the exam on his desk and pushed it towards her. She slid it into her notebook. *Oh, God, he thinks I'm white.* "Thank you for being so kind, Professor Fuchs," Lilly Pearl said. *I've got to pass this course,* she thought sadly.

"Believe me, Miss Ealy, Melville would turn in his grave at the thought of having his ideas abused in this manner. In my opinion," Professor Fuchs said, "such a treatise is psychologically unhealthy."

On her way to meet Ricardo in the library, feeling quite dejected, Lilly Pearl remembered her dear friend Kenny. *He couldn't have lasted here one semester,* she thought. *This is a dog-eat-dog institution. He's probably laughing at all of us silly fools, struggling to stay alive. He's got his Tina, and Seymour's got Waupon. I hope they'll keep him this time.*

Ricardo sat at a corner table waiting for Lilly Pearl. "I have a fantastic idea," he told her. "Let's go by my place and work on our research paper."

"But we can't do research at your place," Lilly Pearl said.

"Sure we can. We'll check out several resources and read them while we're there. Tomorrow we'll come back to the library and find other material."

"That does make sense," she said. "But what about our next class?"

"We'll skip today--in the name of research," Ricardo told her. "Instructors are lazy. They don't lecture much right after exams."

She knew he was lying, but her ordeal in Professor Fuchs' office that morning had left her with a reluctance to sit through his class.

"I'm parked on Downer near Kenwood," Ricardo told her. "Bring your car around and follow me."

A certain thrill rose in Lilly Pearl's chest, and her stomach stirred strangely at the though of being alone in Ricardo's apartment. She experienced mixed emotions-- afraid to go and afraid not to go. They had known each other for only five weeks, but she wanted to become intimately closer to him. Over the years, she had abstained from sexual activity. But her imagination had often entertained the possibility of sexual satisfaction with a man to whom she could give herself willingly.

Lilly Pearl followed Ricardo down North Avenue to Twentieth Street where he turned left and drove to Brown Street, and turned right. His ragged, rust corroded Olds chugged along, ejecting puffs of blue-white smoke from its exhaust pipe. After driving another three blocks, he stopped at a fairly decent duplex between Twenty-third and Twenty-fourth Street on Brown. "Park here!" he shouted back at her.

The sooty layers of dirty snow banked against the curb

had become slippery and hard, making it difficult to park. Ricardo drove around through the alley and parked in the old ragged garage behind the house. Then he walked along the side of the building and beckoned. "Get out! I've got the books."

I do want to be with him, to be a part of him, she thought. *I'm really in love with him. He seems so nice.*

They entered the duplex through a side door and walked up the squeaky stairs. Lilly Pearl was surprised when they reached the second floor and he continued up to the attic apartment. The first room at the top of the stairs was the kitchen. The bedroom was second and the small living room was up front. "You'll have to excuse the mess," he said. "I could use a maid, or a wife." They both laughed. "A wife is cheaper," Lilly Pearl told him.

Ricardo took her coat to the bedroom. She could hear him moving things around, seemingly in an attempt to make the room presentable. "Just take a seat," he called out. "I'll be back in a second."

Lilly Pearl looked about the sparsely furnished room. Everything there apparently had come from Goodwill or the Salvation Army, excluding the modern stereo set that was stacked with albums. The springs in the sofa strained against the under padding, and the cocktail table and two lamp tables were not of the same design. The tattered shag carpeting on the living room floor was red. And in the middle of the ceiling was a twirling mirrored ball that reflected about the room when she turned on the light.

In a matter of minutes, Ricardo was in the kitchen clinking ice cubes into glasses. "What're you doing?" Lilly Pearl asked.

"Just make yourself comfy," he said. "I'll be with you shortly."

Feeling strangely impatient, Lilly Pearl walked to the stereo and flipped through the albums. "I see you like Ray Charles," she said loudly.

"Yes. He's my main man," Ricardo told her as he entered the room and set two glasses of wine on the cocktail table. Then he rushed toward the kitchen again and returned with a plate of cheese and crackers. "Kick your boots off," he told her. "I'll put on Mr. Ray."

"You didn't say we'd wine, dine, and party today," Lilly Pearl said teasingly. "You think we'll do research after this?"

"Of course we'll do research. You'll see. Just have faith in me." Ricardo slid a Ray Charles album from the jacket and turned the stereo on. He stood with inviting hands. "Let's see if you can dance," he said to Lilly Pearl, who kicked off her knee-high boots, walked to him and put her arms around his shoulders. She was closer to him than she had ever been. He pressed her closer and began moving slowly and skillfully while the smooth rich sound of *Georgia On My Mind* filled the small apartment.

"Mmmm. I want to hold you like this forever," he whispered. She felt warm inside, but her body trembled uncontrollably. "Take it slow and easy," he said. "Isn't this mellow?" Lilly Pearl shook her head. "Yes. I'm just a little nervous, I guess. It's been a long, long time since I was this close to a man," she said.

"I'll make you forget," he promised. Then he cupped her face and kissed her on the mouth long and hard. She groaned from the painful rapture of his lips. He led her to the sofa and gave her wine. "Do you believe in love at first sight?" he asked. "Yes. I've loved you since the first day," she said.

Ricardo lifted his glass and smiled. "Pearl, will you marry me?"

Somewhere in the back of her head the words echoed. He kissed her face and mouth gently and repeatedly. *This can't be happening to me,* she thought.

"I'm waiting for your answer, darling. Will you be my wife?"

She drank the wine in one long gulp. "What about my son, Jimmy Lee?" she asked.

"Don't you think I'd made a good daddy?"

"Please, Ricardo. Let's dance."

"If you insist." He took her empty glass, went to the kitchen and refilled both glasses. Again, they danced in a reciprocal embrace. The thought of becoming Ricardo's wife whirled in Lilly Pearl's head like the reflections off the mirrored ball. *I do need a good man,* she thought. *I want to belong to someone, and Jimmy Lee needs a father.*

When the record ended, Ricardo quickly flipped it over and Ray Charles began singing *For The Good Times.* The enchanting bachelor was filled with a puissant desire to possess Lilly Pearl. He kissed her wrists passionately and ran his tongue, in a tremulous manner, deep within her hands. The experienced lover poured wine into her palms and methodically licked it out, while some of it trickled between her fingers, dripping onto the carpet below. She withdrew impulsivily. "I won't hurt you," he said, as he continued sucking the wine off each finger, nibbling the tips and kissing them. Lilly Pearl was frightened because of what she felt, but she hadn't the desire nor the strength to retreat. Her legs no longer sustained her enraptured body. Slowly, her knees gave way and he went down with her. She opened her mouth to speak and hot saliva dripped onto the side of his face. "Please, Ricardo. Let's dance some more."

"If you say so, Pearl."

Ricardo held her hands and lifted her to a standing position. Their bodies became one as they moved sensuously.

Beads of perspiration covered Ricardo's face. He held Lilly Pearl's body plastered to his. Tears from her eyes blended with the sweat on his shirt. She clung to him, feeling his penis press hard against her. Large inflated veins stood on his forehead. His nostrils were flared like a wild stallion. He exhaled heavily into her ear. Suddenly covering her ear with his open mouth, he inserted his tongue hungrily into it, holding it there. She quivered. She secreted so generously that her panties adhered to her clitoris, manipulating with each movement. Lilly Pearl tenderly turned Ricardo's warm, wet mouth toward hers and pressed her parted lips to his. He sucked her tongue firmly and lifted her upright, clearing her feet off the floor. In an instant, she was lying beneath him on his bed. "Take me, darling," she cried. "I need you so very much! Love me, please."

"Will you marry me, Pearl? Will you. . ."

"Yes! Yes! Ricardo, I'll be your wife. I want you. I need you."

Fervency possessed him. His searching fingers found the zipper. He slid her jumpsuit off. She lay spralled beneath him in black leotards that revealed every curve in her body. His entire body was erected, except for his puzzled hands. "How do I get this damned thing off?" he asked excitedly. Before she could answer, the stitches gave way and ripped below her full breasts. The sound of ripping seams and the sight of Lilly Pearl's nipples, beckoning like carmel coated ecstasy, robbed him of any remaining balance. He squeezed her breasts close together, to suck both avariciously, at the same time.

Lilly Pearl became fanatically anxious for the fulfillment of Ricardo. Her vagina contracted ravenously for his presence.

He ripped her panting body bare and lifted her legs to his slippery shoulders. Lilly Pearl's rapid breathing and Ricardo's long hard heaving added new meaning to Ray Charles' singing.

Ricardo slid his tongue down her hot, damp thighs, occasionally nibbling at the sensitive area between them. *Oh, God!* Lilly Pearl wondered. *Is he doing the sixty-nine?* "Darling I've never. . ."

"Don't be square," Ricardo told her. "Relax! You're mine now. There's nothing a man and wife can't share."

I do love him, she thought.

Like a huge muscular cobra, his tongue was quick. He manipulated her erected clitoris--fast, vigorously, without stopping. Lilly Pearl entangled her fingers in his hair, holding tightly, afraid he'd remove the ladder, and she'd tumble painfully from paradise. "Keep it there! Please, Ricardo. Keep it there!" she pleaded. As she became more frantic, he became more determined to send her higher, to a level of euphoria she'd never experienced before.

Lilly Pearl's panting gave way to unintelligible whispers, coarse groaning, and ecstatic crying. She experienced an overwhelming sensation totally unknown to her. He held her there until it seemed he'd explode. Then he brought his body in unison with hers, and his aching penis slowly eased into her. With a quick jerk of his buttocks, he was deep within a world where his entire body became a huge penis, and she became a gapping vagnia--swelling, trembling, rising to the ultimate conflagration of sexual bliss. Simultaneously, they reached climatic glory that brought thunder, lightning and extinguishing rain. Then, the only sounds to be heard were sighs of fulfillment and Ray Charles singing *All of Me.*

- *10* -

Pink Champagne and Chocolate Cake

"You haven't given this matter as much consideration as the purchase of a new dress, Pearl," McCray said. "People spend too little time seriously choosing a mate," he told her. "You'll look at a suit, try it on, and buy if the price is right. Maybe a car you'll think a bit more about, because of the cost. A major investment like a house gets more in-depth concern--most of us buy only once or twice in a lifetime. But, Pearl, you're talking about another human being, another mind, another personality, possibly a different set of values that you're going to give yourself to--live with, sleep with, have as father of your child, supposedly until death do you part." McCray held her hand and looked into her eyes as he spoke. "One afternoon alone with him, knowing nothing more than how he made you feel, is not enough to qualify for the dedication of your life and your son's. Do you understand what I'm trying to say, my dear?"

Lilly Pearl, Jacqueline, and McCray had met in the student union. She had called them the night before, thinking how delightful it would be to have them embrace her when she shared the exciting news. The happy bride-to-be felt they'd be extremely elated that she was about to become Mrs. Ricardo Lewis.

"I'm in a state of shock," Jacqueline said. "Pearl, what do you know about this guy?"

"What is there to know?" Lilly Pearl asked with a shrug of the shoulders. "For the first time, you two, I'm in love."

"Where does he work?" Jacqueline asked.

"The Wisconsin School for Boys--Wales," she said, "about thirty-three miles west of here, past Waukesha. He's a third shift cottage counselor."

"Counselor? How could he be a counselor without a degree?" Jacqueline asked. "He doesn't have a college education."

"It's a non-professional position," McCray told her.

"So what if it is? He has an honest job and he's trying to improve himself," Lilly Pearl said. "We're non-professionals too. I'm on welfare. How could I turn my nose up at a working man?"

"What I've said to you has nothing to do with the kind of work he does," McCray explained. "I've heard some unfavorable remarks about your friend Ricardo but never given it much thought until now. Do you know Louise Fortee?" McCray asked Lilly Pearl. She thought for a few seconds. "I don't think so. Is she a student here?"

"Yes." McCray told her. "She's in my Spanish class."

"Who the hell is she?" Jacqueline blurted out.

"She claims to have been engaged to Ricardo."

"Engaged?" At that moment, Lilly Pearl's eyes grew large and round.

"She says the guy isn't playing with a full deck," McCray told them.

"What did he do?" Jacqueline asked excitedly.

"On this job he has, working with boys, he's been verbally reprimanded for certain types of abusive behavior," McCray said.

"What kind of abusive behavior?" Jacqueline nudged him on.

"I don't want to hear this!" Lilly Pearl said. "I refuse to listen to gossip about the man I love."

"I'm not trying to spread malicious rumors about this man, Pearl. Please believe me. I wouldn't have mentioned it if you weren't planning to marry him. You're my friend," McCray told her. "I feel you should know a little more about him before taking the big step. Date him for a while. If it's meant to be, it'll happen with my blessings."

But I might lose him, she thought.

"Pearl, you're too trusting," Jacqueline said. "You think everybody's honest like you."

Why are they all against me marrying Ricardo? Lilly Pearl wondered. Bea's words were still echoing in her head: "If you marry that man, you'll never finish college." And

Sweet Nancy had called her a fool for the first time. "You're putting your neck in a noose," Sweet Nancy had told her. Even Joe told her, "You don't really know that Mexican-nigger. You don't know what the hell he'll turn out to be."

The day dragged for Lilly Pearl until *Human Behavior* class. Ricardo greeted her with a kiss outside the door, and Professor Fuchs was pleased with the revised essay she had turned in earlier. He laid the exam on her desk with the large *A* showing. Lilly Pearl quickly slid it between the pages of her notebook.

"What was that?" Ricardo asked.

Lilly Pearl pretended not to hear.

"Pearl," he whispered loudly, "what was that?"

"Oh, just my mid-term." He looked at her strangely, as if to wonder why hers hadn't been returned with the others.

"Now, class," Professor Fuchs called out with a wave of his hands, "today we will listen to Ahmad discuss certain customs and how they relate to human behavior in Saudi Arabia, his homeland." The class grew quiet and attentive, listening to Ahmad discuss the moral behavior of young women in Saudi Arabia. Most of the females in class sighed disapprovingly and made defensive statements when he explained that any girl proven not to have retained her virginity, before her wedding day, could be returned to her family and stoned to death. A bride, on her wedding night, must produce blood on the bed sheet that the groom would put on a pole and parade through the streets the following morning. Urshan, the only Iranian in class joked that many pigeons had been sacrificed for the cause. The class had a hearty laugh. And Lilly Pearl thought of all the girls in her neighborhood who would die under a pile of stones. She also thought of herself. "Suppose someone robbed her of her virginity?" she asked Ahmad. He smiled and shrugged, but he never answered.

Urshan was a Persian Jew. His family had gained great wealth through real estate. Prior to the birthday party that he had given and invited the class, everyone in class, excluding Professor Fuchs, had assumed he was poor. Many had joked that at his party he would serve sheep's eyes, floating in tomato sauce, poured over rice, and that he would live in a cheap rooming house near the University. But, when they arrived at the address he had written on the board, it just happened to have been Prospect Towers, overlooking Lake Michigan. The security guard directed them to the twentieth floor.

When Urshan greeted his guest, they were stunned. He wore a burgundy, velvet and satin smoking jacket and white slacks. The complete east wall of the apartment was glass, giving an uninterrupted view of the beach. The walls and plush carpeting were a soft white, and along the back wall of the dining area were three long tables lined with extravagant cuts of meat, hors d'oeuvres, magnificent aged wine, and champagne. Lilly Pearl, Jacqueline, and McCray tasted caviar for the first time.

The class had been surprised to see Professor and Mrs. Fuchs at Urshan's party. They didn't imagine that the diamond dinner ring Mrs. Fuchs wore was a gift from Urshan. And at home under her cheap cocktail table was a luxurious Persian Prayer rug, also a gift from him.

Urshan's greatest ambition was to be admitted to the doctoral program. He was now finishing the final semester of his master's degree. Professor Fuchs' *Human Behavior* course carried undergraduate and graduate credit. And Professor Fuchs was the chairman of the doctorial committee.

Several weeks after the party, Urshan told McCray how disgusted he had become that strange girls came to his door to drop their panties. To avoid them, he'd get in his Buick, ride along Lake Michigan and downtown, having become completely satiated with sex.

It was 2:15 on Friday afternoon. The fast falling sleet tapped chillingly on the courthouse windows--a typical November day in Milwaukee. Bea and Sweet Nancy stood in the back of the room, each holding Jimmy Lee's hand and crying silently. Finally, Judge Nikolakopulos concluded. "I now pronounce you man and wife."

Ricardo smiled and kissed Lilly Pearl's wet face. She was afraid and uncertain. But two weeks had passed since the proposal, and Ricardo had set the date. No persuasion could convince her to prolong the courtship. "You're mine now," Ricardo whispered.

I wish Jacqueline and McCray were here, Lilly Pearl thought. She felt a severing pain within her heart--the breaking away of two precious relationships.

"You'd better take good care of my girl," Nikolakopulos told Ricardo as they shook hands. The judge kissed the bride on the forehead. "I hope you'll be happy, dear. If you need a shoulder, call Uncle Niko." Ricardo looked at him with a suspicious roll of the eye.

Dear, God, please let this marriage work, Lilly Pearl prayed. *I wonder why Nancy's wearing black,* she thought. She moved hurriedly toward the back of the room and embraced Bea and Sweet Nancy. Then she lifted her child, kissed him on the face several times, and hugged him close to her chest. "Oh, Jimmy Lee, the three of us are gonna be so happy."

Bea kept the child with her so that the bride and groom could celebrate. "I'll keep him all weekend," she told them. "Yall have a good time." Jimmy Lee looked over his shoulder with a sad expression when his mother walked away, clinging to Ricardo's arm. "There's something about that man I just don't like," Sweet Nancy said to Bea.

"I reckon he's alright, Nancy. But I wish she had waited a little longer, to know him better."

"Well, I suppose you never really know a man until you're living with him."

"What're you ladies whispering about?" Nikolakopulos approached them. "I guess you're a little concerned about your cousin's happiness?" he said to Bea. Bea tried to sound optimistic. "She'll be fine, Your Honor."

Sweet Nancy chuckled. "You don't have to say *Your Honor* to Niko. He lost his honor at my house." The three of them laughed while Jimmy Lee looked up at them in a state of bewilderment.

The inquisitive neighbors peeked from behind their soiled, tattered curtains and cracked doors while Lilly Pearl and Ricardo hauled his boxes and stereo into her apartment. It suddenly dawned on Lilly Pearl that she was now Mrs. Ricardo Lewis, a married woman. When they had finished, the handsome groom made one last trip downstairs and returned with a bottle of pink champagne and a small chocolate cake.

"It's time to celebrate!" Ricardo said, popping the cork against the ceiling. "Here's to you, Mrs. Lewis!" He held the bottle high, "Let's drink to love and happiness."

A thrilling sensation surged through her body. The joy of being in love and belonging to someone made Lilly Pearl's face glow with a tinge of red. Sitting, facing each other on the bed, they drank the champagne from the bottle and ate the cake with their hands. The two of them became intoxicated by the aura of the moment.

Still sitting on the bed, they undressed each other, kissing and embracing in the nude. Lilly Pearl ran her tongue over his body with a feathery touch. She wanted so much to please him. "Does that feel good, Ricardo?" she asked. "I want to give you everything."

"You're great, darling," he told her. "I'll teach you how to make love to me." He pushed her head down toward his groin. "Just run your tongue around it slowly. Breathe on it and rub my testicals gently."

I never thought I'd do this, she thought. She remembered how detestable she had imagined it would be. *But anything to please my husband,* she vowed.

They had hung the mirrored ball above the bed and it filled the room with twirling, sensual reflections. Lilly Pearl enjoyed the fragrance of his body and the rigid firmness that filled her mouth. Ricardo smiled and stroked her hair. "Tell me who you belong to, Mrs. Lewis." He pulled her up and kissed her.

"I'm yours for ever and ever, darling," Lilly Pearl said,

"until death do us part."

Curled in his embrace, she rested her head on his muscular shoulder and snuggled her face under his chin.

After receiving her welfare check on the first of December, Lilly Pearl reported to her caseworker that she was married. The amount of Ricardo's salary was just enough to make her ineligible for a supplement. Although, Jimmy Lee would still receive an allowance, since he was not her husband's child and was now attending public school.

Ricardo laid down all of the household rules. His father, Jesus "Mike" Morales, had counseled him well--a man must rule his domicile with absolute authority. Thus, their lives were under his control, including the spanking of Jimmy Lee and the driving of Lilly Pearl's car. He would leave his unreliable vehicle for emergencies she might have. Sweet Nancy vowed to repossess the Cadillac each time she'd see him in it. But she prayed Lilly Pearl would soon tire of his domineering nature and kick him out. Lilly Pearl remained faithful, overlooking his authoritarian attitude towards her and the child. Corporal punishment was Ricardo's only method of discipline. When Jimmy Lee would arrive home from school in the afternoon, the terrified boy hardly moved or spoke in the presence of his stepfather. And Lilly Pearl had found suspicious bruises on her son after leaving him in the care of her husband. Ricardo would explain the injuries as accidental--the boy had fallen on the corner of the lamp table, or he had bumped his eye on the doorknob.

The Spring semester had begun and Lilly Pearl was

entering her senior year. She would do her practice teaching at Auer Avenue Elementary School. "I'm almost there!" she said happily, showing the assignment to her husband. He read it without facial expression, folded it three times, tore it crosswise and dropped it in the kitchen garbage. "Honey, I meant to tell you, we can't attend school this year," Ricardo said. He burned her Student Financial Aid awards letter and flushed the ashes down the toilet. "Being a married lady, your student financial aid would be insufficient for tuition, books, supplies, and transportation. I can't afford to repair the other car, so I'll need the Cadillac everyday for miscellaneous business and getting to work at night."

"But why didn't you tell me before now? Why did you let me go to Dean Stanley and get my practice teaching placement?" Lilly Pearl asked.

"You should've gotten my permission first, darling," Ricardo said. "Let that be a lesson for the future. We agreed that I am head of the house. Right?"

"But you know how important school is to me, honey," she said with wet eyes.

"Are you saying school is more important than your husband and your son?" he asked.

Lilly Pearl stood looking at him in shock and disbelief. The premarital advice her friends had given echoed in her head.

McCray: "People spend too little time seriously choosing a mate. . . I've heard some unfavorable remarks about your friend Ricardo. . ."

Bea: "If you marry that man, you'll never finish college."

Sweet Nancy: "You're putting your neck in a noose."

Joe: "You don't really know that Mexican-nigger."

"But, I. . .," Lilly Pearl started to speak.

"There's nothing more to say about it, Pearl." He took a seat at the table. "Warm me a bowl of chili, honey. By the way, I gave that pistol back to Joe this morning. You won't need a gun with me protecting you."

Eight months had passed since the wedding, and Lilly Pearl had been ill for the last six weeks. Her dream of becoming a school teacher had become a painful memory. She missed Jacqueline, McCray, and life at the University. Everday she prayed that God would provide a way by which she and her husband could continue their education. But she had never complained to Ricardo. He demanded unquestionable respect and top priority in her heart. She seldom spoke with Sweet Nancy, and Bea's visits became more infrequent. She'd walk her son to school each morning and spend the rest of the day cleaning, cooking, and catering to her husband's every wish. It seemed that he had become addicted to oral sex from her, but now he never reciprocated. At times he'd ram his hardness deeply within her throat, making her gag. Apparently, he took great pleasure in hurting her, sometimes pretending to be playing.

Four more weeks of feeling extremely ill had passed, and Lilly Pearl's menstruation had become irregular. Bea called and pleaded with her to see Doctor Blackwell. "Roosevelt can stay with Jimmy Lee," she promised. "I'll make you an appointment for tomorrow. Okay?"

Lilly Pearl agreed to see the doctor if Ricardo wouldn't object. "Tomorrow's mop day," she told Bea. "Ricardo hates dirty floors."

"But you need to see a doctor," Bea said. "I've got an idea. You bring Jimmy Lee over here on your way to the doctor. Leave him with me. I'll send Roosevelt over before you leave. He'll mop while you're at the doctor's office."

"That'll be fine if I can get Ricardo's old car started. He's gotta use the Cadillac to drive a friend to work."

The following morning Bea called Lilly Pearl and informed her that the appointment was at 1:15. "Roosevelt will take the bus," Bea said. "He'll be there by 12:30. You'll have forty-five minutes to drop Jimmy Lee by here and get to the doctor's office. When Joe gets off, we'll drive him home and pick up Roosevelt."

Lilly Pearl was happy that Bea still cared. She had begun to feel that her marriage might have been a mistake. Although, she entertained no notions of ending it. *Maybe he'll change,* she thought. *I'll be the perfect wife. Sometimes people do change when you go out of your way to make them happy.*

Roosevelt arrived on time eager to earn the three dollars Bea had promised him. Ricardo had complained about Lilly Pearl's appointment but had agreed to let her drive the Cadillac. She felt light and free driving down Center Street with her son. It had been a long time since she had driven the car that Sweet Nancy had given her. After she had taken Jimmy Lee to Bea, she ran to Sweet Nancy's door and rang the bell anxiously. They embraced like sisters who had been apart much too long.

"Pearl, why haven't you been to see me?" Sweet Nancy asked. "I've seen that asshole Ricardo driving your car all over town, and he's never alone. Girl, I had such high hopes for you. I wanted you to have a good life, to be an educated lady--something I've never had. You let me down. You let Bea down. Most of all, you've let yourself down for that no-good bastard. Pearl, you don't have to take the shit he's putting on you. It's not too late. Get rid of his ass. You don't need him. He ain't made your life no better. In fact, he made it worse. At least you were happy and free. You had the opportunity to attend the University. And you wasn't kissing nobody's ass and being a damn slave."

"I'm okay, Nancy," Lilly Pearl said in an unconvincing tone. "We're happy. Honest."

"You're lying, Pearl," Sweet Nancy told her. "I can look at you and tell. Take a look at yourself. You look awful."

Lilly Pearl looked at Sweet Nancy's watch. "I gotta go, Nancy. I've got a doctor's appointment at 1:15."

"Come to see me when you've got more time. We've gotta have a long talk." Sweet Nancy watched from her porch as Lilly Pearl drove away.

Oh, God, do I hate this, she thought. Her legs were in stirrups and Doctor Blackwell breathed hard, with bulging eyes, while he probed her vagina with his fat, clumsy fingers. Lilly Pearl squirmed from the pain, but he pretended not to notice.

"When did you have your last period, Mrs. Lewis?" the doctor asked.

"I have one every month, but the last three were short," she told him.

"How short?" He pulled off the latex glove and dropped

it into the waste basket.

"About a day or so," she said.

"Mrs. Lewis, from the size of your uterus, you're about three and a half months pregnant," Doctor Blackwell said. He listened to her stomach with his stethoscope. "Do you have other children?"

"Yes. I have a seven year old son, but with him my period stopped the first month."

"Maybe you're run-down, overworked, or both. Here's a prescription for vitamins, and get as much bed rest as possible," he said. "See me again next month unless you have additional complications sooner."

The sky was like a huge comforter, blanketing Milwaukee. White sunrays peeked through light gray patches of fluffy clouds. It was a beautiful day and Lilly Pearl was filled with the joy of carrying Ricardo's child. *Oh, dear God, please let it be a girl,* she prayed. *She'll be so beautiful; we'll have the perfect family. Now that he'll have his own child to love, maybe Ricardo will treat Jimmy Lee better.* She laughed and sang aloud, driving home with the precious news. In her mind, she could see her handsome husband run to her, embracing her, clearing her feet off the floor, whirling her around, laughing loudly.

The scenery swooped by like a continuous kaleidoscope of ghetto colors. She eased her foot off the accelerator, hoping that no cop was nearby. Finally, she parked in front of Ricardo's old dilapidated car. *Oh, good! He's home. He'll be so happy,* she thought. *I'll ask him to drive Roosevelt home and pick up Jimmy Lee. Oh, thank you, Heavenly Father! Everything's gonna be sunshine and roses from now on.*

Carefully, Lilly Pearl climbed the stairs and inserted her key. She could hear the stereo blasting from outside the door. She stuck her head in and said, "Hello in there! Guess who's home?" Coming from the bedroom, she could hear a strange noise. It was Roosevelt's voice, and he was crying and pleading. *Ricardo wouldn't dare whip Roosevelt,* she thought. She closed the door and prayed that her husband hadn't taken a belt to Bea's little brother. She took a quick glance at the living room and kitchen floors and they were spotless. *If he'd hit Roosevelt, Joe would kill him.* Walking slowly toward the bedroom, she felt panic rise in her chest.

"Ricardo," she called softly, pushing the bedroom door open. He stopped and looked at her with rage in his eyes. It was as though the incredible energy that flowed through him had been converted to an overpowering, evil, psycho-pathic, cold-blooded force that filled the room. Thin leather straps had been used to bind Roosevelts frail wrists to each head post of the bed. His nude body was streaked with welts from her husband's belt. Tears, mucus, and saliva strung from his swollen face. He was on his knees, and blood was smeared on his buttocks. It ran from his anus down the back of his thighs--the same blood that covered Ricardo's erected penis and the bed sheet where Roosevelt knelt. Lilly Pearl stood horrified, staring incre-dulously at the nightmare she'd walked in on. Her husband cursed her and lunged at her. His strong hand grasped her throat as he crushed her face and head repeatedly with his fist. The two huge rings he wore ripped her skin like brass knuckles and broke her front teeth in jagged pieces. Roosevelt strained against the straps, to no avail. He squirmed and cried out, begging Ricardo to release Lilly Pearl. But the insane fury, the sadistic passion, grew more intense within him as she screamed and begged for mercy.

Lilly Pearl thought about Tina. *He's going to kill me and then Roosevelt.* Terror shuddered through her body, engulfing her in nameless, sickening panic. The pounding of her heart resounded in her ears. In a state of trauma, moving like an automaton, she crawled towards the phone. His strong hand gripped her wrist, wrenched the receiver from her clasp, snatched the cord out of the wall and crashed the phone down on her head. Roosevelt screamed. Then Lilly Pearl drifted into a painless, soundless, deep blue ocean.

"Bang! Bang! You're dead, Cousin Bea," Jimmy Lee said playfully, pointing his toy gun up at her. "Boy, put that thing back in the holster," she said. "I told you never point a gun at anybody, even if it is a toy." He dropped his head and pouted. "I'm sorry. I forgot. Please don't tell my mommy."

Bea and the boy stood on the porch waiting for his mother to answer the door. Bea had rung several times and banged on the door with her fist. Then she twisted the knob and the door opened. "Pearl!" Bea called out. "You up there?" She held Jimmy Lee's hand and walked to the second floor. The apartment door was standing open. "Maybe your momma and Roosevelt went to the store," Bea said to the child. "Let's just go in and wait."

They entered the living room to take a seat, but a

strange noise came from the bedroom. "Who's that in there?" Bea called out as she walked in that direction. She pushed Jimmy Lee back when she saw the savage devastation of the room. Her twelve year old brother was crumpled at the head of the bed, whimpering like an injured pup, with his wrists still strapped to the bedposts. And on the floor, near the phone, Lilly Pearl lay in a pool of blood, most of which seemed to have flowed from the lower extremity of her body.

"Roosevelt, what happened?" Bea cried. Trying to conceptualize the cataclysm that had swept the room, she wiped his face with the sheet. "Who did this?" His eyes were focused on the floor and his lips moved, but no intelligible words were emitted. Bea knelt over Lilly Pearl and pressed her ear to her chest. Then she screamed out the window to Joe who was waiting in the car.

"Call the police! Get an ambulance!"

Joe was slow to interpret his wife's alarm. "What the hell's going on up there?" he shouted. "Please, Joe, find a phone and call the police. Tell em it's an emergency, to send an ambulance. It's Roosevelt and Pearl!"

"What's wrong with Pearl's phone?" he called back to her.

"Please, Joe, hurry!"

He climbed slowly from the car and proceeded up the stairs. "What the fuck is going on up here?" His wife and Jimmy Lee were crying hysterically when he entered the room. "What in the world happened here? What the hell. . ."

"Please, Joe, get some help!" Bea urged her husband while Jimmy Lee sat on the floor beside his mother, begging her to open her eyes and talk to him. Perplexed by the sight he witnessed, Joe took his pocket knife and cut the straps on Roosevelt's wrists. Then he wrapped the bedspread around him. "Can you tell us what happened, boy?" he asked. Roosevelt's eyes were still focused on the floor where Lilly Pearl lay. He didn't speak.

Joe took a blanket from the bed and covered Lilly Pearl. He felt her pulse and put a pillow under her head. The long copper curls that had graced her shoulders had been cut with a straight razor and left scattered over the floor.

"She's still alive," Joe said.

Thirty-six hours after she had been admitted to Milwaukee County General Hospital, Lilly Pearl awakened in a mass of excruciating pain. In her left arm was a needle secured by a wide adhesive tape. Attached to the needle was a long, thin, transparent catheter that led to an I.V., hanging from a metal hook above her bed. With her free hand, she felt her face that was bandaged with gauze. Suddenly, the tragedy she had experienced flooded her mind, disturbing her, eliciting from her a weak cry. With her tongue, she explored her mouth and found stitches inside her lips, and several missing teeth. She tried to raise her head. A warm, thick fluid gushed from her body. *My baby!* She remembered that she was pregnant. *Roosevelt!* She wondered if he was still alive.

A gentle, masculine voice caught her attention. "Hello, Mrs. Lewis. I'm quite pleased you finally came around. You've suffered a severe concussion and lost lots of blood. They couldn't save your baby.

"I'm Doctor E. Maurice Leatherwood, a plastic surgeon. The hospital called me in to mend your face. You took a serious beating, but we'll get you looking brand new."

I didn't know we had a colored plastic surgeon in Milwaukee, she thought.

"Oh, Mrs. Lewis, I don't want to alarm you," the doctor said, "but the police have been here several times to question you about your injuries. They'll probably come back later today."

"Doctor, do you know my little cousin, Roosevelt?" Lilly Pearl asked.

"The kid they brought in with you?"

"Yes. Roosevelt. Is he alive?"

"Oh, he's progressing just fine," the doctor assured her.

She breathed a sigh of relief. "It was Ricardo." Sarcasm filled her voice. "My Hercules."

"Ricardo? Hercules?" Doctor Leatherwood seemed confused.

"My husband, Ricardo, did this to Roosevelt and me." Painfully, she told him the whole ugly story.

"He's a very sick man," the doctor said. "I hope they'll find him."

"You know," Lilly Pearl spoke angrily, "when we first fell in love, I used to call him my Hercules. Isn't that crazy, doctor?"

"No." Doctor Leatherwood said. "It isn't crazy at all. I'd say that's quite an appropriate name for him. If you'd study the legend of Hercules, you'll find that he was given to occasional outbursts of brutal rage. According to Greco-Roman legend, he killed his wife, Megara, and their children in a fit of madness. But you're safe now." The sympathetic doctor pat her hand with a soft comforting touch and left the room.

Ricardo meant to kill me! she thought. *Dear, God, he really meant to kill me!*

- *11* -

Adios, Cucaracha

Climbing the stairs on crutches was an excruciating task, but the malevolent mess and pungent stench that filled the empty apartment were equally as painful. All of her furniture was gone, the child's toys had been destroyed beyond repair, and the kitchen sink was filled with remnants of garments that had been first slashed by a straight razor and drenched in acid. With no comfortable place to sit, Lilly Pearl crumbled to the floor and wept.

Twenty-six days had passed since she had been taken from the apartment unconscious. Her body was still unhealed and her face was not quite ready for additional plastic surgery.

"Ain't no place to sleep," Bea said. "You and Jimmy Lee can stay with us til you get a bed."

Lilly Pearl visually digested the total devastation of her living quarters. She saw her son examining his broken toys, attempting to repair his favorite truck. She wiped her tears. "We'll stay here," she said in a cold monotone voice. "This is where we belong. But I would appreciate the loan of two pillows and several blankets. We'll sleep on the floor, just like we did the first night." The callousness in her heart reverberated in her expression, filling the room with a defiant determination that was unprecedented. The advice that the social worker, Joan Clarke, had given her seven years ago resounded in her mind: ". . .Life's like a mean man who respects a woman only when she fights back." Lilly Pearl stood up, seeming to have acquired new strength. "Tell Joe I'd like the gun back, please."

"You sure you're gonna be all right?" Bea asked.

"Yes. Of course. Jimmy Lee and I will be just fine. I called the phone company from the hospital this morning. They'll reconnect my services tomorrow, and my new caseworker is coming this afternoon. Honest, Bea. We'll be just fine."

Bea looked at her seriously. "You seem different, Pearl. Maybe it's the work Doctor Leatherwood did on your face. He did a real good job, but you seem like a different person."

Lilly Pearl walked closer to her. "Different, how?"

"Oh, just different--not the same."

"Don't worry, Bea. I haven't changed. In time, you'll see

I'm the same Lilly Pearl with a slightly different face. You'll get used to me looking like this."

"It ain't just how you look that's different," Bea told her. "It's something I can't put my finger on."

"Don't worry about me, Bea."

"Oh, Pearl, I almost forgot. Nancy said they found your car in Racine. Judge Nikolakopulos is working with the police. As soon as they release it, she'll get it back to you. But they ain't found Ricardo yet, and his job ain't seen him neither."

"It doesn't matter," Lilly Pearl said. "Nobody's dying to see Ricardo. I've prayed I never do."

Joe was in the car tooting impatiently. "I gotta go now," Bea told her. "We'll drop off the bedding and a few groceries later. Do you need anything special?"

"Witch hazel and sterile cotton from the drugstore." Lilly Pearl looked in her purse for money. "And don't forget the gun."

Lilly Pearl was now on welfare again. Her caseworker had given her a voucher to purchase certain essentials. After her initial facial wounds had healed, Doctor Leatherwood carefully tested the elasticity of her skin, re-evaluated her health, coloration, facial lines and angles, in preparation for the final phase of cosmetic surgery. Then he made a cast over which chamois was pasted.

Six months had passed since Lilly Pearl's initial release from the hospital, now she had been admitted for the second time. Her broken teeth had been replaced with a skillfully designed bridge by Doctor Miravalli, and Doctor

Leatherwood was quite pleased with his artistic master-
piece.

After he had removed the sutures, Doctor Leatherwood
smiled victoriously. "Beautiful!" he said. "Just beautiful,
Mrs. Lewis."

"May I take a look!" she asked.

"You wouldn't really appreciate it now because of the
puffiness. But, fortunately, I was able to treat your first
wounds when they were fresh," the doctor told her. "The
immediate advantage of using Carrel-Dakin solution, bipp
and ice packs prevented infection and eliminated the need
for debridement."

Lilly Pearl conceptualized very little of what the plastic
surgeon had explained, of course. But the smile on his
face filled her with security.

"Tell me, Mrs. Lewis, what direction will your life take
when you're all well?"

"Back to the University, I suppose."

"You've been on my mind continuously," he said. "I
know you're no longer with your husband. Is that so?"

"I don't want to see him again, Doctor, as long as I
live."

"Have you ever considered leaving Milwaukee, Mrs.
Lewis? Maybe a new city would be good for you. You
might meet someone worthwhile in a more glamorous
environment."

"Leave? But I don't have any money. Where would I
go?" she asked.

"Well, I've been thinking," he spoke in a serious tone.
"I own several condos in Chicago, in the Gold Coast area,
along Lake Shore Drive. I also own a building in the

Bridgeport area near The Boss."

"The Boss?"

"Yes. Mayor Richard J. Dailey. These areas are exclusively white," the doctor explained. "I'd like you to live in one of the condos and manage my properties for me."

"But how could I manage in an all white neighborhood? You'd lose your tenants."

"Have you taken a good look at yourself lately--your color, your features?"

"What do you mean, Doctor?"

"Mrs. Lewis, no one would ever know you're a Negro if you didn't tell them. Any Negroid features you might have had were altered during surgery." She stared at him for a moment, thinking of what Joan Clarke had said: "You're young, beautiful, and could pass for white."

"Doctor Leatherwood, are you suggesting that I move to Chicago and pass for white?" He cleared his throat and looked at his watch. "When I was a young man in college, here at Marquette University, I applied for the medical program. I was directed to the pharmacist program instead. Their contention was that Negroes were in dire need of pharmacists. So, I became a pharmacist. Later, I applied for the medical program again and was told that I should become a dentist. So, I did. They'd rather have my hands in a white woman's mouth than between her legs," he said jokingly. "For the third time, I applied to the medical program and was advised to re-apply in several years. Consequently, I ended up in Switzerland where I earned a medical degree. After returning to the States, I wanted to practice in Chicago, but was denied rental in areas that I found most appealing. My wife and I were denied rental in one of the condos you'll be managing."

"Is that the only thing I'll do everyday?" Lilly Pearl asked. "That could become boring."

"Well, if you feel the need to work, you could study for your real estate broker's license and work for my friend Todd. He owns the agency through which I acquired these properties. He'll teach you the business. There are big bucks in real estate."

"But I don't have the money to make such a move."

"I'll provide the necessary finances," he promised. "I won't press you for an answer, but I wish you'd consider accepting my proposal. Take time to weigh the advantages that Mother Nature and I have bestowed upon you. Based upon the choices you make, your life could be significantly better. I want a Negro to live there and manage for me--one who can pass."

"But what purpose would it serve if they don't know I'm a Negro?"

"The personal gratification will be mine," the doctor said. "Just knowing I own the properties, and a Negro is living among them, would please me greatly," he told her. "I lifted myself by the bootstrap, paid all the dues this system demanded, met every challenge they confronted me with, and leaped all the hurdles. Now, in my own way, I'm demanding the benefits. America is my home and I'll remain here, for better or worse. However, I feel the need to fight back, in my own devious way," he laughed. "Even if they don't know, the satisfaction would be mine."

"Do you really think I could live with whites without them knowing I'm not one of them?" she asked.

"Thousands are passing in this country, Mrs. Lewis.

You're an exceptional woman. You'll soon get the hang of it. Believe me. They'll never know if you don't tell. But you'll have to sever your relationships here. We couldn't take a chance on your relatives or friends knowing where you are and possibly visiting you. Knowing that you can't communicate with certain friends and relatives will probably be the most difficult aspect of your decision. Our people can't keep secrets, you know. This has to be something shared only by Todd, yourself, and me."

"But what about my son? He knows we're colored."

The doctor sank into a chair in the corner. "I'm very sorry, Mrs. Lewis. I forgot about your son. The apartments are for adults only. I guess we'll have to scratch the whole idea," he got up and walked to her bed. "Please promise me you'll keep this conversation strictly confidential, Mrs. Lewis."

On her way home Lilly Pearl thought about Doctor Leatherwood's appealing proposal. *Whites have enjoyed the good life in this country since it first existed. Like the doctor, even an educated Negro with money isn't guaranteed racial freedom and happiness. Living as a single colored woman, on a teacher's salary, might keep Jimmy Lee and me in the same neighborhood for the rest of our lives.*

Lilly Pearl picked up her son from Bea and stopped to say hello to Sweet Nancy. Her car had been deliberately dented by Ricardo. And he had slashed the seats before he abandoned it. Sweet Nancy offered to have it repaired and painted, but Lilly Pearl insisted on keeping the dents and slashes to remind her of the bitter pain that made her strong.

"Pearl, you've become somebody I don't really know," Sweet Nancy told her. "You not only look different, you're not the same sweet girl. Bea and I were just wondering if something inside you snapped."

"Oh, Nancy," she said, "it's just your imagination. You and Bea think I'm different because I don't look the same."

"No. That's not it, honey," Sweet Nancy assured her. "You've changed."

"Maybe I'm wiser," she said. "The Bible says a wise man changes--a fool changes not."

"I don't mean that kinda change. I mean a coldness about you. Maybe you need to see somebody."

"Somebody like who?" Lilly Pearl asked.

"Like a psychiatrist. Maybe you were hurt more than we know. After all you did have a terrible head injury."

"Nancy, are you saying I'm a little nuts?"

"Well, no, Pearl. I don't think you're batty. It's just that sometimes people need to see a professional when they've been hurt really bad. Niko knows someone who's very good. His daughter visited him after her abortion."

"I'm not crazy, Nancy. It's just that I see life differently now. Momma and Papa taught me if you be nice to people and live by the Golden Rule, everything would be all right. But they forgot to tell me about all the other people in the world who don't give a damn about the Golden Rule. I'm not mentally disturbed. I see the world the way it really is. I'm no longer Alice blundering through a non-existent wonderland. Nancy, I still love you and everybody who's worthy of my love. Your kindness will never be forgotten." Lilly Pearl embraced Sweet Nancy and kissed her on the cheek. "You have a permanent place in my heart."

"I can remember the day when reality slapped me in the face too, Pearl," Sweet Nancy told her. "I pray you won't take the wrong path like I did. Everything we do meets us further up the road. Please promise me you won't do nothing you'll be sorry for."

"I promise, Nancy," Lilly Pearl said with her right hand raised. "I promise."

Lilly Pearl checked her mail when she and Jimmy Lee arrived home. In a sealed envelope without a stamp or address, was a note from Leslie Logan: "I knew you'd be home from the hospital today. Please call me, Pearl. I need to speak with you. It's urgent."

What does she want? Lilly Pearl wondered. She and Jimmy Lee had climbed the stairs and entered the apartment when the downstairs doorbell rang. It was Leslie who had been parked in the alley waiting. Startled by her presence, Lilly Pearl invited her in. "I got your note. What's the problem?"

"It broke my heart to hear about your calamity," Leslie stroked Lilly Pearl's arm lightly. "I've wanted to offer my services. You need help, Pearl. So, here I am."

"Everything's okay, Leslie. I'm all well, getting ready for school again."

Leslie reached into her purse and took out a thousand dollars. "This will get you started," she said. "Take it."

Feeling extremely awkward, Lilly Pearl lied. "No. Thank you, Leslie. My parents sent me money in today's mail. But it's very sweet of you to offer me such a generous loan."

"It's not a loan, Pearl. It's yours."

She tried to avoid Leslie's piercing eyes. They looked straight through her head, down her body and undressed her.

"Please take it, Dear. No strings attached."

"Honest, Leslie. I don't need it."

"You're a fool, honey," Leslie said. "I know you're lying. I saw your mail today--no letter from Mississippi."

The thought of Leslie holding her and kissing her like she had done in the powder room made Lilly Pearl shudder, frightfully. "I appreciate your concern, Leslie, but I can't be your friend. I'm not ready for any kind of relationship now."

Leslie backed out the door. "As I said, Pearl, you're a fool. You'll never make it alone. I could make you forget Ricardo."

"I don't need anyone to make me forget Ricardo. I'll accomplish that on my own."

"If you need me, you know where I am." Leslie walked slowly down the stairs.

Lilly Pearl stood at the window and watched her drive away. Then she walked to the phone and made two calls--the first to Doctor Leatherwood and the second to Pearl City, Mississippi.

Crying from the depth of her soul, she clung to Neallie Ealy with her face pressed between her breasts while Neallie's husband, Elton, sat in a rocking chair by the old potbelly wood stove, bouncing the eight year old boy on his knee. "Momma, life's been so hard for me," Lilly Pearl said. "Thanks for letting me come home."

"No need to say thanks, child. You's always welcome to home."

"I'm your papa, boy," Elton was saying to Jimmy Lee. "You's a mighty big man now. Ain't ya'?"

Elton took Jimmy Lee out back to ride his favorite horse, Patsy, and play with Simon III, the family's bloodhound. He was the great grandson of Ol Simon who once saved Elton's life. Lilly Pearl used to ride Ol Simon's back when she was a toddler. Elton had brought him home when he was a pup and named him Ol Simon, because of the loose skin and wrinkled look on his tiny face. Jimmy Lee stroked Simon III's back, but the lazy old hound only raised a brow and continued lying motionless in the shade under the back porch.

"Can you hoe, boy?" the old man asked teasingly.

"I don't know," the child answered.

"Well, I'll teach ya. You and me is gonna plant some collard greens over yonder behind the chicken coops.

"You ever seen a real live hog, young man?"

"On TV, I did."

Elton held the boy's hand as they walked to the pig pen. "How come you're crippled, Grandpa?" Jimmy Lee asked.

"Well, that's a long ugly story, little fellow. Can you shoot a sow between the eyes with a rifle?" he asked Jimmy Lee.

The child stopped and looked up at Elton. "Why would you shoot her, Grandpa?"

"You've gotta kill em before you eat em. Where'd ya think pork chops, bacon, and sausages come from?"

"My mommy gets it from Johnson's Meat Market," he said.

Elton laughed. "You ever had any chitterlings, son?"

"No. What's that?"

"When you's talking to old folks like me, you supposed to say: *No, Sir* or *Yes, Sir.*" Elton spit and wiped his mouth. "Now, chitterlings is the best part of the hog, boy. You'll see."

"Okay, I mean, yes, Sir."

The happy retired farmer chuckled. "You'll learn everything soon enough."

Inside the house, still sitting in her rocker, Neallie stroked her daughter's hair as Lilly Pearl rested her head on Neallie's lap. "Just let it all out, Pearl. I know life's been cruel since you left home, but you gotta face it like an eagle facing a storm--rise above it's fury.

"My papa used to work in a foundry," Neallie told Lilly Pearl. "He said pain is like the forging of steel. They had to keep increasing the heat, making the scum and impurities rise to the top. Then, he said they'd skim it all off til a strong, pure metal was left. Life's hardships, like the forging of steel, bring out the best in us and make us strong.

"In my heart, I know Chicago'll be good for ya. And Jimmy Lee's gonna be just fine livin down here. Him and Elton's buddies already."

Lilly Pearl knew her son would be loved and treated well living in the extended family setting. She explained to her family that she looked strange to them because of the plastic surgery. But they hadn't seen her since she was fourteen. So, it didn't matter to them. They were happy to see her again.

Fearing that somebody might find her and foil her plans, Lilly Pearl asked her family never to reveal her whereabouts to anyone, not even to Bea and Joe. "When I get situated, I'll send my address and phone number," she told her mother. "I've got a good job waiting for me. I'll send money for Jimmy Lee too."

Three days later, at the airport in Jackson, Mississippi, Lilly Pearl squeezed her son in a motherly embrace, saying goodbye. She smiled to camouflage the mental pain she presently suffered. *This is for his own good,* she rationalized. *It's not like losing him forever.*

Jimmy Lee's curly red hair blazed in the sun. He had already begun to resemble his father, J. D. Trodder. With a look in his eyes that transcended a child's understanding, Lilly Pearl knew that her son felt safe. "Grandpa's gonna let me drive his tractor, Mommy."

"Just don't get hurt," she said, remembering J. D.'s crippled leg. "You be a good boy, sweetheart. Mommy's gonna work very, very hard and make lots of money, so we can be together again soon." To conceal her tears, she turned and ran toward the waiting plane.

They met in the Pfister Hotel for dinner. Todd and Doctor Leatherwood stood as she approached the table. She felt like a princess in the elegant suit that the doctor had delivered the night before. Doctor Leatherwood introduced Lilly Pearl to his friend, Todd A. Bonnell, who extended his right hand for what she thought would be a handshake. Instead, Todd took her hand, bowed at the waist and kissed it. "The pleasure is all mine, Mrs. Lewis," he said.

Lilly Pearl blushed. "I'm pleased to meet you, Mr. Bonnell."

Doctor Leatherwood gloated with enormous satisfaction--he would prove triumphant in retaliation. Todd was impressed with the weapon his friend had chosen.

The doctor signaled the waiter who came with a bottle of Piper-Heidsieck champagne. Lilly Pearl felt awkward and somewhat nervous when they raised their glasses. "Mrs. Lewis, here's to a new life, filled with happiness and success," the plastic surgeon said.

"I'll drink to that," Todd added.

"Thanks, both of you," she said. "Oh, Doctor Leatherwood, the flight was exciting. I had never flown before."

Todd was a handsome brunette of medium height, with dancing blue eyes that said, *Trust me.* He was dressed in a dark blue suit and wore a diamond ring that said, *I have money.* His smile revealed well kept teeth and deep, friendly dimples. Unlike Doctor Leatherwood, the way he looked was indicative of his wealth.

As she scanned the extravagant menu, Lilly Pearl had no idea what to order. "I'm not very hungry," she claimed. "Something on the light side would be fine."

Sensing that she wasn't familiar with the menu, Todd asked, "May I order for you?"

With a discreet sigh of relief, Lilly Pearl said, "Yes. Please."

"Escargot for the lady," he told the waiter. "And I'll have the same."

"Would you like the appetizer, Monsieur, or the entree?" the waiter wanted to know.

"The entree, of course," he said.

"Nothing fancy for me," the doctor told the waiter. "I'm a simple man. Give me the combination plate--the steak and lobster, please."

"Thank you, Messieurs," the waiter responded with a phony French accent. He poured more champagne before he left the table.

With his tall weak frame, adorned in tan, uncreased, corduroy pants, a plaid shirt, and an avocado cardigan, Doctor Leatherwood looked as if he didn't belong in the Pfister Hotel.

This is really a classy place, Lilly Pearl thought. *It's like something out of a romantic movie. Who wouldn't choose this life?*"

She enjoyed the escargot without the faintest notion of what she was eating. She was too embarrassed to ask. While they were eating, Lilly Pearl noticed a familiar face staring at her from two tables away. It was Judge Nikolakopulos having cocktails with the police chief and the mayor. He appeared to be puzzled and uncertain that it was she. After all, he had never seen her with short blond hair.

After dinner, they took the elevator to Todd's suite. The large suite was decorated throughout with French provincial furniture.

"Take a seat there," Todd pointed at the plush sofa. She sat on it carefully, as if she might damage it.

Doctor Leatherwood sat beside her. "I was most delighted when you agreed to do it, Mrs. Lewis. We've got so little time to make plans."

Todd served them a glass of Piper-Heidsieck from a

bottle he had chilled in a large silver bucket on the bar.

"My friend here," nodding his head in Todd's direction, "will have everything ready when you arrive," the plastic surgeon told her. "In fact, your apartment's already furnished. He'll take you shopping for a wardrobe when you get there." Doctor Leatherwood gave Todd a six thousand dollar check. "You'll know the right stores," he said. "Dress her well. And lease a nice car for her. I'll send the monthly installments."

Happy, for the first time, to give his money freely, he ran his long slender fingers through his coarse, ragged curls. "Here's a thousand dollars, Mrs. Lewis, to clear any loose ends you might have." Next, Doctor Leatherwood handed her a cashier's check for four thousand dollars. "Open a checking account when you get there. This will cover your living expenses, educational costs, and incidentals for the first three months. You'll owe no rent or utilities, of course."

Never having seen checks of that magnitude, Lilly Pearl found it difficult to maintain her composure. "What educational costs?" she asked.

"Do you recall the conversation we had concerning Todd hiring you at his real estate agency?" the doctor asked.

"Yes. I'd love that," she said.

"You must first study and pass the state exam to become a licensed broker," he explained.

Lilly Pearl walked proudly to Sweet Nancy's door thinking, *She'll love the way I look.*

Sweet Nancy answered the door and looked surprised.

"What have you done to your hair, Pearl? And where did you get that expensive suit?"

"Oh, a friend." Lilly Pearl walked in and spun around to show off the garment she wore.

"But, your hair. Why did you bleach it?"

"Just for the heck of it, I guess. You don't like it?"

"Honey, you look so white. What's happening to you?"

"I've told you, Nancy. Nothing's wrong with me. Can't a lady change her hair without her best friend thinking she's gone wacky?"

"I guess so. But a feeling deep inside tells me you've got something up your sleeve, girl--something you ain't telling. I hope you ain't getting into anything you'll be sorry for."

"It's nothing, Nancy. Honest," Lilly Pearl swore. "I came to return the car and say goodbye."

"Goodbye? Where the hell are you going?" Sweet Nancy asked.

"I'm going to school, but not in Milwaukee."

Sweet Nancy looked worried. "Where the fuck are you off to?"

"I can't discuss it now. I'll write you when I'm there."

"This is really crazy, Pearl." Tears were in Sweet Nancy's eyes. "Something's snapped inside your head. You need to see a psychiatrist."

"Please try to understand, Nancy." Lilly Pearl embraced her. "I'm sorry to disappoint you. Don't cry." She wiped her friend's tears with her hand. "You see, I've learned that life's a big grab bag," Lilly Pearl explained. "I'm gonna reach for the top and take what's mine."

"Don't talk so high and mighty, Pearl." Sweet Nancy got

a tissue and wiped her face. "I said those identical words when I met Niko. Believe me. You'll be sorry, girl. Does Bea know?"

"I'm not going to tell Bea, Nancy. She's not strong like you. I couldn't stand the pain of saying goodbye to her." She reached into her purse. "Please give this gun to Joe and tell him thanks. I won't need it where I'm going."

"You're not saying goodbye to Bea?" Sweet Nancy looked at her with disbelief. "How could you be so cold?"

"It would be too painful for both of us. Please, Nancy, tell her not to worry about me. And don't say anything until I'm gone."

"When will you leave?" Sweet Nancy asked.

"Early tomorrow morning," Lilly Pearl said. "Tell Bea I love her, and I love you too, Nancy. You've been so kind to me. I'll never forget what you've done. God bless you Sweet Nancy." Lilly Pearl gave her the car keys, held her in a long, affectionate hug, kissed her cheek, and walked out the door.

The night was still, eerie, and unusually quiet, except for the familiar scratching of rats in the walls. Lilly Pearl was lonely for her child and wondered if he might be thinking of her. *Does he hate me for leaving him?* She took his picture off the shelf, kissed it and held it close in her arms, as if it were he. "I love you Jimmy Lee," she said aloud. Lilly Pearl lifted the receiver to call her son, but the phone company had already honored her disconnection request. She wrapped Jimmy Lee's picture in a large heavy towel along with those of Elton and Neallie. Then she placed them in the large Samsonite suitcase she had purchased that day at Boston Store.

The drab apartment seemed more depressing than ever now that Lilly Pearl had dined at the Pfister and sipped champagne in Todd's suite. Choosing what she would take on this trip was more than merely packing a suitcase and trashing unwanted items. It was the exclusion of a cruel lifestyle and the systematic acceptance of a dissimilar environment with a different set of values. She was severing five years of dreams that had festered. Lilly Pearl walked to the window and looked out at the old dilapidated buildings under the dim street lights. She heard echoes of broken men bragging of sexual conquests and angry young men swearing and marring the vehicles of neighbors they hated. In her ears were the voices of fat, unkempt, inebriated housewives screaming at undisciplined, ragged kids. Her nostrils seemed to be filled with smokey Bar B Q's, lingering from Memorial Day and the Fourth of July. She peered down at the black owned corner store with its stale meat and molded bread. Lilly Pearl counted the outdated Fleetwoods that lined the streets. *The people here buy old Cadillacs for prestige,* she thought. *They have no dreams beyond their front doors. My people. My people. Sometimes I hate you as much as I love you. Thank God this is my last night in hell.*

This miserable hole in the ghetto had been Lilly Pearl's home, and now it would become a vacant trap for some poor welfare recipient who would know the same frustrations, sorrows, and tears she had experienced. Looking at the four thousand dollar check Doctor Leatherwood had given her, Lilly Pearl wondered what life in Chicago would be like.

On the verge of entering a new life, in a world where she would be white, Lilly Pearl suddenly became engulfed in guilt and fear. She looked at her reflection in the mirror. *Dear, God, is this a blessing--this option to pass?*

The clock alarmed at 5:00 a.m. She had to be at Mitchell Field by 7:45. Getting a cab in the innercity took an hour or more, if one decided to come. Lilly Pearl ran upstairs and paid Bulah two dollars to use their phone.

Excitement fluttered through her stomach as she bathed and dressed hurriedly. *I'd better check the closet and drawers again,* she reminded herself. Before finishing her coffee, she poured a glass of milk. *Just what I need to calm my stomach.* She ran to the window to look for the cab. *Not here yet. I'll drink my milk.* She returned to the kitchen, and in her glass was a large roach heavy with eggs, struggling to be free. "You pregnant bitch!" Lilly Pearl shouted and ran for the roach spray. She held it over the glass and emptied the can. "That'll cure your appetite for milk," she said. By the time the roach had died, there was a loud horn blast outside. *It's the cab! Thank God it came!* Dressed in a winter-white suit, she raised the window and called out to him, "I'll be right down."

For the final time, Lilly Pearl checked herself in the bathroom mirror and grabbed her purse and suitcase. She laid the door key on the kitchen sink near the roach, floating feet-up. With three clicks of her heels and her head held high, she said, "Adios, cucaracha!"

PART II

CHICAGO

- *12* -

The Golden Threshold

She had hardly leaned back in her seat and closed her eyes when the metallic voice of the pilot came over the intercom to announce that they'd be landing in Chicago in five minutes. She looked at her watch. Seventeen minutes had passed since take-off. The plane shuddered as the wheels were lowered and it started its descent. From the window, Lilly Pearl could see the giant city spread out below, bounded along the northeast by Lake Michigan. It reminded her of Milwaukee in only one way. Both cities, about ninety-five miles apart, followed the curvature of the

165

Lake. *Somewhere down there,* she thought, *I'll live a stone's throw from the beach.*

She felt a stirring sensation in her groin when the plane made a sudden dip. And in a matter of seconds, they touched down at O'Hare International Airport. Remembering when she was fourteen, how long it had taken her to travel from Pearl City, Mississippi to Milwaukee by Greyhound Bus, Lilly Pearl promised herself that from now on she'd travel first class. In the terminal she was overwhelmed by the swift-paced, modern, sophisticated facade of O'Hare. Out of the buzzing crowd loomed a familiar smile. "Welcome to Chicago, Mrs. Lewis. Did you have a smooth flight?" Before she could answer, he asked for her claim check. "Let's get out of here," he said. "I left my car in a restricted zone." Todd seemed elated that she was there, and she could see he knew the place quite well.

"Am I walking too fast?" he asked. Then he held her hand like she was a child. She followed, half running. When they had almost reached the exit, he stopped. "I forgot to ask. Did you have breakfast?"

"No," she said, visualizing the pregnant roach.

"Stay here," he told her. "I'll put your baggage in the car. We'll eat in the airport."

This time she wasn't frustrated by the menu. She ordered bacon and eggs.

"What do you think of the Windy City, Mrs. Lewis?" Todd asked.

"Well, I. . ."

"Oh, this is silly," he interrupted. "I feel so uncomfortable calling you Mrs. Lewis. We're going to call you Lilly. Do you mind?"

"Lilly sounds nice to me." Lilly Pearl agreed.

"Now, back to my original question. Do you think you'll like Chicago?"

"Much better than any place I've ever lived before," she said.

"We'll shop for your wardrobe tomorrow." Todd looked at his watch. "Today I have a 3:30 appointment."

"Tomorrow's fine. I could use the rest."

"There's food at the apartment, Lilly. I dropped it off this morning."

"That was kind and thoughtful, Todd. Thank you." Lilly Pearl wondered how a man as busy as he could shop for groceries.

"I'll stop by tonight after I leave the office," he told her. "We'll have you settled in a few days."

Lilly Pearl felt safe, knowing that Todd would look after her. *I wonder if he's married,* she asked herself.

"Maurice told me you have a son, Lilly."

"Yes. Jimmy Lee."

"How old is he?"

"Eight," Lilly Pearl said proudly.

"Oh, he's the same age as my son, Jason. Jason is the spoiled one. He's the one we didn't expect."

I guess he must be married, she thought.

Todd pulled out his wallet and displayed a snapshot of his family. "That's Todd Junior, twelve, my oldest. Becky, my ten-year-old daughter. Jason, the little blond tiger there, and Beth, my wife." His chest seemed to swell as Lilly Pearl complimented him on the beauty of his children, and his attractive wife. Beth wore a chubby smile and appeared to be hiding behind the three children.

"Thank you," he said, seeming to sense what Lilly Pearl was thinking. "Beth used to be your size." He put the wallet away. "She talks a lot about dieting."

"It isn't easy to lose weight." Lilly Pearl sipped her coffee. "Bea tries all the time."

"If you try, you lose," Todd spoke dryly.

From the tone of his voice and his immediate mood change, Lilly Pearl could detect that it was a sore subject for him.

Todd cleared his throat and shifted in his seat. "Tell me about your son, Jimmy Lee. What is he like?"

"Are you asking if he could pass?"

"No, Lilly. That thought hadn't entered my mind. You're being overly sensitive. I was wondering if he's a fun guy."

She was embarrassed and felt she'd made a fool of herself. "I'm sorry, Todd. Please forgive me." *Oh, God, I don't want him to hate me.* "Yes. He's a nice kid. We have fun together. He's rather grown-up for his age, but Papa will probably spoil him like you did Jason."

"What about his father, your ex-husband? Does he know where he is?"

"My ex is not his father." Lilly Pearl ground her teeth slightly and took a deep breath. "Tell me about Chicago, Todd."

"Well, it's my home--a rather complex city," he said. "Illinois is both a northern and southern state in attitude. Are you interested in politics?"

"Yes, but I've been struggling too hard to get involved. Are you politically active?" she asked.

"Me? No. This city is extremely divided, socially and economically. There's too much distrust between races and between nationality groups. You might say that Illinois is a swing-state," he told her.

"What's a swing state?" She looked at him with wide-eyed curiosity.

"Oh," he chuckled, "votes often mirror the fluctuation in socio-economic tension," he explained.

"I think I understand," she said. "It's like all the other states."

"Yes." Todd laughed. "Maybe it isn't unique in that respect. But you'll love living in the Gold Coast area."

She smelled the roses and touched them gently, afraid she'd awaken to find it was just a pulchritudinous dream--the long-stemmed red roses Todd had brought, the luxurious apartment furnished with a rich Mediterranean flare, and the bottle of champagne.

Remembering where she had been five hours earlier, Lilly Pearl was afraid to trust reality. With the passing of a few hours, she had left a life of poverty and crossed the threshold of the upper middle-class. *By now Bea knows I'm gone,* she thought. *I hope she'll forgive me.*

After two glasses of wine, Lilly Pearl felt light, young and exhilarated. She scrambled through her suitcase and found the new silk robe she'd bought. Standing in the spacious, beautifully designed bath, Lilly Pearl stripped. *I do feel different,* she said to herself as she looked at her nude body in the huge, full-length mirror that covered the wall. Her life had been so filled with pain, she had forgotten the physical, desirable Lilly Pearl. Looking back at her were two gray eyes that suddenly sparkled with life. She thought of Todd and what it would be like to have his lips pressed firmly against hers. *But he's married,* she told herself. *Shame on you, Pearl.*

The naked body in the mirror was that of a woman, well formed. Standing at attention were two full, rounded breasts with cherry-sized nipples. Her firm, flat stomach sloped delicately down to a soft patch of brown. An erotic image of white satin projected off the wall. She was alive again inside and desiring the presence of a man. The impassioned blond pressed her fingers to her lips fantasizing that her lover was kissing her. She cupped her breasts and sighed.

Lilly Pearl left the mirror and stepped carefully into the shower. She lathered her body until it was slippery with foam. The heat intensified as she ran her long, slender fingers repeatedly over her hungry flesh. With her eyes closed, Lilly Pearl enjoyed the appeasing force of the warm water, while the fragrance from her body filled her nostrils with the scent of lilac.

This was the first time the phone had rung in her new life. "I'm calling to congratulate the first Negro to live in the Lake Shore Condos," he said. "How do you feel, Mrs. Lewis? This is Maurice."

"Doctor Leatherwood! I'm so happy you called. Everything's fine. The place is just devine."

"You have my number if you need me, Mrs. Lewis. But Todd's a dependable individual," the doctor said, "I don't think you'll meet a more responsible person."

"He's been awfully nice, Doctor. I'll tell him you called."

"No need," he said. "I just called to say hello."

The hours passed swiftly and at 9:50, on the evening of

Lilly Pearl's arrival in Chicago, Todd was with her again, having a glass of wine in her apartment. As he explained all of the necessary things they'd do for the next few days, their eyes met with startling electricity. She quickly regained her composure and he continued talking. When Lilly Pearl walked to the bar to refill their glasses, Todd's eyes followed her. And she recalled her fantasy. The room was filled with an unusual air of wonder and magnetic interest. Todd nervously stroked his hair off his forehead and shifted his position on the sofa. Lilly Pearl felt embarrassed because of the aching passion in her chest and abdomen. Suddenly, Todd stood. "Lilly, I'll see you at 8:30 tomorrow morning. We'll have breakfast and go shopping."

On her second day in Chicago, Todd picked her up early as he had promised. The weather was unseasonably warm for October, and Chicagoans took advantage of the bright sunshine. The morning traffic was heavy with tie-ups when they reached Michigan Avenue. They'd had breakfast at the Palmer House. Now the exclusive shops on North Michigan would be open. Lilly Pearl felt extremely anxious, thinking of buying a wardrobe that day. Todd, who skillfully threaded his way through the mass of impolite drivers, seemed to be in serious thought.

The morning passed quickly and the afternoon found Lilly Pearl and Todd still running from shop to shop. He would smile approvingly or shake his head from side-to-side when she'd model a garment or shoes. Finally, when his trunk and back seat had been crammed with boxes, he suggested calling it a day. "We'll look through what we have and decide what else you need."

Todd and Lilly Pearl dined that evening at Don Roth. During the meal, he detailed their plans for the coming day.

With chattering teeth, Lilly Pearl ran from the bathroom thinking, *I'll see him again today. What shall I wear?* She sang *Misty* as she walked into the closet, trying to remember how she had looked in each outfit. From her new wardrobe, she chose a navy blue tailored suit and accentuated it with a string of cultured pearls.

"Aren't we glamorous today," Todd told her when she met him at the door. The magnetism between them propagated with each passing hour. But they denied the existence of it.

"Off we go again," Todd said, driving toward the Lake. On Lake Shore Drive, he parked in front of an ultra-modern building. Everything grew quiet and all eyes were on Lilly Pearl when they entered the outer office. On a folding table near the window were assorted doughnuts and coffee. "Welcome to the gang!" she exclaimed gregariously. "You must be Lilly?"

Surprised, she managed to say, "Yes. I'm Lilly."

The tall pregnant lady with soft hazel eyes walked over and shook her hand. "I'm Blair. Blair Janquet," she said. "Nice to meet you, Lilly." Then the secretary stood at her desk. "I'm Eve Smythe," she said. "Hi, Lilly."

Lilly Pearl was speechless. Todd had told them she'd be there and hadn't prepared her for the surprise.

A short stocky fellow came out of his office and called to someone in the adjacent room. "This is Peter Smyth,

Eve's husband," Todd told her. "And the lady with her head poked out the door is Lisa Stark."

"Hello, Lilly," Lisa waved to her. "I'll be out in a minute."

Peter Smythe adjusted his blazer and tie with his left hand, offering his right hand in a clammy grip. "How do you do, Lilly? Happy to have you aboard. Just call me Pete."

Lilly Pearl heard the muffled sound of a toilet flushing and a door opening from somewhere down the narrow hallway. "That has to be Chuck Anderson," Todd announced. "Here he is folks--the one and only Chucky, the office manager!" He was red with embarrassment. "Howdy, Lilly. Glad to meet ya'."

Then slowly the large mahogany door with *Todd A. Bonnell* printed on it in gold captions opened. Todd stood frozen, waiting to see who'd emerge from his private office. Everyone stood motionless with their eyes on the boss. Lilly Pearl recognized her from the snapshot. "Beth! I didn't know you were here," the real estate lawyer said to his wife. "Why didn't you tell me you were visiting the office today?" She looked as if she enjoyed the stymied expression on his face. "I'm Beth," she told Lilly Pearl, with a wry smile. "Mrs. Todd A. Bonnell," she said, ignoring Lilly Pearl's extended hand.

"Does your wife know I'm a Negro?" Lilly Pearl looked worried.

"Of course not," Todd assured her. "You, Maurice, and I are the only ones who know you're passing. I can't imagine what got into Beth."

"Did you tell her I'd be in the office this morning?"

"No. I told no one except my staff."

"How did she find out?"

"I have no idea who informed her," he said, "nor the reason why."

"Maybe I shouldn't work for you, Todd."

"What I'm doing for Maurice is a business transaction between friends."

Lilly Pearl thought for a moment. "Is that what I mean to you--an item in a business transaction?"

"Please, Lilly," he pat the back of her hand, "let's drop this conversation. I'll get things straight with Beth tonight."

Before they reached the motor vehicle department, Todd reminded Lilly Pearl that she must write *Caucasion* or *white* in any space on the application denoting *race* or *nationality*. After she had received her driver's license, they went to the dealer where her new car was waiting.

She ran her hand over the cool leather seat. *Oh, God, I can't believe all of these wonderful things are happening to me.* On the front seat beside her was a map of Chicago. She tucked it into the glove compartment and turned on the ignition.

"You'll follow me," Todd said. He drove slowly back to her apartment and told her to park in the spot marked *manager*. Night had fallen and the sporty Thunderbird glowed in the lights of the underground garage. Still sitting in his car, Todd called out to her, "Take the elevator up and rest tonight. We'll get you enrolled in real estate classes tomorrow."

"I know what Maurice did for you!" Beth shouted. But must you pay forever?"

"Please, Beth. I promised to help her get situated," he explained.

"You have enough to do without playing big brother to this woman," Beth said angrily. "What is Lilly to Maurice?"

Todd knew quite well that he couldn't renege on his promise, nor could he tell Beth who Lilly Pearl really was. Although, he feared that the secrecy surrounding Lilly Pearl's being there might further arouse Beth's suspicious nature. Todd had been a visiting instructor in the Law school at Marquette University when he and E. Maurice Leatherwood met in 1960. During that time, the Green Bay Packers were leading the Western Conference of the National Football League. The Spartan-like Vince Lombardi and his warriors were the major attraction in Milwaukee and Green Bay. One was most fortunate to get a fifty-yard-line ticket for any game during the season. However, through one of his fellow visiting instructors, Todd had managed to acquire three such tickets to a game in Green Bay between the Packers and the Vikings. After a delightful day at Lambeau Field, watching the battle between the mighty Packers and the *Purple People Eaters,* Todd and two of his co-workers drove back along Highway 41 toward Milwaukee. A thin sheet of ice covered the road and a dry flurry of powdery snow filled the night sky. Suddenly, a deer with glassy eyes reflecting in the beam of his headlights jumped in the path of the car. Todd swerved on the slippery road, struck a bridge and flipped over. Fortunately, for him, E. Maurice Leatherwood had attended the same game. He happened along just in time to drag Todd, who was unconscious, from the burning car that exploded before he could free the others. Leatherwood examined Todd carefully in the sub-zero weather; then he placed him on the padded floor of his station wagon and carried him to Mount Sinai Hospital in Milwaukee. That was the birth of their friendship. And during the next five years, Todd developed an empathetic understanding of the psychological pain and frustration his black friend had experienced. He made a personal commitment to rectify certain societal wrongs through his loyalty to Leatherwood.

"I can't give you an indepth explanation of Maurice's personal affairs," he told his wife. "You'll have to trust me, Beth. Lilly is an intelligent young lady. She'll soon be independent of my help."

Dubious, Beth reverted back to her initial anger, snatched a pillow from the bed and slept on the sofa that night.

Beth never approved of her husband's allegiance to Doctor Leatherwood. Previously, she had never thought seriously about their business transactions. She hadn't decided whether she liked the doctor or hated him. Having grown up in the Bridgeport area of Chicago, she never had to contend with racial differences. But now a black man had asked a favor of her husband that proved abrasive to their marital relationship. She extended her protest by moving into the bedroom with Becky.

Inexorably time went by, and almost three months had passed. Lilly Pearl and Todd had become very close platonic friends. Todd's one consolation during this time was that Lilly Pearl had successfully completed the real estate courses and passed the state broker's exam. He had tutored her well. However, for Todd, it was a bittersweet feeling. The more she learned, the less he'd have a reason to visit her evenings. Her work at the office was excellent, and she had no problem collecting rent for the doctor. Now he feared she might seek a job at another agency.

There were only a few days left before Christmas. Todd had a real estate transaction that required a trip to Palm Springs. He decided that this would be the ideal exposure for Lilly Pearl. If he could make her job more glamorous, he believed she'd remain in his employment. Lilly Pearl was Todd's creation. He felt like Pygmalion. Todd had chosen her clothes and tutored her. He had taught her where to eat and what to eat. Lilly Pearl had quickly absorbed it all. Todd had taken a black welfare recipient out of the ghetto and molded her into a well dressed, intellectual, middle-class white lady. His friend, Maurice, had financed the venture, of course, but it was he who had performed the metamorphosis.

Todd was convinced that Lilly Pearl would learn a lot about selling commercial buildings during their trip to Palm Springs. From Palm Springs, she would fly South to spend Christmas with Jimmy Lee and return to Chicago before Blair would have her baby.

Blair had been extremely anxious about giving birth before she knew that Lilly Pearl would be with her. She was five months pregnant when they first met, and her husband, Cory, had died of a congenital heart defect three months earlier.

On the first day that they met, Lilly Pearl and Blair had

seen an understanding of pain and loneliness in each other's eyes. Lilly Pearl helped Blair to remain strong through her pregnancy. She had sat with her through Alcoholic Anonymous meetings, never questioning her past. They ate lunch together daily, went to a movie on weekends, and shopped together frequently. From the very beginning, Lilly Pearl found in Blair a sincere warmth that was most rare. Unlike Lisa, Blair never tried to pry into her background and her personal affairs. Unlike Lisa, Blair never told nigger jokes, nor did she laugh at them. Lilly Pearl concluded that whatever Blair's problem in the past had been, concerning the abuse of alcohol, she was still a classy lady. They both looked forward to the baby.

"There's Mount San Jacinto," Todd pointed to the left of the plane. The snow capped mountain reached into the blue sky above them. "Isn't it beautiful?" he said. Hot saliva flowed from under her tongue. The four hour flight from Chicago had Lilly Pearl's stomach churning. "I think I'm going to vomit," she said.

"Breathe deeply and look at the ground," Todd told her. "We'll be landing soon."

Lilly Pearl looked at the brown desert that extended as far as she could see. *Not a patch of green,* she thought. *How could anyone live out here?*

Over the intercom the pilot apologized for the rough ride and assured the passengers they'd be landing soon. He got a light applause from the crowded plane.

Todd had reserved two adjacent pool side suites at the El Mirador on Indian Avenue. From room service, he ordered food and wine for Lilly Pearl and suggested that she rest until evening. He would contact his client.

Looking out the window of the hotel, Lilly Pearl could see why people were so excited over Palm Springs. *It looks like a picture post card,* she thought. *I'm impressed.*

She slept. And, as night crept over the desert, Palm Springs came alive as if by one master switch. Soft floodlights illuminated the tall palm trees that lined Palm Canyon Drive. And tourists filed along the sidewalks ducking in and out of tiny shops that looked like Spanish adobe huts.

Seven hours had passed when Todd phoned Lilly Pearl to dress for the evening. They would dine with his client. For the occasion, Todd had bought her a sleek black gown with a teasing split from the hem to the knee. To accentuate it, she wore one-carat diamond studs, silver pumps and an autumn-haze mink stole.

Todd was breathless when she answered the door. "My, are you beautiful!" he said. They walked arm-in-arm, returning the warm smiles of people they met. His client was waiting in the lobby. He was a robust fifty-four year old Texan, about six-four, with a reddish complexion. He wore a white ten-gallon hat, tan cowboy boots, and a fancy western outfit. Clinched in his teeth was a giant cigar with ashes an inch long. When he spoke, his high pitched Texas drawl filled the lobby. "This here must be Miss Lilly," he said, with a handshake that unbalanced her. "Why, you're as cute as a new born Jersey. I'm B.T.--Big Tom Tuckey!"

"Nice to meet you, Mr. Tuckey," she said.

"We'll have none of that Mister formality. My friends call me B.T."

"Okay, B.T.," Lilly Pearl smiled. "I'd love to be your friend."

"She's a precious little gem, Todd," Tom said as he opened the door for Lilly Pearl.

Immediately outside was a white Cadillac limousine with long steer horns mounted on the hood. From behind the wheel bounced a wiry black man in a chauffeur's uniform. He opened the doors and stood until they were seated. Lilly Pearl guessed his age to be about forty-nine. He was graying at the temples and bore a strong resemblance to her cousin, Willie Ray. She was about to say, "Good evening," but caught herself.

Tom talked continuously as they sped southward on Palm Canyon Drive. "We'll eat at Las Casuelas. Go through that light, Isaac" he'd say to the chauffeuer in an audacious manner. Or he'd instruct the driver to blow the horn for pedestrians crossing the street. "Too many people in Palm Springs these days." He chewed on his cigar. "A few years back I did fifty down this here street. The snow birds are ruining this damn town."

Lilly Pearl's heart beat rapidly. *Where are the police?* she wondered. *The things rich whites get away with. The whole world is their playpen.*

Isaac's gaze caught Lilly Pearl's eyes for a split second in the rearview mirror. She felt he knew her secret. At that moment, she hated him for being there, filling her with guilt. For the very first time, she hated her own blackness.

- *13* -

Empathy

It was 4:22 a.m., and the waiting room was quiet. Lilly Pearl sat alone wondering how much longer Blair would be in delivery. Deeply concerned about her friend's condition, she walked to the nurses' station again, but found no one there. In a tiny side-room was a metal stand on which a pot of coffee was brewing. Lilly Pearl poured herself a cup and pushed a folded dollar bill under the sugar bowl. Someone had left yesterday's Tribune lying on a chair in the corner. She took the paper and coffee back to the waiting room and tried to relax. *Babies take their own sweet time,* she reminded herself.

As her eyes casually scanned the newspaper, the word Milwaukee jumped out at her. She quickly brought the paper close to her face and read: Race Riot in Milwaukee Destroys Upper 3rd Street, Black Male Killed. Lilly Pearl dropped the paper and ran to the phone in the corridor. The long distance operator asked her to deposit ninety-five cents. She took a deep breath. Her fingers were trembling so badly she could hardly dial. After several long lazy rings, Joe's gritty voice sounded in her ear. Lilly Pearl opened her mouth to answer him, but her throat was tight and frozen. "Who the hell is this?" Joe growled. "Hello! Hello!" She quietly placed the receiver on the phone. *Oh, God, I hope nothing's happened to my relatives and friends in Milwaukee,* she prayed. *Joe Junior was always protesting and marching. But it couldn't be Junior they've killed. His daddy was too calm. I'll call Momma when I get home. She'll know if anybody's hurt.*

The nurse looked at Lilly Pearl sympathetically and told her that the Janquet baby had died at birth.

"Where's Blair?" she asked. "I've got to see her."

"I'm afraid she's still under," the nurse said, "but I'll take you to her."

Blair looked pale and fragile, almost lifeless. Lilly Pearl wondered if she knew her baby was dead. She held her cold white hand, kissed her forehead, and whispered, "God bless you, Blair. I love you."

The nurse brought Lilly Pearl a chair and said it would be a good idea for her to be with Blair when she awakened. She'll recall the death of her baby.

What shall I say to her? Lilly Pearl wondered. *What do you say to a woman who has lost her dead husband's baby?* She knew how much Blair had wanted Cory's child. It was the only thing he'd left her.

Before Cory, Blair had dropped out of college and married Ted Schultz, who was divorced with two children. Their marriage had been quite comfortable for the first five years, but she became obsessed with having her own baby. Ted had dreamed of expanding his one-hour cleaning business into several chains throughout the Chicago area. Having another child to support would not be conducive to gaining great wealth. After five years of marriage, Blair learned that Ted had gotten a vasectomy three weeks before their wedding. His friend, Mike, had convinced him that she would settle for mothering his two children. Blair felt betrayed. Facing the realization that with him she'd never know the fulfillment of motherhood, her anger grew into depression. Her depression grew into a dependency on valium and alcohol. Ted watched while her self-worth deteriorated. And when she had become shamefully helpless, he left her in the Bay Side Rehabilitation Hospital.

"I can't live without my baby," Blair spoke weakly.

"Sure you can," Lilly Pearl told her, fighting back the tears. "People do it all the time."

"But you don't understand. Our baby was all I had to live for."

Lilly Pearl took a deep breath and kissed Blair's hand. *God, please don't let me cry. I've got to be strong--to say the right thing.*

"Time," she said. "It'll take time, Blair. You'll recover and meet someone really nice--someone like Cory."

Blair stared at the ceiling with a look of pain on her face. Lilly Pearl knew she'd need her friendship more now than ever before.

During the following eighteen months, Lilly Pearl had proven to be Blair's only friend. And Todd had become a strong shoulder for Lilly Pearl and Blair, while at the office someone kept Beth up to date on all current events. Todd found it impossible to nail the culprit. Although, he knew it had to be someone on his staff. Beth knew that Lilly Pearl had gone to Palm Springs with Todd. For a year and a half she had hounded him and accused him of infidelity. Anonymous phone calls to Beth from the office came frequently, inventing tales of suspicious behavior between Lilly Pearl and Todd. After each call, Beth would consume a large bowl of ice cream and a package of oatmeal cookies. She had managed to add twenty-eight pounds to her stately posture since the Palm Springs trip. Todd could not convince his wife that the calls were filled with malicious lies.

The phone rang violently in the pit-black room. "Miss Lewis?" the voice coming from the receiver inquired. "Is this Miss Lewis?"

Puzzled, she answered, "Yes. This is Lilly Lewis."

"This is Pleasant View Rehabilitation Hospital calling. We have Mrs. Blair Janquet here. She's asking for you. Are you a relative?"

"No. A friend. I'll be there right away. What's wrong with Blair?"

"Her condition is serious, Miss Lewis."

I must go to her, Lilly Pearl thought.

When she entered the small sterile room, Blair was straining against the unyielding leather straps that imprisoned her in a world of wretchedness--a world woven with threads of valium and alcohol. She squirmed, screamed, and pleaded with the doctor to end her life, to rid her of the excruciating pain.

"You must try to relax, Mrs. Janquet," the doctor was saying. "We're trying to help you."

Lilly Pearl stood staring in disbelief at the traumatic sight of Blair's spasmodic, undernourished body, twisting and jerking beneath the merciless strips of cowhide. Two years had passed since Blair's baby had died. Since that night, she had seldom drawn a sober breath. Lilly Pearl moved close enough to touch Blair's face. "I'm here, Blair. It's Lilly. Can you hear me?"

Wrying, she opened her eyes. "Lilly, I want to die," she said. "Please tell them to let me die."

"You can't die," she told her. "You're my friend." Blair's nails cut into Lilly Pearl's palm, but she didn't mind the pain. *This too shall pass,* she thought.

The office was quiet when Lilly Pearl arrived. Peter Smythe and his wife Eve usually stayed quite late, but they had gone for the day. She'd spent several evenings a week studying certian folders trying to familiarize herself with closing procedures. Todd, Chuck Anderson, and Smythe were the only brokers authorized to close property. They earned substantially more than everyone else. Todd had suggested that Lilly Pearl prepare herself to handle residential closings. After she had pulled several folders and poured herself a cup of coffee, the phone rang. An enraged former client was trying to reach Peter Smythe. He related a confusing story concerning an agreement between he and Smythe, whereas Smythe had reduced the initial commission on the sale of some property from 8.5 percent to 6.0 percent. The client had paid Smythe 1.75 percent under the table, after closing. Mr. O'Brien, the client, learned that Smythe had only charged his brother-in-law 1.25 percent in a similar transaction. Lilly Pearl took his phone number and gave it to the boss.

Todd had his suspicions about the late hours the Smythes had been spending in the office. Lisa had often complained that she'd lost clients to Smythe. And many times he'd lowered her commission shortly before closing. Now Todd had to prove that Smythe was collecting a portion of the reduced commission after the closing, thus stealing from the agency and the broker for whom he closed. Todd contacted Mr. O'Brien and his brother-in-law and learned that Smythe had been doltish enough to accept personal checks from both men. Hoping to avoid negative publicity, Todd reimbursed Mr. O'Brien and his wife's brother. Quietly, the Smythes were dismissed.

Lilly Pearl felt somewhat guilty watching the secretary and her husband leave the office with their personal effects in cardboard boxes. She had been the informant. *But they were stealing,* she reminded herself.

Polly Young replaced Eve Smythe. She was a fifty-eight year old veteran secretary who had worked for Todd before the Smythes came to the agency. She had been there before Blair, Lisa, and Chuck Anderson. Todd was comfortable with her. She knew the real estate business better than most of the brokers.

Polly tapped nervously at Todd's door, then she opened it. "Please excuse me, Mr. Bonnell. It's Becky on the phone. She sounds upset."

"Excuse me, Barney," Todd said to the prospective employee who would fill Peter Smythe's position. "I'll take the call in the outer office." He followed Polly to her phone. On the other end, Becky was crying and speaking unintelligibly. "Sweetheart, calm yourself," he said. "Tell me what the problem is."

From her gibbering, he managed to conceptualize that something quite serious had occured at home--something involving Beth. "I'll be there immediately," he told his daughter. "Try to calm yourself."

Blood was on Beth's gown and spotted the sheet where she lay. She appeared to be lifeless. Becky and Jason sat on the bed beside their mother crying. Todd Junior was away at summer camp. The frightened real estate lawyer stood momentarily glued to the floor while conjectures whirled through his head. Never diverting his eyes from the gruesome sight, he moved slowly forward. "Beth," he said softly, "what have you done?" He could see the cut on her wrist and the empty pill bottle on the night stand. His face felt hot, tiny beads of perspiration appeared on his forehead, and the sound of his heartbeat filled the spacious room. He touched Beth's temple, trying to get her pulse. She was still alive. He dialed Doctor Mac Knick's office, but the doctor was in surgery at St. Michael's

Hospital. "Take her to County Emergency," Doctor Mac Knick's nurse told him. "I'll let them know she's coming."

Todd called an ambulance and tried to change his wife's bloody gown. Due to the superficial nature of the wound, Beth's wrist had stopped bleeding. Soon the ambulance was there and the cumbersome task of putting the unconscious lady on the gurney began.

"Do you know how many pills she took?" the paramedic wanted to know. Todd shook his head, "No." The tall muscular medic put the empty bottle in his pocket. "They'll want to know what she swallowed."

Todd rode in the ambulance with Beth, holding her hand and wondering how he could make things right again. He could not reveal Lilly Pearl's secret and the reason why he felt obligated to watch over her. He accepted the full responsibility for the chill that had pervaded his home and drove his wife to commit such a desperate act. Todd prayed a clumsy prayer for Beth, the woman he loved. If she survived this ordeal, he'd make her want to live.

- *14* -

Diary of a Fat Woman

Todd did not smile when he walked in the door. He spoke slowly, trying to choose his words carefully. "Lilly, I've grown to love you like the sister I never had, but our friendship has to end. I've been a narrow-minded fool, expecting Beth to trust me and love me unconditionally. Maurice and I never considered the potential problem our arrangement could cause in my personal life."

Lilly Pearl looked into his eyes and knew he meant it. No longer would he come running when she needed him. Suddenly she felt frightened and alone. Todd had been the stabilizing force in her life. She thought he'd be her friend forever. The blood drained from her face. She wasn't prepared to lose him now--not at a time when Blair was in the mental health ward at Metropolitan Hospital, and she hadn't another friend in Chicago. When Lilly Pearl had wanted to seek employment at another agency, Todd had discouraged the move. "Why are you saying this to me, Todd?" At that moment she felt faint.

"It's Beth." He explained what she had done. "I've been at the hospital all day. She's out of danger, but they kept her."

Lilly Pearl studied him a moment. "Are you all right?" she asked.

He shook his head. "Yes. I'm fine, but I'll have a drink. A double, please."

Todd walked to the sofa and slumped heavily on it. Lilly Pearl poured brandy into two large snifters and handed him one. The tormented expression on his face made her feel as if her heart were in a vice. Tears rolled freely down her face. She dropped to her knees before him and wept.

"What will happen to me now?" A feeling of panic washed over her.

"You'll have to find new friends, Lilly." He wiped her tears. "Please don't make this more difficult. I've taught you the real estate business. You really don't need me now. I'm not free to be your friend nor to accept your friendship."

"Does Beth know I'm passing, Todd?" Her voice trembled when she spoke.

"No, Lilly. Your secret is safe with me."

Lilly Pearl stared at Todd. Every cell in her body ached. She had allowed herself to grow dependent on him. His words were like thorns of steel that pierced her soul. *I wonder how many frienships have died this way--severed like the chop of a guillotine?* Lilly Pearl watched Todd as he walked out the door. Then with unsteady steps she strolled slowly into the bathroom and stared into the large mirror. "Who are you?" she croaked aloud. Lilly Pearl stood there frozen, looking at her mascara-streaked face. She began crying hopeless, empty tears.

When he pulled the sheet from the bed, he heard a muffled thump. It was a tan leatherback book that must have been tucked under the pillow. Todd picked it up and saw *DIARY* written on the cover. Apparently, Beth had left it there. He had no intentions of snooping, but he wanted to know why she had tried to kill herself. Becky and Jason were asleep and the house was quiet. He thumbed through the book until the line, *Dear Diary, I want to die,* caught his eye. Three months earlier she had written: *The mental and emotional pain that I now suffer is so extremely excruciating that I no longer want to live. I'm in hell living in this fat body. I cannot endure this agony for a lifetime.*

The guilt that Todd felt swelled in his chest and brought tears to his eyes. He laid on the bare mattress and turned another page. *Dear Diary, I am an embarrassment to my family. I hate myself for living in such a narrow world. I feel completely helpless. I eat because of what is eating me.*

Todd knew that what she had written was true. He had

avoided social events because of Beth's obesity and their children never brought friends home. Reading until his eyes had become heavy, he fell asleep with the book on his chest.

"The human psyche is a delicate thing, Mrs. Bonnell," the psychiatrist said. "When one's anxieties become too acute, certain defense mechanisms come into play, whereas the psyche escapes into hidden recesses of the mind. Your present state of sadness, inactivity, and self-depreciation has contributed to overeating. You eat to alleviate momentary frustrations, and it's having a manipulative influence on your mind."

Groping for a defense, Beth squirmed in her seat. "I become ill when I starve myself, doctor. Most times I eat like a bird. But sometimes I eat because I'm bored, lonely, or just plain scared."

"Birds eat their body weight in food each day, Mrs. Bonnell. Food is a necessity, but with you, it has become an addiction. You eat to escape."

Beth twisted her lace handkerchief around her finger tightly. She could feel the biting perspiration gathering in her armpits. He carefully pushed the huge leather recliner back. "Just relax," Doctor Gerhardt told her. "I'm going to hypnotize you, Mrs. Bonnell. Do you mind?"

The burden of her body caused the chair to emit a groaning sound. With her under hypnosis, the psychiatrist discovered that Beth actually walked in her sleep and raided the refrigerator each night. Although, she was not conscious of this behavior.

Before she left his office, Doctor Gerhardt handed Beth

a card with Doctor Harvey Lamb's address on it. "I want you to get a thorough physical examination," he said. "Then we'll begin a sensible diet program, using hypnosis once a week. Starting immediately, you'll walk two and a half miles everyday."

"But I get out of breath when I walk." Beth looked as if she wanted to cry.

"You'll have to do this, Mrs. Bonnell." The doctor's voice was commanding. "No one else can do it for you. Begin by walking a few blocks at first. Then increase the distance gradually. In a few weeks, you'll feel so much better. I expect you to lose eight pounds the first two weeks, then two pounds a week thereafter. It'll take time, but as you begin liking the person in the mirror, you'll be motivated to lose more. And your husband will be pleased, I'm sure."

Beth took a deep breath. "I want that very much, Doctor Gerhardt, if it isn't too late." She tried to hold her stomach in, thinking she'd look more slender.

"Just don't try anything drastic, Mrs. Bonnell," he said.

"I promise never to try that again, Doctor. I know my husband still loves me."

Now that her friendship with Todd was over and Blair would never return to work, Lilly Pearl considered finding a job at another agency, but the thought of leaving was too painful. Polly sensed her agony and fussed over her like a mother hen. "You're working too hard," she told her. "You need a young man to go out with. Barney seems nice enough, but you don't like him. Do you?"

"Oh, he's okay," she said, "just not my type."

Barney was a forty-three year old man of average height and adequate intelligence. He wore cheap, Robert Hall suits--the kind that had two pairs of pants and a reversible vest. The old Chevy he drove had weak springs that caused the car to lean, and he'd been married three times with four children to support.

Lilly Pearl had non-intimacy dates with Barney a few times when he first came to the agency. Each time he'd visit her, she'd miss certain pieces of lingerie. But she had charged it to her own carelessness. One evening after she had visited Blair, Lilly Pearl arrived home and found Barney lying on her sofa, drinking a martini, adorned only in her tightly fitted silk panties. She tried to understand his behavior but concluded that it was rather weird. Feeling extremely sorry for him, she never revealed his little quirk.

Polly was most discreet in discussing her boss' personal life. She was quite fond of Todd. Lilly Pearl and Blair were also on Polly's good side, but Lisa had rubbed her feathers the wrong way. Polly warned Lilly Pearl that Lisa Stark (nee) Starski, was a vicious gossip with a poison tongue. She had heard Lisa on the phone with Beth the same morning she attempted suicide. Now Lilly Pearl knew who had kept Beth up to date on everything that had happened in the office.

"She's been in love with Todd since her very first day here," Polly spoke in a whisper. "But he never gave her a second look. She'd go shopping during lunch and return with expensive gifts until he stopped her."

And Beth thinks she's her friend, Lilly Pearl said to herself.

"You know, she's really from a trashy family." Polly

thumbed through papers on her desk. "I knew Todd would never become interested in her. He's a gentlemen. He'd never cheat on Beth. Although, she's too sick to trust him."

"Did Todd know how Lisa felt?" Lilly Pearl found herself whispering too.

"The whole world knew how she felt, except Beth, of course. But she's suspicious of everyone."

Lilly Pearl shook her head in wonder. "I'm surprised she kept working here."

"Lisa would do anything to stay near Todd."

So would I, Lilly Pearl thought.

"This is the best thing that ever happened to her," the secretary said. "She grew up in the Cicero area, but her folks used to live next door to me in Joliet. Old man Starski is a beer guzzler. He wakes up with a bottle in his hand and goes to bed the same way. In fact, I've never seem him without one. Sometimes I think he was born with a bottle in his right hand, and during the day he just refills it."

Chuck Anderson walked into Lilly Pearl's office wearing a big grin and carrying a shoe box under his arm. "Happy birthday, Lilly!" he said. "Guess what I have for you?"

The box he held had holes in it and no lid. Sitting at her desk, it was impossible for Lilly Pearl to see the contents of the box.

"Oh, Chuck, how did you know it was my birthday?" she asked. "I almost forgot it myself."

"I never forget important days," he told her.

She heard a faint shuffle. Then he set the box on her

desk. Inside was a three week old white Toy Poodle. The sight of the dog brought tears to her eyes. "This little fellow needs a home," Chuck said. "Can you accommodate him?"

Lilly Pearl carefully lifted the puppy from the box and held it against her chest. "You're so thoughtful, Chuck. He's just precious. Where did you find him?"

"Anne's uncle had three. She and I took one. We brought this one for you."

"Please thank Anne for me, Chuck. Tell her I love him." She raised the pup and looked under his stomach. "It's a boy. Isn't it?"

"What's that you've got there?" an unfriendly voice from behind Chuck asked. Without looking, they knew it was Beth. Doctor Gerhardt had convinced Todd that she'd have more success controlling her weight if she worked. Beth liked the idea of being in the office, keeping an eye on Todd. She watched every member of the staff as if there were some combined conspiracy to take over the agency. Beth and Lisa were bosom pals, but she was suspicious of Lisa too. She had noticed the wanton stare in Lisa's eyes whenever Todd was near. Everyone in the office was careful never to mention the word *obesity*.

When Beth wasn't being nosey, she sat at Todd's desk and wrote in her diary.

Lilly Pearl kissed him on his furry head and set him on the sofa. "I'm going to call you Little Simon," she said to the puppy. "You'll never be as big as Ol' Simon, but we're gonna take care of each other. Right?" The tiny dog whined and shivered as he looked about the room. Lilly

Pearl stroked his tiny head and remembered how she used to ride Ol' Simon's back when she was a child.

- *15* -

Paradoxical Choices

It was December 1973, Lilly Pearl brought coffee-cake and doughnuts to the office in celebration of her eighth anniversary at Todd A. Bonnell's Real Estate Agency. In January, the United States, North Vietnam, South Vietnam, and the Provisional Revolutionary Government of South Vietnam had signed a cease-fire agreement in Paris. By August, the U.S. Congress had prohibited further U.S. military activity in Indochina. Vietnam veterans had come home and some of them had purchased low priced houses within the Chicago area. Under Beth's watchful, suspicious eye, Lilly Pearl and Todd seldom exchanged words in the office. But Todd delegated more responsibility her way. Lilly Pearl's commissions were outstanding, but she had no friend with whom to share her financial success. Lilly Pearl directed most of her energy and time to her job--burying herself in her work, drinking too much at night, and overspending on luxury items.

Now that she possessed material wealth, she had no other identifiable goal in life, other than the acquisition of more money. With her mounting wealth, the most critical aspect of her being lie within the fact that it had been impossible for her to reprogram her subconscious mind. It kept raising its ugly head reminding her, "I know who you are no matter what your lips might say." She remained out of sync and void of emotionally positive strokes.

Todd had been her only carryover from her family and friends in Milwaukee. Without him, she had become a ship without a rudder, experiencing the harsh manifestations of loneliness.

There are certain ties that bind us to reality, Lilly Pearl thought. Her reason for being in Chicago had denied order within her life. She had no genealogical roots there. Lilly Pearl worried about her future, wondering what she'd do if something happened to Todd or Leatherwood.

The long evenings alone had become her worse enemy. She hadn't been aware of it at first, but day and night blended into endless periods of intimate unfulfillment. Thinking back over the almost six years without Todd's visits and phone calls, Lilly Pearl remembered that her only contentment had been the evenings she spent with Blair, talking to her, even though Blair had seemed oblivious to her presence. For three years Blair had sat in the mental ward of the Metropolitan Hospital, staring at her empty cradled arms, as if she were holding her dead baby. Her long silky hair hang from her bowed head like a shawl surrounding her fragile shoulders. Now a year had passed since Blair's parents had come and taken her to Duluth, Minnesota.

The fears and emotional pain to which Lilly Pearl had become a prisoner had grown and closed in on her like threatening dark clouds. Sometimes, during the loneliest hours of her misery, Lilly Pearl would close her eyes and envision a phantom lover's muscular physique over her, perspiring, dripping sweat onto her body and into her eyes, making them burn, as the world with all its challenges became insignificant. Then the dry scaly presence of reality made her curse the night. She'd drink brandy, play *Misty*, and lull herself to sleep while images of nude men swam through the deep whirlpool of her mind.

A day seldom passed when Lilly Pearl did not consider leaving Chicago, but she had no place to go. She thought of returning to Milwaukee, but remembered that she had nothing there. *What kind of work would I do?* she would ask herself. *Everybody there knows I'm colored. I've become accustomed to having the finer things in life. I'd probably end up in the ghetto again when my savings are exhausted. Money and freedom go hand-in-hand, except when you're colored.* Lilly Pearl thought of her rich friend, Doctor Maurice Leatherwood. *The pain of exclusion is more excruciating when money is no longer a factor, and the mere color of one's skin acts as a barrier, dictating a definite place in society that one must assume. I'll never wear the badge of blackness again,* Lilly Pearl vowed. *I can't let Doctor Leatherwood down.* She remembered Bea and Sweet Nancy--how they had held such high hopes for her, encouraging her to do the things that they had only dreamed of doing. She could hear their voices saying, "You're gonna be a great lady someday."

Lilly Pearl thought about Ricardo. Sweet Nancy had worn a black dress to their wedding. She seemed to have known that he'd be a deadly force in Lilly Pearl's life. The tragic experiences she suffered with Ricardo had annealed and somewhat hardened her forever. Time had brought her pain, and people had brought her pain. Lilly Pearl's son, Jimmy Lee, had accused her of not loving him. But her life in Chicago could not include a son who had lived for sixteen years as a Negro. Even though he could *pass,* she feared he'd never agree to live a lie. At sixteen, he wasn't mature enough to adjust to the consistent demands of covering one's background. She had learned that profound sophistication was required to hide one's real self and exist entirely on a superficial basis.

Why was I born with the choice to pass? she asked herself. *Whose blood is this that rushes through my veins, making me hate who I really am? I feel two opposing ancesters at war within me--one fighting to be free, the other maintaining a position of control, dictating the denial of my true identity. I'm torn into. When I visit my son, I'm Black. When I return to Chicago, I'm white again. Like Pavlov's dog, I'm conditioned to wag my tail on cue. I have taken on the values of the people who would squash me beneath their heels if they knew. With all the things that passing has brought me, it never brought me pride. But living as a Negro robbed me too. I cannot find wholeness in any role. It is only human that I'd choose the most rewarding existence.*

The freedom to make choices, living under the umbrella of favorable ethnicity, was greater than the frustrations of passing. For Lilly Pearl, being white had been filled with certain anxieties, but being black had been hell.

- *16* -

Aloha

Todd dreaded losing his best man in the office, but
Chuck Anderson had saved enough money to start his own
real estate business. Lilly Pearl and Polly were teary-eyed
during the entire dinner given in his honor at a small
Italian restaurant. Beth over ate, as usual, and Todd
forced a pleasant expression across his face. His chubby
wife spent the entire evening watching him and analyzing
each statement he made. Todd had taken great care to
keep the conversation centered around Chuck and his
contributions to the agency. Casually, he pointed out the

success that he and Chuck had shared. Then he stood and made a toast, wishing Chuck well in his new business. "You're joking," Beth spoke with a mouth full of food. "He's going to be our competition." They all, excluding Beth, raised their glasses and wished him success. Chuck smiled and kissed his wife Anne on the cheek. "Anne and I have sacrificed many luxuries for this day. I'm a lucky man that she's worked with me, done without trips and extravagant clothing to help me realize this dream." Anne blushed and squeezed his hand lovingly.

"We're going to miss you," Polly spoke wetly. "Take good care of him, Anne."

From under the table, there was a faint whine. "Did I hear something?" Beth gulped down her drink. Everyone grew quiet. Then Lilly Pearl reached down and got the large straw purse she had been carrying. "Chuck, I couldn't let you leave without saying goodbye to Little Simon." Four years had passed since they'd given him to her. Lilly Pearl lifted him across the table to Anne. She caressed him as he wagged his stubby tail and licked her face.

"How gross!" Beth protested. "A dog at the table. I'm sure that isn't allowed. Really. This is outrageous!"

"For once in your life, Beth, please be quiet," Todd told her.

"Of course, you would side with her," Beth retorted.

"No. Please." Lilly Pearl said. "I'll leave. I should've known better. Please forgive me for ruining your party, Chuck. I thought you and Anne would like to see Little Simon. How foolish of me," she apologized and quickly excused herself.

During the next six weeks, Todd was away a great deal. He had taken Chuck's clients in addition to his own. There was always plenty of work to keep everyone busy, and yet the office seemed lonely and empty with Chuck gone. A continuous stream of potential clients, most of whom were men, called Lilly Pearl and bombarded her with dinner invitations that had little to do with real estate. She had accepted a few promising invitations, but found that most of the men were interested only in taking her to bed. She was aware of the barrier she had invented for herself, but she felt safe within her emotional corner.

Lilly Pearl had been working late, preparing a closing, when Todd came back to the office with someone whom he apparently would be interviewing for Chuck's vacant position. She could hear their voices but never saw them. Later that night, as she lay in bed, Lilly Pearl prayed that Todd would hire a man who'd be as nice as Chuck had been.

Early the following morning the phone rang. It was Polly. "We'll have a new man in the office today," she said. "He's been in Chicago ten years, but he used to live down South. It seems that Todd knows him quite well. He used words like handsome, efficient, upper-middle-class, and eligible bachelor in describing him."

In spite of what Polly had told her, Lilly Pearl was not impressed. "That's nice, Polly," she replied. "Today we shall see what Mr. Wonderful is really like." She had failed to share Polly's enthusiasm. There was a vague, disquieting thought in the back of her mind that made her feel somewhat apprehensive about meeting this new man.

He was just over six feet tall and had the slim muscular body of an athlete. He had wavy black hair that was graying at the temples, bright gray eyes, and a strong, rather austere jaw line. "Hello. Who are you?" His voice was deep and authoritative. His eyes swept over her with encompassing scope. He shifted from one foot to the other, trying to maintain a professional air. His reddish complexion was deeper than usual--the beginning of a tan.

He wore a white suit with a pale-blue shirt and a white tie. Lilly Pearl's face grew hot. She felt embarrassed because of the tender aching in her bosom and her abdomen. Her heart pounded rapidly against her chest, but she was experienced at hiding her emotions. He held his head high, looking down his long narrow nose at her. With long strides, he strolled slowly towards her, smiling, with his right hand extended. "You must be Lilly," he said.

Nervously, she shook his had, staring at his deep dimples. "Yes. I'm Lilly. Lilly Lewis."

"Grant Gilley," he replied.

Their eyes caught with startling electricity. The office was filled with an unusual air of wonder--a magnetic whirl-wind, the center of which Lilly Pearl and Grant were rapidly being drawn. Then she withdrew her hand and started towards her office. "Nice to meet you, Grant. I hope you'll be happy here." As Lilly Pearl walked away, she could feel his eyes follow her. The white linen slacks she wore adhered to her slender body, and her narrow hips moved slightly, stopping just short of bouncing. She wore a white off-the-shoulder blouse. Her hair hang loosely down her bare back and sprang with each energetic step she took.

She looked back over her shoulder at Grant whose eyes glittered with life and lust.

Lilly Pearl and Grant had coffee together almost every morning while chatting over light matters. Polly had nudged Lilly Pearl on, trying to play Cupid, but she had sworn she'd never fall in love again.

Three weeks after Grant had been hired at the agency, he walked into Lilly Pearl's office. "I hope you won't think I'm rushing things," he said. "You're a very nice person, Lilly. Would you please accompany me to the Mill Run Theatre tonight? I have two excellent seats for the Sammy Davis, Jr. show."

"I'd love to," she said without thinking. Leaving work early, she rushed home, washed her hair, set it, and took a long luxurious bath. When he called for her, she could see approval in his eyes.

At the theater, they sat on the front row. Near the end of his one-man show, Sammy sang "Mr. Bojangles"--how he grew too old to dance, and how his aged dog had died. Lilly Pearl's luminus eyes pooled over with large tears. She felt terribly sad. *Bojangles was an extremely tragic figure,* she thought. *Oh, God, what would I do if Little Simon died?*

For Lilly Pearl and Grant, the days in the office were filled with magic and stolen moments of touching and kissing. But Polly's sharp approving eyes missed very little. She was pleased and eager to witness their budding romance. The passing months had been filled with idyllic moments of enchantment that foreshadowed a trip to the altar. And after six months of sharing Lilly Pearl's body and cherising her companionship, Grant proposed.

"You'll have to give me time to adjust to the possibility of becoming your wife, darling," she told him. "We hardly know each other."

"We've been together everyday, making love every night. We are intellectually compatible. We have so much in common. So, what is there to know?" he asked. "You do love me. Don't you?"

"Yes. Of course I love you," Lilly Pearl kissed him hard and long. "But that isn't the problem."

"Is it your son you're worried about?" he asked.

"No. It isn't Jimmy Lee. Please give me time to think."

In the cold darkness of the night, her thoughts burned and blazed until her mind was empty of every emotion except one: There was no future for her in marriage. She wept for herself. The overpowering reality shook her body until she was sick inside. *I can't live without love forever,* she thought. *But he'd despise me if he knew who I really am.*

Lilly Pearl loved Grant, but it wasn't the blind young love she'd wasted on Ricardo. It was a mature, comfortable, ardent affection, based on respect and enjoyable companionship.

Grant tried to understand her apprehension. Although, his ego was deflated. He had never been married before. No one else was ever right for him.

Attempting to influence Lilly Pearl's decision to become his wife, Grant sent flowers with a card attached: *I have two tickets to Southern California for Valentine's Day. One ticket has your name on it.*

Lilly Pearl hadn't taken a pleasure trip since Todd took

her to Palm Springs eleven years earlier. She visited Jimmy Lee every year or so, but she never enjoyed the trips to Mississippi. *I'll go,* she thought.

When their plane landed at the Burbank airport, she was filled with excitement. Grant rented a Lincoln at the airport. They drove down the sunny, broad streets that were lined with palm trees, stretching tall against the sky. The beauty and uniformity of them were overwhelming. Grant drove her past Warner Brother's Studios - a brick building that looked like a huge factory. They passed the enormous Hollywood Bowl and turned off Highland Avenue, traveling west on Hollywood Boulevard. He pointed out the Egyptian Theater and two blocks west was Grauman's Chinese Theater. Grant drove down Sunset Boulevard and headed for the Beverly Hills Hotel where they stayed. It was the most beautiful hotel Lilly Pearl had ever seen. After five days there, Grant revealed his surprise. "You've never lived until you've seen Hawaii. Guess where we're headed tomorrow?"

"It can't be! Not Hawaii!" Lilly Pearl covered his face with kisses. "Grant, you're spoiling me."

"I love to travel," he told her. "We're going to get away as often as time permits."

During the four hour flight from Los Angeles, Lilly Pearl wrote Jimmy Lee: *My darling son, I'm writing this letter while flying somewhere over the Pacific Ocean on my way to Hawaii--wish you were here. . .* And when Grant wasn't sleeping, he made a list of the sights they'd see and the things they'd do while visiting Oahu--the *Aloha Island.*

They stayed at the Waikiki Gateway/Aston Hotel,

between Olohana and Kalaimoku on Kalakaua Avenue, a two mile walk to Waikiki Beach, past Fort DeRussey Military Reservation.

For the eight days they were there, they strolled the beach and enjoyed the warm surf creaming over the white sand while the hibiscus and orchard-laden breezes fanned the palm trees in the gentle tradewinds. Grant would bask in the sun, seeking a tan, while Lilly Pearl hid under a large umbrella afraid she'd turn brown.

Grant rented a small car and showed Lilly Pearl the popular sights. She felt like a small child in Disneyland, seeing the Royal Palace, the Punchbowl National Cemetary, and Diamond Head. But tears filled her eyes when she stood in the Pearl Harbor Monument, looking down on the Arizona, knowing that seventeen hundred young men lay entombed in it's hull. She watched the thin oil slick on the water that still seeped from the ship below.

The third evening on the island, Grant took Lilly Pearl on the Windjammer Sunset Sail. They dined, danced, and viewed the lighted, mystic shoreline of Waikiki from the moon bathed Pacific. The following day they joined seven hundred tourists at the Paradise Cove Luau. Lilly Pearl took pictures of the sexy brown islanders as they dug the baked pig from a skillfully designed underground pit. She was deeply touched when they all held hands for grace before indulging in the Polynesian feast.

On their fifth day they shopped for gold jewelry. They bought "his" and "hers" bracelets. Later that evening they attended the Don Ho Show. And, on their final night in Hawaii, the two exhausted lovers went to the South Pacific Review. "You're going to enjoy this," he told her.

They sat at a table near the stage drinking Mai Tai's. "How many times have you been to Hawaii?" she asked.

"I've lost count," he said jokingly.

The room grew dim, and spotlights of red, yellow, and blue flashed slowly about the stage like search-lights, casting a hypnotic spell over the quiet audience. Casually, six hula dancers with swaying hips and bare feet ascended to the platform, smiling and weaving a tale with their hands. "Do you know what they're saying?" Lilly Pearl whispered in Grant's ear. "Yes. Of course I do. They're saying that Grant Gilley loves Lilly Lewis. He'll marry her soon and live in a little grass shack on Waikiki Beach." Lilly Pearl kissed him and laughed. "You're impossible, Grant."

Suddenly, with a thunderous beat of the drums, three male dancers appeared with flaming torches. They whirled them and tossed them in the air skillfully, stomping their feet as the drums and music combined a wild rhythm that grew faster and faster until the dancing became a form of sensual excitement. Their costumes were fascinating, sexy and exotic. The frantic pace increased and became so encompassing that the audience became caught-up in the sexually inspired performance. The male and female dancers moved their nearly-nude bodies apart and came together in a magnetic frenzy of desire. Without touching, they were making heated, passionate love. Lilly Pearl sipped her Mai Tai in an attempt to subdue her sexual arousal.

Her life had entered a new phase in the sense that she now constantly rubbed shoulders with the elite. Grant had introduced Lilly Pearl to judges, politicians, businessmen, and educational administrators. She had reached a higher level of emotional stability--a heady exhilarating peak. When she was with Grant her life was most gratifying. Lilly Pearl had never experienced Chicago before on such a high emotional level. Although, she had always considered it to be a central and vital area with incomparable strategic advantages. She now saw it as the real core of America and the pulsating center of power. No longer was she bewildered by her restricted life at the agency. This was the city that held in its hand her fate, the potential for great wealth, and the possibility of acquiring her own real estate agency. Her son would finish college and she'd teach him the business. He'd be mature enough by then to understand why she had chosen to pass. Even if Jimmy Lee would choose not to pass, she felt that things were beginning to change for black people. The 1963 March on Washington had proven that blacks and whites shared a dream of racial equality in America. And President Johnson's signing into law the Civil Rights Act of 1964, forbidding institutionalized racial discrimination, provided hope that certain social and economic ills would eventually be nullified in America. By the early 70's people of color no longer identified themselves as Negroes or colored. The word was *Black*. Young children and adults had been brainwashed with a new concept of ethnic identity by black militants and the entertainment industry. Over the radio, on T.V., and in black taverns, James Brown's record "I'm Black and I'm Proud" blasted loudly and repeatedly. *By the time Jimmy Lee finishes college, it'll probably be okay to be a Negro,* Lilly Pearl thought, *especially if he has a wealthy mother. With the implementation of Open Housing laws, maybe he will be able to live anyplace he chooses. But, that's in the future. Why worry about it now? My major concern is to get rich,* she concluded. *If Jimmy Lee wants to live here after college, the racial sentiments of "the powers that be" will probably affect his decision to pass or not to pass.*

- *17* -

Deja Vu

"Happy anniversary," Grant said with a broad smile. "Make a wish." Then he blew out the three candles. The waiter cut the cake and gave each a slice, after which he popped the cork and poured a bit of champagne into Grant's glass. He tasted it and shook his head. "Yes, it's perfect." The waiter filled both glasses, pushed the bottle into the silver ice bucket, and dismissed himself. Lilly Pearl and Grant raised their glasses in a toast. "We've been in love three years, my darling." Grant winked and sipped his wine. "Here's to many more."

Lilly Pearl noticed the warm expressions on the faces nearby--the smiles and nods of approval. "They think we're married," she whispered.

"What they don't know won't hurt us," he said, jokingly. "So drink up and look like a happy wife. If you'd say yes, we wouldn't have to pretend."

"I'm not quite ready to marry again," darling. "Our relationship is perfect the way it is. Don't you agree?" A chilly feeling was stealing over her. She could feel her tension rise. Lilly Pearl wondered how much longer he'd wait.

"It's perfect because I love you madly. We belong together. Tell me. When will you agree to become Mrs. Grant Gilley?" He stared into her eyes; it seemed as if he had known her forever.

There was one frozen moment of silence. She swallowed and took a deep breath but could not find the appropriate words to tell him that she could never be his wife.

"Would you like to go with me to Washington Monday?" he asked.

Happy to change the subject, Lilly Pearl's eyes lit up. "Gee! I've never been to D.C. I'd love to go."

"Todd wants me to meet someone there who's in the market for a commercial building."

Grant drove her home in silence. She was relieved that he had dropped the subject of marriage.

When they were alone in her apartment, Grant took Lilly Pearl in his arms and kissed her hard, repeatedly. The presence of his maleness pressing against the pit of her stomach sent delicious sensations of ecstasy coursing through her body. With his lips on hers, his hands moved slowly down her body, undressing her. He lifted her, laid her on the bed, and slowly, methodically ran his fingers down her stomach, touching her vagina tenderly, gently easing his finger in and out until she was wet. Very wet. Frantically, she wrenched and pleaded, "Take me now, Grant!" Then he plunged deeply inside her, with a powerful rhythm, until she became wild, wildly pleading, "Please don't stop, Grant!" Then with one masterful, trembling thrust deep inside her, he exploded. "Lilly, darling, I love you." She lay beneath him panting, knowing someday she'd lose him.

Driving from Washington's Dulles Airport, the chauffeur pointed. "Look! There's the Lincoln Memorial."

"Oh, my goodness, there's the White House!" Lilly Pearl was filled with excitement.

They moved up Pennsylvania Avenue, surrounded by world famous landmarks. Lilly Pearl thought: *This is where the President lives.*

Grant had reservations at the Riverside Towers, a small family hotel with comfortable, nicely decorated suites, which was only one block from the Watergate complex.

After they were settled, Grant called his client to inform him that they'd meet at his hotel.

The Grand Hotel was indicative of its name. When they arrived, Lilly Pearl was astounded. Heads of state and diplomats from all over the world stayed there. Lilly Pearl and Grant waited in the elegant, imposing lobby with its Italian marble floors and gracious columns that stood under a circular ceiling.

Lilly Pearl had no idea who Grant's client would be, other than he was a man of great wealth from Dallas who wanted to purchase a commerical building in Chicago. She also knew that he and Grant had been partners in real estate when Grant lived in Dallas thirteen years earlier. It was he who had recommended Grant for the job at Todd's agency.

Suddenly, Lilly Pearl heard a familiar voice calling out to them. When she saw Tom Tuckey her facial expression was one of puzzlement. He shook Grant's hand and said, "Howdy, partner!" Then he looked at Lilly Pearl closely. "Don't I know you, Miss?" Her hair had grown to her shoulders and she had matured in the fourteen years since he had seen her.

"Yes, Big Tom. It's me--Lilly. Remember the fun we had in Palm Springs?"

He grabbed her in a wild bear hug and spun her around. "Why you're prettier than ever, gal! How in the hell did you end up with Ol Grant here, in Washington D.C.?"

"I came here to see you and the White House, of course." They laughed and Grant blushed. He had no idea she knew Tom.

"So, what did you think of the White House?" Tom asked.

"It's not as white as I thought it would be," she said. "It could really use a paint job."

They went to the Congress Club to dine--one of the most exclusive clubs in Washington. Tom was a member, because his father had belonged. Lilly Pearl was in awe as she beheld the brick building discreetly nestled behind a wrought-iron fence. *This is really the elite,* she thought.

The maitre d' seated them. Grant and Tom discussed the commercial building that Todd had located for him. While they talked between bites and sips of wine, Tom rubbed Lilly Pearl's knee under the table. And when Grant excused himself to call his boss, Tom took her hand and pressed it against the hardness between his legs. She withdrew it quickly and pat him on the hand. "Now, Big Tom, we'll have none of that."

He chuckled and said, "Just testing the temperature of the water, my dear. I reckon you and Grant's got a thing going. Hey?"

"Well, I guess you could say that."

"Seeing as how me and Grant's such good friends, I reckon an apology's in order."

"No need," she said. "You and I are old friends too."

"You ever seen the Big Apple, gal?" Tom asked Lilly Pearl.

"No. Never."

"We'll have to fix that," he said.

Grant returned to the table and Tom insisted that the three of them fly to New York after dinner. "One day is all we need to show the little lady the Statute of Liberty." Grant couldn't say no, of course. No one ever said no to Big Tom Tucky.

The city was mind-boggling. Lilly Pearl's neck ached and she became dizzy from continuously looking up at the skyscrapers on Manhattan Island. The sidewalks and streets crawled with people and cars like a giant ant colony. Hustlers stood at stop lights with plastic bottles filled with diluted Windex, clutching dirty rags, wiping windshields for handouts. It seemed like an organized conspiracy--at one corner your windshield was fairly cleaned. At the next corner it was smudged again--by men who were supposedly trying to earn an honest living.

His strong skillful hands massaged her tired nude body. She was happy to be in her own bed again. She had called Polly to let her know she'd pick up Little Simon after work the following day. "How was your trip?" Polly wanted to know. "I think Little Simon knows it's you. He's climbing all over me."

"I'll tell you all about New York and D.C. later, Polly. Give Little Simon a big hug for me. And tell him mommy's home."

Grant had poured two glasses of burgundy. He gave her one and kissed her long and hard. "You belong to me, Lilly. Your eyes look so familiar. It seems I've known them forever."

"Of course they're familiar, silly," she said teasingly. "You've looked into them for the last three years."

"No. It's something much more profound. I've seen them before. It's like deja vu."

Lilly Pearl laughed so heartedly that she spilled her drink. She was in a euphoric mood. Then the phone rang. *Now who could that be,* she wondered.

"Pearl." Her mother's weak, teary voice entered her ear. "You best get home on tomorrow's plane. Elton's dead, child."

She gripped the receiver. "But, Momma, that's impossible." Her forehead felt as if it would burst. "What's the matter?" Grant walked to her and held her in his arms.

She took several deep breaths, trying to control herself, then said to Grant, "I'll talk to you later."

She wept. She wept for the loss of Elton Ealy. She wept for the cruel twist of fate that would change her life forever. She'd never be able to make Grant understand why she had to fill Elton's shoes and become the head of his extended household--a black household. He had never known where she was born, nor had she ever questioned his background.

"I have to leave early tomorrow," she told him. "My father died today."

"Oh, darling. I'm sorry," he said. "I'll go with you."

"No, Grant. *Oh, God. He shall never know I'm Black.* I'd rather be alone," she said. "Please try to understand."

"But you shouldn't be alone at a time like this." He pleaded with her, "Let me spend the night with you."

"Please, darling." She held him tightly, in a long embrace. "I need to be alone." When Grant had finally left, Lilly Pearl called Todd. He'd contact Leatherwood and send her personal effects to Mississippi by freight. Now Polly would own Little Simon that she loved dearly. And Lilly Pearl would sorrowfully say farewell to a lifestyle, a chosen ethnicity--fourteen years of adjustment, dreams, memories, success, and love.

Grant called when he had reached home. "Will I see you before you leave?" he asked.

"No," she said. "I'll take an early flight. There's no need to get you up."

"But when will you return?"

"Soon. Very soon," she lied. But in her heart she cried, *Goodbye my darling forever.*

PART III

PEARL CITY

- *18* -

Black Again

Her body jerked violently as if it had suffered a shock of electricity when the earth reached up and broke the flight of the huge jet. Then she swayed in her seat like the other passengers while the pilot maneuvered his airplane towards the terminal in Jackson, Mississippi. She was on southern soil again. She was home again. She was Lilly Pearl Ealy again.

She was Black again.

Lilly Pearl felt cold and resentful. Her behavior was as mechanical as that of a trained front-line soldier. She had been designated by fate to defend the territory of her family, and she dreaded the degradation that she would face--the harsh contrast between being a Black woman in the small town of Pearl City, Mississippi and what her life had been for the past fourteen years in Chicago where she had passed for white.

Behind her were the luxury, the acceptance, and the advantages that she could never expect in Pearl City--the town where she was born.

The town that knew her.

Her life in Chicago had not been altogether free of frustrations, of course. She well remembered those moments of inner-rage when her Chicago friends would tell "nigger" jokes and she would be compelled to laugh as heartily as they. She had also lived with fear--the fear of discovery. Some people, especially other blacks, seemed to possess an uncanny insight into certain tell-tale, minor, racial characteristics that expose those who are passing.

She had made herself appear to be the most racist member of her white peer group. Lilly Pearl had avoided all social settings that included blacks. They tended to stand too close, she felt, invading her personal space. Because of their suspicious nature and sometimes uncanny insight, Lilly Pearl feared that they would look beyond her gray eyes and see the Black in her.

In the doorway of the sweltering airplane she stood looking around, briefly wondering who'd be there to meet her. In the early autumn sun she could see the heat that erupted from the tail of the 727. A soft westerly breeze brought the engine fumes past her long narrow nose. The large, expensive sunglasses she wore made her look exotic and mysterious under the wide-brimmed, beige straw hat. Her long copper hair hung free, its large, loose curls touching her shoulders, forming an almost perfect "U" in back. Lilly Pearl's beige silk dress had a narrow belt, pulled daintily at the waist, and a full skirt gave her walk a swan-like flow.

Subconsciously, Lilly Pearl kept rearranging the triple string of pearls she wore and twisting her ring as though to make sure that its eighteen small diamonds showed.

She stood as tall as her slender five-foot-seven frame would allow and carried her head as if she looked down on anyone or anything that did not come above her classically-lordy cheekbones.

"Ma! Over here!"

Her eyes surveyed the crowd. "That's Jimmy Lee!" she told herself aloud. "That's my baby! Oh, God, that's my baby!"

Then she saw him.

Her baby had become a tall, handsome young man who swept her off the bottom of the gangway, whirling his mother in a playful embrace that caused her hat to slide off her head.

"Get my hat, Jimmy Lee! Get it before someone steps on it!"

A sky cap who happened to be passing caught Lilly Pearl's hat. With a hopeful smile, he handed it back to her and said, "May I help you with your luggage, Mam?"

"Thanks. Thanks a million. We'll wait until the crowd has cleared."

Jimmy Lee held his mother at arms length, behaving as if only the two of them were there.

"I'm a man now, Ma! Look at me. I can lick salt off your head!" He laughed and kissed his mother in the center of her forehead. "Look at me. You got a man for a son now. Ain't I something?"

"You sure are, Jimmy Lee. You really are. I can't believe you've changed so much since I last saw you."

"Well, four years is a long time, Ma. It's been a little more than four years since you've been down here."

"Yes. That is a long time, Jimmy Lee. I missed you. I missed you so very much."

Lilly Pearl looked at her son. She saw joy and innocence in his dancing eyes. Then, like a hard, dry scab pulled suddenly from an old wound, Jimmy Lee's face brought back the horror of twenty-four years past. There, staring into her eyes, were the blue-grey eyes of J.D. Trodder. Jimmy Lee's strong square face, his curly red hair, and his six-foot-three stature had been passed down to him by J.D. Trodder. Trying not to remember, Lilly Pearl forced a smile. "Who else is here, Jimmy Lee?"

"Just me, Ma. Just me. Hey! Have I got a surprise for you!"

"What is it, Jimmy Lee?"

"You'll see."

"Tell me."

"I got it for my birthday. It's really something."

"Okay. Where is this fantastic surprise?"

"Over yonder on the parking lot."

"Jimmy Lee, are you talking about a car?" Lilly Pearl carefully placed her soft, closely-weaved straw hat on her head.

"You really gonna love it, Ma."

"I'm sure I will, dear. But what about the car I bought you five years ago? It is still in good condition. Isn't it? I bought it new."

He made no response as they walked slowly, hand in hand, towards two long baggage trolleys where all luggage from the airplane had been stacked.

Lilly Pearl's full skirt waved lazily as it was gently stroked by a gust of the warm, morning breeze. Her sheer dress became an elegant umbrella revealing shapely, tanned legs and thighs that looked like fresh cream.

"God, do I hate this place!"

"What?"

"Oh, nothing, dear. I was just thinking aloud."

Tucked into the zipper of her large leather purse, Lilly Pearl found her claim checks. Jimmy Lee took them.

"I'll get your luggage, Ma."

"But they're so heavy, Jimmy Lee."

"Oh, Ma! The girls call me Muscles."

"Okay. We'll see how strong those buttermilk and chitterling-muscles really are."

"Now, Ma. You know I don't eat no hog guts."

Lilly Pearl squeezed her son's well-developed shoulders and arms, teasing him.

"Oh, I suppose you have grown up a little in the past four years. Now, tell me what kind of grades are we getting in college this semester?"

"We? Oh. Pretty good, I reckon. But I'm gonna do much better now. You'll see."

"Does that mean we haven't yet made the Dean's list?"

"I've been doin okay, most of the time. I ain't too good at English yet, but you can learn me how to speak correct

English."

Lilly Pearl flinched. She tapped her son in the middle of his left palm and said, "Now repeat after me, 'I'm not doing well in English, but I will study diligently to improve.'"

They laughed.

"Okay, Momma, I'll do better. But you know I won't hardly be talking like you. I mean, you talk like them northern white folks. I ain't hardly gonna be talking like that, never."

"We don't have to be white to speak the King's English."

"What king?"

Lilly Pearl chuckled, "Oh, Jimmy Lee, you're impossible."

She thought of how much she loved him and how immature he was at twenty-three. Lilly Pearl compared Jimmy Lee's life to what her experiences had been when she was his age.

"I'm glad you've come home to stay, Ma. I've really missed you. Everything's been okay, but it wasn't like having you here. Know what I mean? I mean, it's gonna be real nice having my own momma here all the time, like everybody else."

Trying to conceal her resentment over having to move back to Pearl City, Mississippi, leaving a life that she had learned to like, a life that was a great deal more rewarding than what she knew was facing her, Lilly Pearl faked a smile.

"Yes, Jimmy Lee. I know exactly what you mean."

She tried to be jolly as she and Jimmy Lee walked

through the terminal holding hands. He enjoyed walking beside his mother. Her hand felt warm and soft inside his.

"Back to the subject of school, honey. I want you to have the best education possible. For so many years, our people were almost totally illiterate."

"Momma Neallie and Papa know how to read."

"Yes. They read well enough to get by. That kept the whites from robbing them blind. But black people have suffered a lot and lost a lot because of ignorance. The white people down here used to say, 'If there's something you don't want niggers to know, put it in writing.'"

Jimmy Lee dropped his head like a sulking child. "Okay, Momma. I'm gonna make you proud of me. You'll see."

"You'll have to do well, honey. You'll have to take over when I'm gone."

"I don't want to talk about you being gone, Ma. I don't want to talk about death--not now." He suddenly wrapped his left arm around his mother's shoulders, letting her hand drop from his, squeezing her close to him. "Look over yonder in the parking lot! Look in the front row. I'll bet you can't tell which car is mine."

"Mmmmmmmm. Let me see. Is is that raggedy old blue truck over there with the back window all shattered?"

"Now, you know that ain't it, Ma. Oh, I mean, you know that isn't it."

She was pleased that he was making an effort, but she could see she had a difficult job ahead. She wondered how many young people at the university spoke like her son. "Well, if it isn't that beat-up old truck, it just couldn't be that neat little blue and white Cougar setting there beside it, looking like it might belong to you."

"Aw, Ma, you guessed. . ."

The brim of her hat bumped lightly against his shoulder. She pressed it more securely on her head.

He had her suitcases now and was showing off with them, swinging his arms as if they contained nothing but feathers. At the car he made a production of loading them into the trunk. By then she'd started worrying; the Cougar was a late model, practically new.

"Oh, it's really cute, Jimmy Lee. Can you afford it?"

"Old man J.D. Trodder gave it to me for my birthday. Ain't it something?"

The blood froze in Lilly Pearl's veins. All of the hate and anger she'd felt for J.D. Trodder over the last twenty-four years suddenly seemed to paralyze her, and she experienced fear more intensely than she ever had before. Then the cold fear turned into flaming anger she desperately tried to control. Through her clamped teeth she demanded, "What do you know about him? Why would he give you a car?"

Jimmy Lee could see through her dark glasses. Her eyes were wide open, blazing with emotion. He blinked and instinctively took a step back.

"It was my birthday, Ma. And Mr. Trodder said. . .He said I seem like, you know, like a son to him. And he. . ."

"Like a son?"

A frightening spasm shook Lilly Pearl's body. She heard herself saying loudly, abrasively, "These fucking white bastards down here don't stop until they've rubbed dog shit in every black face they come near."

"What do you mean, Ma?

"That son-of-a-bitch ain't gonna ruin your life too,

Jimmy Lee!"

Lilly Pearl brought herself up short, *I'm acting like a nigger,* she thought. *Oh, God. I'm acting like a damned nigger.* She realized that her rage had whirled her back through a time tunnel. She had no use for the King's English. She'd become the Lilly Pearl who swore viciously when angered. She'd talked like she had before she'd passed for white. Jimmy Lee stood staring at her open-mouthed. "Hey, what's so bad about Mr. Trodder giving me a car? He's rich. He likes me a lot."

Still fighting to regain her composure she could see that he was frustrated, bewildered, unable to make sense of her outburst. "What's wrong, Ma?" he was asking quietly. "Please tell me. What's the matter? Did I do something wrong? I'll make it right. I'll take the car back to Mr. J.D."

"Oh, Jimmy Lee." She shook her head and sighed. "It's not just the car."

He stood facing her with outstretched hands resting on her shoulders, trying sincerely to understand. With a steady gaze, Lilly Pearl searched her son's questioning eyes. Within the dark chambers of her mind, the anguish that she had suffered was once more concealed.

"It's not the car?"

"No. It's more than that, honey."

She decided that Jimmy Lee would never know that J.D. Trodder was his father and that she'd do anything necessary to protect her son. *He's such a happy, handsome young man,* she marveled and thought. I love him more than anyone in the whole world. He is the only person alive, other than Momma Neallie, who'll help me to maintain the capacity to love.

"I'm sorry, dear. You'll just have to forgive your old mom."

She had learned long ago to change facial expressions without must effort. She quickly evoked a mask of grief. "I really can't imagine what came over me. Maybe it just hit me that Papa is dead. He won't be home when I get there. He's in Brown's Funeral Home, dead. My papa is dead, Jimmy Lee. All at once it hit me."

"But what about Mr. J.D.?"

With a slight shrug, Lilly Pearl turned from Jimmy Lee and got into the car.

"Oh, it's just that I never liked that old man. He used to raise sweet potatoes when I was a kid."

"He still do, Ma."

"We used to buy sweet potatoes from him when we had a grocery store. I can remember how Momma had to tie Ol' Simon's Son behind the counter everytime old J.D. Trodder came into the store with those big, dirty bushel baskets full of sweet potatoes. You know, Jimmy Lee, the old folks believed that dogs possess a special sensitivity that allows them to sense the true character of human beings. I took heed of Ol' Simon's Son's reaction to Trodder. Ol' Simon's Son knew somehow that J.D. Trodder was a snake in the grass."

Getting behind the wheel Jimmy Lee looked at his mother thoughtfully. "Did he ever do anything wrong to you or any of our family, Ma?"

Lilly Pearl dropped her eyes. She sat there like an abused child, rubbing the palm of her left hand with the thumb of her right hand. She answered in a low voice that sounded bitter, old, and cold.

"Nothing to mention, Jimmy Lee--nothing worth talking about."

- *19* -

The Cherry Picker

As Jimmy Lee weaved his way through traffic, leaving the airport parking area, Lilly Pearl sensed her son's curiosity. She was forced to accept the fact that he had changed from a tooth-fairy child into an intelligent, analytical, young man--a young man who sought a logical answer to his mother's illogical behavior.

"Momma, I been working for Mr. J.D. for about eighteen months--mostly on weekends."

Lilly Pearl's anger had begun to rise again.

"Nobody told me that you were working for Trodder! In

239

fact, nobody told me you were working anywhere. I've been sending money for your support, Jimmy Lee."

"I know you sent money. Momma Neallie gives me money every week. But Mr. J.D. offered me a job to help with college."

She had to make an effort not to shout at him. "Hell, Jimmy Lee! I take care of your college expenses. And I send you an allowance."

"I know, Ma. But I wanted a better car. I mean, I wanted a pretty car like my friends got. And Mr. J.D. needed somebody he could depend on. Besides, I'm a man now. I oughta be working."

"Yes. But why you, Jimmy Lee?"

"Well, see, when Teddy Joe went and got himself killed, Mr. J.D. was pretty broke-up. You know, he ain't got no son now, Ma. Teddy Joe was his only son. And them two girls of his left home soon as they got grown. They living up North now."

"Killed? How'd Teddy Joe get killed?"

"He was hauling sweet potatoes up to Memphis for Mr. J.D. You know Mr. J.D.'s business is really big now. Teddy Joe used to drive one of them three-quarter ton pickup trucks for his daddy. He delivered to lots of towns. . ."

"What happened?"

"Well, see, Teddy Joe took to drinking like his daddy. Some say he could out-drink Mr. J.D. I reckon he just wanted to be like his papa. . ."

"Dammit, Jimmy Lee, get to the point!"

"Well, they say that Teddy Joe was driving over yonder in Tennessee one night, and it was pouring down rain. With him being drunk like usual, he lost control of that big pickup truck, full of all them sweet potatoes. They say he hit that bridge where you go over the Mississippi River into Arkansas. So where he ended up was in the river-- him and the truck, with all them sweet potatoes. It took them three days to find the body, cause the river was high. I guess he got throwed outta the truck when it flipped over."

Her first thought was, *Vengeance is mine, saith the Lord.* "When did this happen, Jimmy Lee?"

"Bout two years ago. In the spring when the river was high. The whole thing was really strange. When they lifted that truck outta the water, they found the body of a woman buried down there under Teddy Joe's sweet potatoes."

Lilly Pearl bit her lips. "Who was she?"

"Didn't nobody know who she was."

"Are you saying no one ever found out? They never found out how she got into the river under the sweet potatoes?"

"I don't know, Ma. I never heard no more about her. Wasn't nobody round Pearl City missing at that time. All I heard, she was young and Black, and pregnant."

"Do you think she might have been in the truck with Teddy Joe?"

"I ain't heard nobody say."

"Was Teddy Joe married, Jimmy Lee?"

"Not him! Not that ol drunken Teddy Joe."

She felt a sense of victory. She believed that God had pierced J.D. Trodder with some of the thorns he had sowed in his earlier years.

She was only fourteen and in the early blossom of her life, Lilly Pearl recalled in silent memory. It had happened in the fall, the season when J.D. Trodder went cherry-picking. He used to love the fall, because that was the beginning of the first semester at Rankin County Junior High School.

Rankin was the largest Black junior high near Pearl City. And every fall, there was a parade of fresh young ladies in bloom on their way to school.

She well remembered how J.D. Trodder had pleaded with her mother to let her pick sweet potatoes for him when she was still approaching her adolescent years. He had tried every year thereafter, unsuccessfully.

Every Saturday morning J.D. Trodder would deliver four bushels of sweet potatoes to the Ealy grocery store in Pearl City. He was an imposing figure at six-foot-four. His heavy build seemed to be quite burdensome, due to the manner in which he dragged his left leg. It was an old injury from his youth that had occurred when he fell off a tractor his father was driving. In his left jaw J.D. Trodder always kept a huge cut of tobacco which he only occasionally chewed. When his mouth became filled with dark brown saliva, he would throw his large head forward and spit the distance of a stone's throw. Along the driver's side of his truck, there were always streaks of tobacco juice, unless it was a rainy day. On those days, the tobacco juice would blend with the mud on the truck and not appear to be such a repulsive sight.

Whenever J.D. Trodder entered the grocery store, Ol' Simon's Son, the Ealy's elderly bloodhound, would bark viciously and strain his rope, leaping at J.D. Trodder.

"That there dog sure has a big appetite for my last good leg," Trodder would say to Neallie Ealy, Lilly Pearl's mother.

"Oh, don't worry, Mr. Trodder. He ain't ate nobody yet. We keeps him well fed," Neallie Ealy would reply.

Lilly Pearl's mother would move quickly to get J.D. Trodder paid and out of the store. He never failed to try convincing her that she should allow Lilly Pearl to work for him.

"That there gal oughta be starting her own savings for college," he would say.

After Lilly Pearl had reached her thirteenth birthday, her mother could never move fast enough to forestall J.D. Trodder's pleas to get Lilly Pearl in his sweet potato patch or into his home--to assist his wife.

With his eyes gleaming with lust, fixed directly on his quarry, J.D. Trodder would take a comfortable stance by shifting his weight to his right leg, relieving his crippled left leg, and resting his right elbow on the counter. He would plead. "Aunt Neallie, why don't you let that there gal come dig some taters for me and my wife? I'd pay her right nicely."

Neallie Ealy detested being referred to as Aunt Neallie by whites. She would occasionaly respond in a resentful tone, "You ain't got no auntie black as me, Mr. Trodder."

"But you ain't really black--not like them other Negroes."

Neallie Ealy would keep herself busy when Trodder was in the store. She would polish her fruits or rearrange cans on the shelves. And, if her fruits were clean and her shelves were neat, Neallie would drag her shaky old step ladder near the meat cooler. She would climb carefully, three steps up the ladder, so that she could wipe the many cans of molasses stacked on top of the six-foot tall meat locker.

"I declare, you're a neat woman, Aunt Neallie. It ain't a time I'm in here when you ain't busy wipin."

Neallie Ealy never smiled around J.D. Trodder. She would keep busy while she supplied a few logical reasons why Lilly Pearl could not dig sweet potatoes for him.

"You know," Trodder would say, "I think you're a mighty fine lookin woman, for your age."

In a low voice that Trodder never heard, Neallie would answer. "A sweet mouth ain't gettin you nowheres round here, Mr. J.D."

Lilly Pearl usually stood behind the L-shaped counter when Trodder was in their grocery store. She felt like something for sale. It seemed as if Trodder were bartering for her services.

On her fourteenth birthday, Trodder observed Lilly Pearl's growth. She had begun to blossom more rapidly. And Trodder's desire to get her in his sweet potato patch became more intense.

"I'll give her fair wages, Aunt Neallie. If you'd let that there gal come to work in my patch, I'd take right good care of her."

"No sir," Neallie would answer, "I be using her round here in the store every day. Plus, she can't stand much sun." Or at other times: "Like I done tole you before, her Papa don't want her doing no field work. Ol Doc Flowers said she got a touch of that asthma. She wasn't cut out for no field work."

Shifting his weight to his good side, Trodder would not stop his plea. "If you'd be so kind as to let her go, she wouldn be put in the field. For the last eight weeks my wife has been poorly sick. I'm thinkin maybe she's got a growin case of consumption--keepin me wake, coughin all night and lyin round most of the day. Our house is gittin to look like a pig's sty. My wife sure could use some female help round the house with them three kids needin lookin after."

Placing her hands on her hips, Neallie took a stronger stand. "Mr. J.D., I reckon you'll be looking someplace else for somebody to do a woman's work. Lilly Pearl is still a child, you might say. She ain't got no business takin on another woman's wifely duties. There's plenty women in Pearl City lookin for your kind of work. They needs the money."

Finally, Lilly Pearl's mother decided that it would be better for her, and for Trodder, if she would keep Lilly Pearl out of the store on Saturday mornings until the sweet potatoes had been delivered.

Eula Mae, Azell, and Satie Mae worked in the Ealy's cotton field on Saturdays with their father, Elton Ealy. Lilly Pearl stayed home with her mother and her youngest sister, Camille. The grocery store was attached to the front of their house. It was easy for Lilly Pearl to hide in the bedroom that she shared with Satie Mae. When Trodder would leave after making his Saturday morning delivery, Neallie would call Lilly Pearl through a window in the wall that separated the house from the grocery store.

Neallie never told her husband that Trodder was causing her problems. She feared the consequences of his knowing. Elton Ealy had served three years in prison for shooting a white man. He still carried the white man's bullet near his spine, just above his waist.

Lilly Pearl was lost in the memories of her past, almost oblivious to the loud rock music that Jimmy Lee seemed to enjoy so much during their ride home. She did not notice that he was driving well over the speed limit while he finger-tapped lightly on his left knee in time with the music. J.D. Trodder had paid extra to have a tape player installed in Jimmy Lee's new car. He now imagined himself playing the keyboard as the leader of a big rock band.

I'll make Jimmy Lee quit that job with Trodder. Lilly Pearl thought. *I'll buy him another car and have this one returned to that son-of-a-bitch. It would give me great pleasure to see his face when I send it back.*

Her hands were resting on her lap. But they were clinched; they seemed to be choking the life out of something that was not there. She was reliving that Sunday afternoon when she had left the Vester theatre. She'd sat through two showings of *Stormy Weather*. J.D. Trodder knew that she was in the theatre. So, like the big-bad-wolf, he'd waited in the cafe next door.

Lilly Pearl ran for her bus which sped past the theatre just as she walked out. Not seeing J.D. Trodder's truck parked discreetly around the corner, she sat on the bench at the bus stop, waiting for the next one.

The big potato farmer gulped down his beer and limped, half staggering, out of Evelyn's Cafe.

"Hey there, Gal! I seen your bus go past. You just missed it by a hair. I'm goin right near your house. It don't make no sense for ya to wait forty-five or fifty minutes for another bus. You could be home playin with Ol Simon's Son. Lordy, I swear, that's a vicious dog."

The left shoulder strap flapped loose on the filthy overalls he wore. He pulled a sweatstained handkerchief from his back pocket and blew his nose into it. It sounded loud, like old rags tearing in his head.

She had been petrified with fear.

"Ain't seen much of you since your fourteenth birthday, gal. Where you been hidin?"

His faded blue shirt had a hole at each elbow. All of its buttons were missing, except the second and third from the top. He had used his shirt collar to wipe perspiration from his face and neck. And there were several streaks of tobacco juice down the front of his clothes. The sole of his left shoe was very thin. He dragged his left foot when he walked.

"I ain't been hiding, Mr. Trodder." *Oh, God, I'm scared,* she thought.

"Now you just stay right there. Old J.D.'ll take ya home. . ."

"Thank you very much, Mr. J.D., but I ain't in no hurry. I mean, I'm not in no hurry."

She could feel the hot sun on her face and arms. It bit her small body like a thousand ants. The many layers of yellow paint on the bench had cracked and popped off in spots. It felt rough beneath her hands.

"I know you ain't scared of old J.D., gal. It ain't like some stranger askin you to accept a ride. I been doin business with your folks ever since they opened up. Stop actin stubborn now. I'm gonna pull my truck right over here and drop you off home."

Run! Lilly Pearl told herself. "I'm scared," she whimpered like a pup.

J.D. Trodder walked toward his truck.

She thought, *Oh, God. He's going to hurt me!* She would have hidden from him, but she could think of no place to run. She was alone with him. Not even a stranger was in sight. Her teenage sisters, Azell and Eula Mae had left the theatre with their boyfriends long ago. Satie Mae, her retarded older sister and Camille, her youngest sister, were at church with her parents. In vain, she desperately wished for a brother. Her heart seemed to shake her body when it beat. Azell and Eula Mae had promised to drop by and pick her up. *Oh, God. Please let them come, right now,* she prayed.

J.D. Trodder's red hair looked aflame with the bright fall sun striking sparks from the large, fleecy curls that he habitually stroked back off his broad forehead. Behind the wheel, his eyes dancing with glee, he beckoned her commandingly. Experience had taught him that he would be able to look under a girl's dress when she put a foot on the running board of his truck.

Lilly Pearl felt herself blush. She knew that he had seen her pink panties. When she sat down beside him he reached across and slammed the door, then pushed down the handle that locked it. Lilly Pearl jumped like a frightened bunny when his elbow bumped the buds of her breasts as he secured the door and rolled up the window on her side.

"You ain't scared of me, are you, gal?"

"No. . .no, sir."

"Old J.D. ain't gonna hurt you none. You'll see."

After he turned off Main Street, he increased his speed. Lilly Pearl held on to the dashboard while the truck bounced and juggled her light body. She tried to brace herself with her feet. But the slick new patent leather shoes she wore provided no traction on the bare metal floor. Her black pleated skirt and the back of her dainty, white shirt-blouse were cleaning layers of brown dust from the tattered passenger seat.

The man behind the wheel, glancing at her, saw the tears welling in her wide, gray eyes that slanted slightly upward over high cheekbones. The summer tan on her fair complexion partially disguised a spray of freckles across her short, pinched, turned-up nose. Narrow pink lips formed a small, inverted valentine above the dimple in her chin. Her short copper curls looked like large, new pennies framing the delicate oval of her face.

"Where. . .where you taking me, Mr. J.D.?" she stammered.

"Well, now, I thought we'd take the long way home. You don't mind looking at them pretty trees turning all them different colors, out yonder on Pristine Pike, do you?"

Afraid that she would anger him, Lilly Pearl tried to choose her words carefully.

"I think I need be heading home, if you don't mind, Mr. J.D., sir. Momma Neallie and Papa don't like me out by myself after sundown."

"You ain't by yourself, gal. I'll have you home long

before sundown."

The man turned his head away and spit a mouthful of tobacco juice through the window. Most of it landed on the door of the truck and on the running board. He used his left arm and the back of his left hand to wipe off the excess saliva that strung from his chin down to his stomach.

When they had reached the wooded area on Pristine Pike, he turned into the woods and drove along a narrow trail that led into the shady trees of the Mississippi forest land.

Dear Jesus! Mary's Baby! Please save me. I ain't gonna see my momma and papa no more. Mr. J.D.'s sure to kill me in these woods. Oh, Heavenly Father, please save your child, Lilly Pearl prayed silently.

She could hear branches scratch the top and sides of the truck as Trodder forced his way along a path that had not been cleared. The tires broke dead twigs and occasionally spun on soft wet grass. The motor strained while the man wrestled with his steering wheel. "Damn! This here trail sho do grow-over quick," he complained.

He stopped, set the brake, and turned off the ignition. Birds and small animals had fled the area. Everything grew quiet. The afternoon sun failed to penetrate the heavy over-growth.

"What-what you gonna do, Mr. J.D.?"

"We're just fixin to have a little fun, gal--you an mé."

The man was laughing at her, wetly. Using the back of his right hand, he wiped off the saliva that had crept out of both sides of his mouth. Then he wiped the back of his hand on one leg of his overalls.

Lilly Pearl started to cry. The man turned to her and ran a hand under her dress, between her legs. With his right arm he held her trapped against the back of the seat.

"Please Mr. J.D., sir, I wanna go home!"

Lilly Pearl cried harder. She knew something was about to happen that she had never experienced.

She sensed the end of her youth--the end of her innocence.

"I'm takin you home, gal, soon's I bust that little cherry here I got my finger on." His dirty hand and his rough, broken nails explored the crotch of her panties.

She tried to bite him and he laughed. "Now, don't you fight and struggle like that, gal. It ain't gonna help you none. The sooner I git what I come here for, we can be takin you home. I been waitin too long for this here little black pussy to let it git away."

He took his hand out from between her legs, reached back to open the door at his side, slid over that way and pulled Lilly Pearl with him, forcing her down against the seat, tugging her panties off. He shrugged off the right-shoulder strap that kept his overalls up, let them drop and fumbled at his shorts until his erected penis stood free.

Lilly Pearl screamed at the sight of it. She wildly groped with both hands trying to open the door that the top of her head was pressed against. The man laughed at her fruitless struggles, raised himself and spit through the open window above her head.

"Now you just stop tryin to git away from Ol J.D. I ain't gonna hurt ya. I'm what you might call one of them experts at breakin-in young nigger gals."

He forced her left leg over his right shoulder and her

right leg up between the steering wheel and the dash-board. Then with all the force he could muster, he rammed his penis into her.

Lilly Pearl fainted.

Briefly, mercifully, she became no more than half aware that she'd been brutally torn open where the man's penis still moved inside her, back and forth, faster and faster. His squeeky old truck rocked from side to side in time with his movements. Suddenly, he squealed like a stuck hog and slumped heavily upon her, covering her body, panting into her face. She was invaded by the stench of stale liquor, cheap tobacco, and unclean human sweat. Hot liquid ran from her, between her thighs.

When she came fully back to consciousness her first conclusion was that she was bleeding profusely. She knew then that she would die there, and the man would dump her body where she might never be found.

She watched him reach into his pocket to get out the handkerchief he'd used to blow his nose. He wrapped his bloody penis in it and got off her, pushed her legs toge-ther, shoved her to one side, then moved himself under the steering wheel again.

She was afraid to move. She was afraid to look in the direction of her pain.

"Please take me home, Mr. J.D. Oh, please don't leave me out here to die."

J.D. Trodder leaned back in his seat and burst into laughter until he coughed violently, like his sickly wife.

"You ain't dyin, gal." He lightly spanked her on her bare left hip. "You gonna come to like this good ol dick I got here." He tried to make her look at it as he unwrapped it and pulled back the foreskin.

She felt her stomach heave against her diaphragm. But she managed not to vomit as he wiped himself and said, "Just look at this pretty pink head rarin to git hisself another black cherry."

He sat back again and got out his tobacco pouch to treat himself. Chewing made him contemplative.

"As I recollect, the first pussy I had was black. That's when I learned how to fuck on you little colored Herefords. Come to think of it, I'll bet I done had more black cherries than I got taters in my fields. Yep! If I could stack all of them little black cherries up to all my taters, that there cherry pile would be the tallest."

J.D. Trodder rolled his damp, dirty handkerchief into a crumpled ball and pushed it between Lilly Pearl's legs. "Here, gal. Clean yourself up."

He gazed off through the windshield down the trail and shook his head. "You know, I'll bet your little pussy ain't black at all. I'll bet I just got me a red cherry, seein as how you're bout as white as me. And you tryin to save that pretty little pink pussy for them damn black nigger bucks! I already done seen em smellin after your skirt tail. Now that wouldn be right for no big ol black nigger-dick to be the first to break-in that nice little pink pussy you got there. No, siree, it just wouldn't be right."

- *20* -

To Live And Die in Dixie

Lilly Pearl's palms were wet. Perspiration covered the nail prints in her hands. She shared her horror with no one. *Oh, God, I hate J.D. Trodder,* she thought. *But I do love my son.* She looked at him and smiled.

"Ma!" She saw an alarming expression on his face. "We're being stopped!"

"What?"

He gripped the steering wheel. "I think we're gittin a ticket."

They heard the short bellow of a siren. "Oh, Jimmy

Lee! You were speeding! He's pulling us over. Stop!"

Jimmy Lee slowed down, pulled onto the shoulder of the road, and turned off his tape deck. Behind them, the highway patrolman had stopped. He looked young and full of spring. With one pounce he was out of his car, pad and pen in hand. He looked almost gallant in the brown and tan uniform that accentuated his blond hair. He was over six feet tall, and he carried himself with evident pride. He approached the window where Jimmy Lee sat nervously waiting. He adjusted his large sunglasses with a finger on the bridge of his nose while he chewed gum, rapidly flexing the muscles in his jaws. In a slow southern drawl he accosted Jimmy Lee.

"Hey, buddy. Where's the fire?"

"Uh. I reckon there ain't no fire, Sir."

"The hell there ain't. I know you ain't flying like this for nothin. Now, I'm askin you one more time. Where is the damn fire?"

Shrugging his shoulders, Jimmy Lee clung white-knuckled to his steering wheel. "Officer, Sir, I reckon the fire's in me. I got to listenin to some music and kinda forgot how heavy my right foot is."

"How long you been drivin this here Cougar?"

"Bout three months. I guess you could say I ain't used to it yet."

"Is it yours?"

"Yes, Sir. She's mine."

"You got a license to be drivin?"

Jimmy Lee reached for his wallet with a jittery hand. "Oh, yes, Sir. Here they is. . ."

"Officer," Lilly Pearl interrupted, ". . .this is my son, Jimmy Lee Ealy. I'm Mrs. Lewis. We didn't realize we were speeding. But, you see, my father has died, and we're under pressure to get on with the funeral arrangements. I just arrived from Chicago, and I'm exhausted from my flight. Maybe fatigue has dulled my senses. Otherwise, I'm sure I would've been aware of my son's unintentional breaking of the law."

The patrolman leaned over, looked in at her, and touched the bill of his cap. "Howdy, Mam. Nice day, ain't it? I'm mighty sorry to hear about death in your family and all. But your boy here's got a mighty heavy foot."

Jimmy Lee sat holding his driver's license, hoping the patrolman would take it. But Lilly Pearl knew that the man thought she and Jimmy Lee were white. She hoped he would not look at her son's driver's license and see Negro written there. With her most dazzling smile, she distracted him.

"Thank you so much for your concern, officer. . .Officer?

"Oh, I'm Patrolman Tillman, Mam--Bill Tillman."

"Well, Patrolman Tillman, thank you very kindly. I'm home to stay now, and we're going to be very careful from now on. I hope you'll please take our difficult circumstances into consideration before you write that ticket."

He pushed his heavy uniform cap toward the front while he scratched the back of his head.

"Mam, you'll find Bill Tillman is the most considerate patrolman on the force. I'm gonna let you and your boy go home to your dead papa. Now, Jimmy Lee, you just keep your mind on where you at and what you doin behind that there wheel. This is a dangerous instrument you got at the mercy of your hands an feet. You take heed, now, boy. If I catch you with your foot in the gas tank again, I won't be lettin my heart out on a string."

Lilly Pearl was getting bored and feeling sorry for her son who sat beside her looking straight ahead, clutching the wheel with one hand and his license with the other.

"Yes, Sir. You sure right about that, Sir."

"Sometimes we let things control us," Tillman said. "That ain't no good. Those things can lead us straight to hell, know what I mean? I done witnessed tragedies too many times in my job. What you got to do, you got to keep your mind on what's important, boy. Gittin there fast ain't important. Gittin there in one piece, that's important.

"I'm lettin you go this time. But you remember what I'm tellin you. You got to pick out what's important in life. Or else you gonna be a man who drives like a bat outta hell ever time somethin makes you happy or gits you riled."

"Thank you, Mr. Tillman." Jimmy Lee, putting his driver's license back into his wallet, sounded overly sincere. "Believe me, I'm gonna take heed to your advice. Everything you said is true."

Please don't overdo it, Jimmy Lee, thought Lilly Pearl. She waved at the patrolman as he tucked the ticket pad back in his pocket. "Thank you so much, Officer Tillman. God bless you."

Tillman smiled and walked back to his car. She listened to him humming to himself. *In Dixie Land I'll take my stand, to live and die in Dixie. . .*

I hate this damn South! thought Lilly Pearl. "Jimmy Lee,

you watch it now. I don't want to be stopped again. Just how fast were you going?"

"I don't quite know, Ma. This here little Cougar does git outta hand sometimes. But that Bill Tillman is a strange one. He's said to be really tough on colored folks."

"Black folks, Jimmy Lee. Don't ever say *colored folks.* That's out. It was the whites decided to call us colored people. Remember that."

"Well, that Tillman's got a reputation for being really tough on us. I heard talk of how he never give a B-B-Black man a break. But he's a pretty fair guy after all. He never even looked at my driver's license. He seems to be a real nice man."

He thought you were white, thought Lilly Pearl. "Well, honey, sometimes luck just runs your way. Maybe he was in a good mood, to let us Blacks get by without a speeding ticket."

"I guess I was lucky, Ma. But you sure talked to him like a real city lady. That's what throwed him off his feet."

They were passing a long, weed-infested tract of land with an old, weatherbeaten farmhouse on it. "Isn't that the Honeysuckers' place, Jimmy Lee? It looks neglected."

"No, Momma, that ain't the Honeysuckers' house and land no more. They moved to Texas. They been gone ever since Jessie Mae was found dead in the woods off Pristine Pike."

"The woods off Pristine Pike! Oh, no!" Lilly Pearl whispered. "Who killed her, Jimmy Lee?"

"Sheriff don't know who done it. She'd been raped, her head cracked open. They found her layin under one of them big pine trees off the trail. Her clothes was all tore up and blood all over ever thing. And. . ."

"When? When did this happen?"

"Bout twelve years ago, I reckon."

"Jimmy Lee? Exactly how old was that child?"

"Uh. . . maybe thirteen or fourteen, they say."

"Oh, God! That's horrible. Why hasn't someone told me about this. I've been home several times during the last twelve years. Nobody ever mentioned it." She cringed inside, remembering how she'd feared death in those same woods twenty-four years ago.

Her son glanced at her puzzled. "Guess nobody thought of telling you all the strange things that's goin on down here. You always came and went so fast."

"Who lives there now?"

"Ain't nobody living there now. Ever body says it's haunted. They say Jessie Mae's ghost can be seen strollin through the house and cross the yard on a bright night."

"Maybe she has a story to tell, Jimmy Lee."

"There's unpaid taxes on the house and the land that put it in the courts. I believe Mr. Trodder owns it now. But it's just setting there empty like that--looking kinda sad and all." He shrugged if off. "Jessie Mae, they say, was homecoming queen that year. She was the last one they had at Rankin. She was the Honeysuckers' only daughter--a real pretty girl, they say."

He turned off the highway onto a coarse gravel road. The rattle in the wheel hubs of the Cougar startled Lilly Pearl enough to make her catch her breath. Her son gave her another worried look, not understanding. He was used to it. She forced herself to change the subject. "Have the Stubblefields come in from Milwaukee yet?"

"They might be there now. But they hadn't got there when I left. They done sent word they had to rent a car to drive down in. They said that beat-up car they own wouldn't never make it all the way from Milwaukee to Pearl City. Pulled out of Milwaukee last night around midnight. It's a seventeen hour drive."

"Did Momma Neallie take Papa's death really hard?"

"She won't eat, Ma. She won't take her medicine. She just sits there in that old squeaky rocking chair, staring at Papa's picture on her dresser, waiting for you."

An aura of sadness suddenly enveloped Lilly Pearl. She detested the very thought of having to walk into the house where Elton Ealy died, to take the reins in hand that he had held for all these many years. Most significantly, she loathed the impending imprisonment of her body and soul. She had been torn from an environment that had satisfied her, that had made her happy. Now she'd have to adjust to a lifestyle that nurtured the very existence of man's inhumanity to man.

She cried softly.

- *21* -

The Wake

Laughter filled the big eleven-room house. Flocks of relatives and friends spilled over onto the porch and into the yard to pay their last respects to Elton Ealy. The old country house had begun its existence as a four-room frame dwelling, but it had grown in size at the same pace that the Ealy family had grown in number.

If it could speak, what awesome tales it would tell, this scabrous old white house surrounded by a white, peeling, picket fence with missing pickets here and there. Its weatherworn face usually displayed an air of life and happiness. Children played daily on the green, flower-patched lawn. But since Elton Ealy's death, the house had been shrouded by a cloud of sorrow, generated by bereavement that lay heavily within the bosom of Neallie Ealy.

A large funeral wreath adorned its front door. The old tire-swing out back was still, looking as mournful as the weeping willow tree from which it was suspended.

Sitting in her bedroom alone waiting for Lilly Pearl, Neallie could hear the sounds of friends and relatives who walked through her house inquiring about her. She was excluded, by her own choosing, from the greetings and embraces that filled her home.

Among the familiar faces that filled the Ealy livingroom was that of Antredious B. Bailey, on military leave to attend his uncle's funeral. His two older brothers, John Henry and Bud Alphus, were the most uncomfortable guests there. Antredious, the family drunk, appeared to be so deeply distressed by his uncle's death that he kept importuning his brothers for a small loan, its purpose the purchase of additional alcoholic solace at Gitter Bug's, a nearby tavern.

Under his large army jacket, he had hidden one of Neallie's fruit jars in which Gitter Bug would be asked to dispense a quart of moonshine. Money was his only obstacle. Thus, the anxiety of his pleading grew as he continued to nudge his brother. "Oh, come on, Bud. Lemme have a couple of bucks. I'll pay you back."

Bud Alphus was afflicted with a rapid stutter. "B-B-B Boy. Uh ruh. I-I-I ain't got no tu-tu-two bu-bu-bucks. Plus, you ain't g-g-got no j-j-job to be payin me back, n-n-nohow."

It was difficult to decide whether Antredious' body was too skinny or if his uniform was the wrong size. He never wore one that fit. He constantly pulled up his pants while tucking his shirt-tail. One could easily have slid three fingers down the neck of his shirt with him in it, wearing a tie.

"What you mean, I ain't got no job? I works for Uncle Sam! You see this here uniform I'm wearin?" He turned around to model for his brothers.

"What's that there lump under your arm, boy?" John Henry asked.

Antredious pushed the fruit jar into a more secure position under his arm and tried to close his jacket over it. "I don't know what you talkin bout, John."

"I'm talkin bout Aint Neallie's fruit jar you got hid under your jacket."

"Hush, John. Mind your own business. I ain't got nothin of yours."

Bud Alphus and John Henry occupied a worn old love seat near the window. Numerous relatives and friends were talking among themselves, paying little attention to Antredious. Satie Mae Ealy sat watching him intently. She knew that he had her mother's fruit jar hidden under his jacket. She wanted to retrieve it. He was the enemy.

"Why you watchin me like that, Satie Mae?" Antredious questioned her.

Without moving a muscle or batting an eye she answered him in a low angry voice. "Shut-up, you ol black dog!"

Satie Mae was tall and slender; she walked with her

head held royally high. She kept a large coffee can by her chair into which she occasionally deposited snuff and tobacco spit. After emitting a huge mouthful into the cup, she would smile, wipe her mouth on the underside of her skirt tail, and cross her legs again at the ankles. She behaved in the fashion of a well-bred lady. Her dimpled smile concealed her angry thoughts. She had promised herself that she would kill Antredious in order to recover her mother's fruit jar.

Antredious stood in front of his brothers prancing like a horse ready to run. "Come on, Bud! Lemme have a couple of bucks."

"Well. Uh ruh. Un-Un-Uncle Sam g-g-got more money than me. Why don't yu-yu-you call him and a-a-ask him f-f-for a-a-a c-c-couple of bu-bu-bu-bucks?"

"Please, Bud. I'll send your little ol two bucks soon's I git back to camp."

"Yeah? That's what yu-yu-you said wh-wh-when I l-l-lent you two bu-bu. . .ah, dollars, the last time you was here on ah-ah-ah furlough. Yu-Yu-Yu-You and yo-yo-your Uncle Sam ain't sent that back yet."

Bud Alphus chuckled and dispatched a mouthful of snuff and tobacco spit out of the open window. It landed across one of Neallie Ealy's bushes of pink roses that had begun to droop from the rays of the blazing sun.

Antredious' brother, John Henry, tried hard to avoid involvement in their conversation. He was the least likely to lend Antredious two dollars for an alcoholic beverage. According to John Henry's philosophy, he would never buy for another man anything that he would not buy for himself.

"Come on, brother. I ain't askin for a million. What's a measly little ol two dollars?"

"It ain't much. B-B-B-But. Uh ruh. It's bout tu-tu-tu-two more d-d-dollars than what you got."

Antredious moved closer to John Henry. However, in doing so, the fruit jar began to slip from under his jacket. He pressed his right arm more firmly against it. He leaned over and now directed his plea into John Henry's ear. "Hey, John! Man, lemme have a couple of bucks? I'll send it back soon as I git to Fort Smith."

John Henry sat chewing on a wooden match, swaying his right leg, habitually, from side-to-side, looking up at the ceiling in a very serious, contemplative mood. "Boy, I ain't got no money." He kept looking at the ceiling, swaying his leg from side to side and chewing on the match.

"John, you know you got money. I seen you give Aint Neallie some while ago. And you didn't give her all you had."

"Well, let me put it this way. I ain't seen your face or read your name on none of my money. If I had'a, I'da give it to you without you askin. All my bills got presidents' faces on em. Ain't got Antredious nowheres. Only writin I done seen was *In God we Trust.* That don't seem to be fittin you none."

Still looking at the ceiling, John Henry found his own words amusing. He laughed.

"John, you just as crazy as you was before you started preachin. Ain't he, Bud?"

Bud Alphus ignored Antredious' statement. He crossed his legs, spit out the window again, and pretended to be interested in something outside.

John Henry seemed not to be overly concerned about his younger brother's verbal attack. He smiled faintly and retorted, "I might be crazy but I ain't broke. And I ain't havin no fit for no rot-gut."

Bud Alphus agreed. "Th-Th-Th-That's all he wa-wa-wants."

"You crazy, John!" Antredious said.

Finally, John Henry looked at him, and in his calm, quiet manner he said, "Speakin about who's crazy, if somebody was to git a buzzsaw and saw the top off that boy's head, what do you think they'd find, Bud?"

"I'll bet it's fu-fu-full of fe-fe-fe-fermentin corn."

Antredious' nostrils flared. "Man, you don't know nothin bout what I got in my head. I got me enough brains to be a medic for Uncle Sam."

"Yea." Bud Alphus chuckled, "Bu-Bu-But they got you wo-wo-workin with them c-c-crazy folks like you. After you f-f-finished cleanin up all them body parts durin the war, you was as c-c-crazy as a b-b-b-bat." He laughed, took off his glasses, and wiped the perspiration from his forehead. "Now, uh ruh, I know wh-wh-what's in th-th-that, uh ruh, flat head. Sawdust an feathers." John Henry and Bud Alphus burst into laughter.

In his attempt to turn the joke away from himself, Antredious touched upon a subject that was a thorn in John Henry's heel. "Hey, Bud," nudging Bud Alphus on the shoulder, "Remember when John used to go in the grave yard and preach to them dead folks?" Antredious became so intent on teasing John Henry that he slapped himself on the knee and lost control of the fruit jar. He scrambled for it as it dropped heavily on John Henry's foot, rolled across the freshly waxed floor, and came to rest under Satie Mae's chair.

"You throwed that jar at me, boy!" Satie Mae shouted. With the speed of a panther she pounced on him and buried her teeth in his scalp. He had instantly become her Siamese twin. Her saliva, darkly mixed with snuff and tobacco, ran down his forehead and dripped onto his chest.

"Hey, somebody! Git this here crazy woman offa me!" Antredious pleaded while keeping his eyelids pressed tightly together. "This woman is strong," he moaned.

Satie Mae and Antredious had acquired the full attention of all who could squeeze into the large room. Willie B. Poe, the fourteen-year old son of Azell and Levester, tried to pull his aunt off Antredious. "Cus'n Antredious, they say if Aint Satie Mae gits her teeth clinched into somethin, she ain't lettin go till it thunders--just like one of them old snappin turtles. Daddy's on the back porch talkin to Momma. You want me to git im?"

"Forgit your daddy! He can't even talk your momma into takin him back!"

Knowing that Satie Mae would listen to her mother, John Henry sent Willie B. to fetch Neallie.

"Hurry-up, boy!" Antredious shouted. His left hand was entangled in Satie Mae's thick hair, but he was afraid to pull. He tried to keep the hot saliva out of his eyes with his right hand.

Willie B. ran to his grandmother's bedroom. "Momma Neallie," he called softly as he tapped lightly on her door. "You in there?"

One of Neallie Ealy's attributes was that she could hear exceptionally well for her seventy-eight years. But, being selective, she often pretended not to hear certain interruptions. Most family members were aware of this. So Willie B tapped again.

"Who's that?"

"It's me, Momma--Willie B."

"Is Pearl here yet?"

"No, Mam. She ain't here."

"What you want?"

"Satie Mae won't let go of Cus'n Antredious' head."

"What she holdin his head for?"

"She ain't holdin it. She's got one of them snappin turtle bites on im."

Neallie slowly got up from her old rocker. "Come on in, boy. Gimme that cane over there." Willie B eased the door open, took the cane from its corner and gave it to his grandmother.

"I wonder what got into Satie Mae?" Neallie mumbled to herself. "Sometimes that gal is too hard to handle, specially on a full moon. She just gits crazier an crazier." She toddled towards the room where she was needed.

When the tap of Neallie Ealy's cane came near, the crowd parted like the Red Sea. "Satie Mae," Theodis Serpentine cautioned his sister-in-law. "Here comes your momma." His wife, Eula Mae, stroked her sister's back, hoping to relax her tense body while step-by-step Neallie made her way to her eldest daughter. "Hold on, Satie Mae!" Theodis called out. "Your momma is here. Uh, I mean, heh! heh! heh! Let go, honey! Momma Neallie is behind you."

Neallie tapped Antredious firmly on his ankle with her cane. "Boy, what you doin to that gal?"

"Aint Neallie, Mam. I ain't meanin no disrespect to your house, but it ain't me that's doin somethin. It's Satie Mae what's got her teeth bit into my head. I'm the one who's in pain. And she ain't thinkin on lettin go no ways soon, seeing as how it ain't lookin like no thunderstorm outside."

Neallie tapped Satie Mae lightly on her head with a knuckle. "Hey, gal. What you tryin to do? You ain't hungry. And iffen you was, his head ain't no fatback. Now, loose that boy an go wash your mouth out. Boy, your head looks like a half-empty cuspidor!"

Satie Mae released her bite. Neallie turned slowly and headed for her bedroom.

"Ain't Neallie!" Antredious called after her. "Please, Mam. Could you lend me six-bits til I git back to camp? I got a mighty bad headache from Satie Mae's bite."

Neallie paused and looked around at him. "If it's a headache you got, boy, I got just what you needs in my room. And you don't need none of my fruit jars to be carryin it in. Just follow me."

Antredious skidded on the wet, slippery, linoleum-covered floor. Everyone laughed at his condition. "Man, you sho do look a mess," Theodis called out.

"Can I help you outta that spit, Cus'n Antredious?" Willie B asked.

Antredious slid quickly past Sadie Mae when she reached for him. "I'm gonna kill you bout my momma's fruit jar, you ugly old black dog."

Eula Mae held her back. "Momma done told you to

leave that boy alone, Satie Mae."

Antredious landed in the corner and sat there rubbing his eyes. Satie Mae stood trembling and biting her bottom lip. Bud Alphus took out a plug of tobacco, bit off a piece and gave it to Satie Mae. "Put this in yo-yo-your. . .Uh ruh. P-P-Put this in yo-yo-yo jaw, honey." Then he took out his snuff box and measured a dip of snuff in the box top.

Satie Mae smiled coyly at Bud Alphus. "I like you, Bud. You can be my boyfriend if you want to." She straightened her dress and ran her hands over her long, thick hair. The dimples in her face made her yellow complexion sparkle.

He backed away quickly, "I-I-I can't, Sa-Sa-Sa-Satie MMMMae. We's f-f-first cousins."

Satie Mae pulled out her bottom lip. Bud Alphus moved towards her again and dumped the snuff into it, filling her lip to the brim. She continued smiling at Bud Alphus. Her hazel eyes glowed.

Eula Mae wiped her sister's chin. "Sit down, Satie Mae," she said softly.

Satie Mae's eyes were still on Bud Alphus. "You can be my boyfriend if you want to, Bud!"

Theodis laughed to himself as he walked towards the corner where Antredious sat holding his head. "Git up, boy. Walk upright like a man. Momma's got some medicine in that big old trunk in her bedroom. It'll cure you or kill you."

"It's good, Cus'n Antredious," Willie B. lied. "We don never git sick. She's got camphor an whisky, calmus root an whisky, and peppermint candy an whisky. She got turpentine an sugar, garlic an whisky, and. . ."

"That's enough, boy," Theodis interrupted. "We ain't got a kid in this here house who's brave enough to play sick."

Antredious was afraid to go to Neallie's room. The small amount of whisky he'd get wasn't worth the trip. He stood wiping his face with his handkerchief, using the corners to clean his eyes. But the handkerchief was not equal to the task.

John Henry and Bud Alphus stood near him. Their grins were tinged with sympathy for their youngest brother.

"Boy, you look a mess! Go out back an clean yourself." John Henry told him, "I'll give you a buck."

"Money! Whisky!" Antredious said in a whisper. "Well, all right, brother John. You ain't as tight as you used to be." He saw John Henry's face and winced. "Uh, I mean, you ain't as tight as you look."

"You gonna talk yourself outta this here dollar, boy."

"Hold it, Brother John. I didn't mean nothin by what I said. You used to be real tight, you know? You used to squeeze a nickel til the buffalo shit. . ."

"Keep on talkin, and this here dollar's gonna stay where it is, little brother."

"Okay, John. My lips is sealed."

"Uh ruh. It's gonna take m-m-more th-th-than Satie Mae's spit to s-s-seal your l-l-l. . .uh, mouth," Bud Alphus added. "I'll p-p-put a-a-a nother buck wit John's."

Antredious scooped the fruit jar from the floor, left the room, and headed for the back yard. Camille Ealy was sitting on the back porch listening to Levester pleading with her sister Azell to accept him back into the family. "I know you gonna let me come back," Levester pleaded. He rubbed his Mo-Joe with his thumb and squeezed it tightly in the palm of his right hand. His hand was jammed firmly into his pants pocket when he told Azell, "You got to take me back. I know it. You got to take me back this time."

Azell had no knowledge of her husband's hoo-doo. Thus, it had no effect on her. "I done told you naw! I ain't takin you back no mo, Vester."

"He ain't worth a damn, nohow," Camille mumbled.

"What did you say, gal?" Levester asked Camille.

"Who? Me? I ain't said nothin," Camille answered in a sweet, innocent tone. She swung her legs back and forth as she sat on the edge of the porch. She kept her hands resting on her stomach so that she could feel her baby move. "Oh, God. Please let it be a boy this time," she prayed in a soft voice. "I hate girls." Camille was startled when Antredious turned the water faucet on. "You scared me, fool! Can't you speak, ol ugly nigger?"

"I could if I wanted to," Antredious shouted back at her.

Camille looked at him with a puzzled expression on her face. The sun half-blinded her, but she could see that something was in his hair and on his shoulders. "My God, Antredious! What in the world is that mess you got on yo self? It looks just like snuff-spit. I bet it smells like dog shit."

"That crazy sister of yours put this stuff on me."

"Which crazy sister?"

"How many crazy sisters you got?"

"You mean Satie Mae?"

"Yeah. That one."

Camille held her stomach as she laughed. "Boy, you look like a toilet stool full of shit."

"Maybe. But if you don't stop makin fun of me, your

baby's gonna look like me when it's born."

"My baby ain't gonna look nothin like you with your ugly skin head. I don't fuck nothin black as you."

"I might be black an ugly, Miz White Lady. But I ain't got no baby in my belly."

"You mind your own business, you ol whisky-headed nigger. This is my belly an my baby. I fucks who I want to fuck. And I ain't no white lady, mother-fucker."

Antredious saw no reasonable end to the argument. He kneeled down and placed his head under the faucet.

"You gonna need some soap and a rag to git all that snuff spit an tobacco offa yo head. You is one *u-gu-ly* black nigger."

Antredious was mumbling to himself. "That whorish bitch always callin somebody black. All them damn Ealy's think they's better'n other niggers, just cause they's got yellow skin. That little bitch done had two babies, and one on the way. Ain't none of em got no daddy."

"What you over there mumblin bout, boy? How come you can't talk out loud? Cat got your tongue? You scared, Corporal Chicken-shit?"

"Camille, why you keep messin wit Antredious?" Azell asked with reproach. "He ain't done nothin to you. You git so evil when you git a big gut."

"I ain't botherin him. Plus, I don't like him nohow."

"Just leave him alone, Camille."

"Hey, Azell, kin I have a rag?" Antredious asked.

Azell had needed a reasonable excuse to get away from Levester who was still pleading with her to take him back. She took Antredious inside to dry himself. Then he returned to his brothers. They were standing on the front porch discussing him. And, as he approached them, they laughed at him.

"Boy, ain't you hot in that there jacket?" John Henry wanted to know. He knew that Antredious was still trying to conceal the jar.

"Uh ruh. Yu-Yu-You still ain't. Uh ruh. Ain't g-g-got that tu-tu-tobacco outta, outta, outta yo head, boy." Bud Alphus chuckled as they looked down at him from the porch.

He made a sweep of his right hand over his hair. "Ain't nothin in my head. Where's the money yall promised me?" He stood there looking up at them with his damp hand presented upward like a small child begging for another cookie. Leaning over, they each placed a worn dollar bill across Antredious' palm.

"God's gonna bless you two greatly, my dear brothers. Angels of mercy, that's what you is. You done just donated to a most worthy cause--me, your patriotic baby brother who's dedicated his life to the service of his country. I thanks ya. And Uncle Sam thanks ya. And. . ."

With a thumbing gesture in the direction of the tavern, John Henry added, "Old Gitter Bug thanks us too, I reckon, almost as much as you. Cause that's who's gittin it."

"It's for a worthy cause."

"The *cause* is you who ain't g-g-gonna know yo ass from a hole in th-th-the ground when you gi-gi-git ba-ba-back."

"Man, I don't wanna hear that shit! I drinks to be sociable."

"Boy, you stop usin them four-letter words in this here yard." John Henry was leaning against one of the eight round pillars that were spaced strategically along the full-length porch. "You know you can't call yo self a sociable drunk, cause when you git full of that moonshine, the only thing you be talkin to is the ground where you be layin."

"I don't have to stand here and be talked about." Antredious headed in the direction of Gitter Bug's tavern.

With a serious expression on his face, John Henry looked at Bud Alphus. "You know. That boy ain't been right in the head ever since the war."

"He's crazy as uh-uh-uh bat now."

"I'da been there too, but they didn't want no man with one leg shorter than the other. That's a funny thing. Mother Nature can save one man by cuttin his leg short, leavin him whole, and cut another man short by makin his body perfect."

Bud Alphus stared at the ground while he brushed his heavy mustache with his finger. "I guess I would'a been there too if I could see good. Maybe we do owe that boy somethin. He done been through a lot." He adjusted his thick glasses. "I guess we f-f-forgit that he is, uh ruh, a man."

278

- *22* -

A Pilfered Melon

Approaching home, Lilly Pearl's heart palpitated like that of an unborn fetus inching its way through the birth canal--forced to face a different world not of its own choosing. She, too, was being thrust from a secure environment into uncertainty.

Glancing back over her shoulder again, she saw that the brown station wagon was still behind them. "Who is that following us, Jimmy Lee?"

Her son seemed pleased that his mother had regained her composure. "Oh. Uh, I don't know that car, Ma. Looks like it has Wisconsin plates."

"Slow down please, dear. That must be Joe and Bea."

Jimmy Lee looked into his rear-view mirror again and reduced his speed. "Yep! I'll bet that's them."

The brown LTD came closer as Jimmy Lee pulled over. When the dusty vehicle passed them, Lilly Pearl recognized her first cousin, Bea Stubblefield and her husband, Joe. She reached over to sound the horn. Jimmy Lee waved his arm out of the window and shouted, "Hey, yall! It's us! It's me and Ma!"

The brake lights on the station wagon flashed. Bea and Joe had recognized them. Before Jimmy Lee could come to a complete stop, both Bea and Lilly Pearl had flung their car doors open and scrambled out onto the road. Like the warm spring rain that rushes toward the sleeping earth, they ran to each other with open arms, re-awakening their mutual love that had slept through a very long winter.

Lilly Pearl, for a long while, had lost contact with the experience of humble joy. And Bea was incapable of restraining her delight. "Oh, my God! Girl, is it really you, Pearl? You look so fine!" She cried.

"Bea! Bea! Oh, it's been so long!"

They clung to each other with lingering ecstatic joy. For a few moments, the two men seemed not to exist. Then all of them were out of the cars, embracing with verbal expressions of happiness.

After awhile, Joe Stubblefield backed off, rubbing his tired, red eyes, "I'm pretty wore down from all this driving, yall. Let's git to the house so we can rest. I ain't had no sleep in two days. And I don't feel too good standin round on this here busy road. You can't never tell who might happen by and make-out who we is."

Lilly Pearl's eyes grew wide with fright. "Oh, Joe, I'm sorry. I forgot."

"Well, I ain't forgot. I ain't never gonna forgit. And I'll bet that damn old cracker, Jim Bob Pickins, ain't forgot neither, specially with his sittin there every day in a wheel chair, just wishin he had a piece of my ass."

"Let's get home," Jimmy Lee suggested.

As he drove ahead of Jimmy Lee, Joe Stubblefield's mood changed from fatigue to anger. His mind apparently stole back to Pickins' Slaughter Pen where he had been employed when he lived in Pearl City. Twenty-eight years had passed, but in Joe's ears, the sound of Jim Bob Pickins' voice still rang loudly.

Who'n th hell stole one of my cold water melons?

Pickins owned the only slaughter pen in the Pearl City area. He hired blacks because they expected lower wages. But Pickins never felt comfortable with his black workers. He was sure that they were making up the difference in their pay by stealing from him. So, Joe and his best friend, Fats McAfee, saw to it that Pickins' suspicions were well grounded. They stole.

Jim Bob Pickins was a man of many vices. He gambled, committed adultery, chewed tobacco, dipped snuff, smoked cigars, drank corn whisky, and frequently fist-whipped young black men.

Pickins Slaughter Pen was a unique business that served Pearl City. It fulfilled many of the residents' needs. On Saturday mornings white people would do most of their shopping. The blacks would shop in the afternoon. Pickins sold freshly killed beef, pork, chickens, ducks, turkeys, geese, and live fish. He also stocked smoked hams, hamhocks, slab bacon, southern style sausages, and salt pork. He sold molasses by the gallon and moonshine by the gallon, disguised in molasses buckets. Moonshine did not appear on the shelves along the walls of the marketing section of his slaughter pen, but those shelves displayed a wide assortment of just about everything from cheap perfume and cheap fabric to pinto beans and watermelons.

Every evening before Joe and Fats were allowed to leave work, their employer would instruct them to put fifteen watermelons in one corner of a large room that he had constructed to serve as a meat-cooler. By morning, the melons would be just cold enough to cool the hottest stomach or the meanest temper.

Jim Bob Pickins was known to indulge heavily in certain contents of his business. And he was never to be taken lightly when moonshine affected his temper. However, his drunken stagger was no clear indication of his ability to keep count of his cold watermelons.

Like a religious ritual, every morning Pickins counted his cold melons when watermelons were in season. Before his business opened for the day, he would cut one for himself. He would stand up in the meat cooler and eat the heart out of a whole watermelon, leaving the remains for Joe and Fats.

Gertie Pickins, Jim Bob's wife, worked exclusively in the marketing section of their slaughter pen. The blood, intestines, old hides, feathers, scales, and general suffocating stench of the slaughter pen were not a part of

Gertie's daily life. There was an invisible door that barred Gertie Pickins from the pen and restricted her to the store and their attached living quarters.

Joe and Fats were the only two employees who were allowed to enter the cooler. When Gertie would see her meat supply getting low, she would call out back to have Joe and Fats bring more meat from the cooler, under the watchful eye of her husband. But Fats' hands were quicker than the eye, especially when the eye was dimmed by moonshine.

So quick were Fats McAfee's hands that Pickins never caught him stealing. And Joe himself seldom did, unless Fats had bragged to him earlier that he would take one of Pickins' prized watermelons during the meat call.

One Saturday morning Fats became ill after working almost a double shift. It was the weekend before Labor Day when an unusual amount of hams, ribs, beef, and chickens were sold. Pickins had insisted that Fats work two shifts since Joe would have to do the same during the weekend before Thanksgiving.

Fats' illness became worse as the day grew slowly towards noon, and for once his boss indulged in tenderheartedness. He agreed to let Fats go home after Fats had assisted Joe in restocking the store for Gertie.

Fats left when the task was finished, but he'd forgotten to tell Joe that he had stolen a cold watermelon. If he had remembered to tell him, Joe would have taken one off Pickins' truck at the loading dock and put it in the cooler to replace the one that Fats had taken.

When Pickins' stomach growled again for the soothing relief that only his watermelons could bring, he went into the meat cooler, thumped several watermelons, took one out of the pile, made a quick count, and discovered that one was missing.

He counted a second time to be sure. Then, with a loud roar, he called Joe.

"Hey, boy! Where you at?"

Joe's heart felt as if it had jumped up against his palate. The anger in Pickins' slurred speech gave full warning of trouble.

"Who'n th hell stole one of my cold watermelons?"

All of the customers in the store with Gertie were trying to peek through the partly opened door that led to the slaughter pen.

Joe laid the sharp butcher knife on the cutting block and walked across the slippery, saw-dust-covered floor. He went in the direction of the cooler where Pickins stood bellowing. "Joe Stubblefield! You come here, boy!"

"I'm coming, Mr. Pickins. I'm coming." Joe was trying to imagine what the problem was. "You want to see me, Mr. Pickins?"

"You mighty damn right. I want to see you, nigger. Where's my fuckin watermelon?"

Joe wondered if his employer might have forgotten exactly how many watermelons Gertie had sold that morning. He felt sure that Fats would have told him to replace any that he might have taken. Joe stood looking at Pickin with a frown of confusion. "What's the matter with this ol drunk bastard?" he asked himself.

"I don't know nothin bout no melon, Mr. Pickins. Did they git counted right?"

"You questioning me, boy? Do you know who I am,

nigger? I'm known to kick niggers asses. You know that? Now, I'm gonna ask you one more time. Go git my cold watermelon from where you done hid it. It better be cold. And it better not be cut neither."

"But I ain't got no watermelon, Mr. Pickins. I ain't seen no watermelon."

"You saw em, nigger. You helped put em in the cooler."

In the store, Gertie Pickins excused herself from the customers to attend to her furious husband. They followed her as if curiosity had lassoed them together in a single loop.

Knowing that he had a wife and a young son to feed, Joe tried to reason with the man. "If I had'a took your cold melon, Mr. Pickins, I'da got a hot one off the truck an put it under the cold ones--if I had'a took one."

"Is that what you been doing?"

"Naw. Naw, Sir. I ain't been takin your melons, Mr. Pickins. Please, Sir. Let's talk this over."

"Jim Bob," Gertie called, "why don't you leave that boy alone? You most likely et that melon yourself."

Pickins stood swaying while his stocky, six-foot-frame was partially supported by the cooler door.

"I been downright decent to my nigger workers. My niggers git paid a good wage for a good day's work. They ain't gonna make no more than this in the cotton field. Don't I pay you good, boy?"

"I reckon you do, Mr. Pickins," Joe replied in a subdued voice. "You do, Mr. Pickins, I reckon."

"You reckon! What the hell you mean, you reckon?"

"I mean you do, Mr. Pickins. You do."

"Well then, git my cold melon. Wherever you hidin it,

it better still be cold and whole, cause that's the one I wanna cut."

Gertie was tugging at her husband's arm. She attempted to pull him away from Joe, back into the door that led to their living quarters.

"Jim Bob, why don't you leave that boy alone. What you need is a good nap."

"Fuck a damn nap! Hell, I ain't sleepy. I'm gonna kick this here nigger's ass. I'm gonna teach him a fuckin lesson bout stealin from Big J.B. Pickins. Hunh! I'm gonna make an example outta this here boy."

Pickins had started staggering towards Joe while Gertie tried to hold him back. But her husband, well over two-hundred pounds, was too much for her ninety-eight pound physical makeup.

Joe backed slowly out of the side door, never taking his eyes off Pickins, who was reaching for the heavy iron rod that was normally used to barricade the door at closing time.

"No, Jim!" Gertie pleaded, "You could kill the boy with that!"

Joe backed slowly down the loading dock. Behind him the parking lot had never been paved or leveled off. There were numerous pot holes half filled with the past week's rain. A dozen pickup trucks and cars that belonged to Pickins' customers were parked at random to avoid the holes. Most of these shoppers had emerged from the store on the dock and stood gawking in anticipation of what was to happen.

"Might as well come back and take your medicine, boy. Gonna kick your black ass today for sure." Pickins turned to the crowd. "I done been real civil to my niggers, but they can't be trusted when a man ain't got his eyes right on em. Most niggers I know can steal the linin outta a bobcat's ass while he's lickin it."

Some of the customers laughed, and there were a few catcalls. Joe kept his eyes on the iron rod that Pickins grasped in his right hand. He held it by its smoothly cut end with the sharp end resting over his right shoulder. The iron looked to feel cool on his shoulder which was bare except for the strap of his worn gray overalls.

"I ain't takin no beatin from this old drunken bastard," Joe told himself. Still slowly backing away, feeling his way with his feet, Joe intended to jump off the dock to the parking lot, hoping to find a clearance broad enough for him to run. But the thought of running was not appealing when he considered the possibility of Pickins throwing the rod so the sharp end would catch him in the back. Joe recalled having seen him throw a hatchet straight between the eyes of a wounded, charging bull. "I ain't turnin my back on him with that rod. That son-of-a-bitch is fixin to kill me," Joe mumbled in a frightened tone. He could feel the sting of his own perspiration as it crept down his temples and seeped into the corners of his eyes, but he was afraid to blink.

Joe slipped off the dock with a loud, crackling sound under his feet. Then he remembered the plank that he had placed over a large mud-puddle that morning. It had served as a bridge for Ginne Sue Pickins, Jim Bob's sixteen-year old daughter, when she got into her car to go take her Saturday morning piano lesson.

Joe reached down, never taking his eyes off Pickins.

The plank had broken into two long parts, one of which Joe picked up. Several splinters from the jagged edge pierced his hand when he grabbed the end of the longest section of the plank. "If I hit im I'm gonna have to run," he told himself.

Pickens had jumped off the dock himself and was closing in on Joe. "Nigger, you askin for a killin now! How dare you pick up a piece of wood, like you fixin to hit me. I'm a white man. You done forgot your place."

Pickins suddenly laughed at Joe. He pointed mockingly at him. "Look at this here black ape, pickin up a piece of wood for to hit a white man. Boy, yall just stopped swingin from the trees over yonder in Africa. You're a monkey, boy. You ain't no man! I'm gonna put you back in them trees where you belong."

With one huge step forward, Pickins swung the rod. Joe ducked, avoiding what could only have been a death blow to the head. He could hear the howl of the iron rod as it slashed through the air where his head had been. There was a shattering crash followed by a tinkle of glass. Jim Bob Pickins had broken the left side-window of his own truck.

"I'm gonna kill you now, you fuckin nigger.!"

The rod whipped high in the air. Joe swung the broken plank with all the strength that he could summons. The wood smacked against one side of Pickins' balding head, almost exactly reproducing the sound of a large watermelon dropped on cement.

"Grab that there nigger!" Someone from the crowd shouted.

Suddenly, Joe's legs seemed to have a mind of their

own. He ran across the parking lot towards a wooded area that was shaped like a huge horseshoe around Pickins' pasture. He ran with such speed that his heels seemed to strike his back pockets.

The veins in Joe Stubblefield's temples were standing out, full and rigid. His teeth were clinched tightly together, causing the muscles in his jaws to flex like tiny ripples flowing under his ebony skin. His palms were perspiring where he gripped the steering wheel of the dust-covered brown LTD. He had just turned onto the road that led to the Ealy's front door.

"God, thinkin bout that shit twenty-eight years ago can fuck up a man's whole system," Joe said to Bea. "The sight of this here town brought all that nightmare shit right back, like it was happenin all over again."

Jimmy Lee's Cougar was close behind Joe when he stopped in front of the old house with the large funeral wreath hanging on its front door. And, for the first time since Elton Ealy died, Lilly Pearl fully realized that he was gone forever.

She and her future looked each other in the eye, like two sworn enemies on a narrow trail--trying to out stare each other. Who'd step aside to let the other pass? The Ealy house had stood longer than Lilly Pearl. And she knew that the old house would never budge. It was more than a building. It was the symbol of a bloodline that would continue long beyond her own existence as its head.

"Well, here we is, Ma!" Jimmy Lee joyfully announced.

"Yes, Jimmy Lee. We're home."

- *23* -

Neallie

Outside a horn sounded three times, rapidly. In the family room someone shouted, "That must be Jimmy Lee, yall!" Willie Ray Gatson limped out the front door and stood on the porch with John Henry and Bud Alphus. For an instant, the three of them gazed at the unfamiliar station wagon parked just ahead of the little blue and white Mercury. "Hey, Bud an John, who's that?" Willie Ray asked.

Before they could answer, Joe Stubblefield got out of the station wagon and called out to them. "What in the hell is you country folks starin at?"

Holding the bannister, Willie Ray walked carefully down the steps from the porch. A broad grin covered his thin brown face as he crossed the lawn to the front gate. "Lawd have mercy! Look who's here!" Willie Ray seemed to be talking to himself at first. "Is that really Joe an Bea?"

"Hell, yeah, it's us, fool. Who else you think we is. I can see time ain't done nothin for you," Joe said, "cept maybe made you uglier."

When Willie Ray reached the gate he called over his shoulder, "Hey, John, tell ever body to come out! Tell Aint Neallie they's here!"

Joe approached him smiling. "Hey, Willie Ray, where's your teeth, man? You ain't got a tooth in your head." He pointed his finger close to Willie Ray's mouth. "I bet you can't bite this, you ol cocksucker."

Willie Ray grabbed Joe's finger and playfully snapped at it with his bare gums. Its owner snatched it back. "Shit, man, I don't want my finger in your nasty mouth. You might have the damn claps-of-the-mouth from suckin on all these tight little young pussies down here."

With a hearty laugh they fell into a strong embrace. "Joe, man, I ain't seen you in a year-of-Sundays. You's lookin good."

"Shut-up that noise out there." Bea pressed the horn lightly, startling them. "Yall help me outta this car."

Willie Ray leaned against the hood and peeked through the windshield of the station wagon. "Git outta that car an give your goodlookin cousin a big hug. Girl, lemme look at you. Turn round. Ooooooweeee! Woman, your hips look like the back end of a Greyhound bus!"

"Oh, stop lyin, Willie Ray. You know I ain't that big." When she pulled him close, Joe put his hand between their faces. "Hold it, Bea. Don't kiss that ugly nigger in the mouth. He might have somethin catchin."

"Joe, you an Willie Ray always did like to tease each other." Bea kissed her first cousin and hugged him gently. "How old is you now, Willie Ray?

"Old as my tongue an a little bit older'n my teeth."

She knew he was several years younger than she. "I know. You're about forty-five." But to her he looked so old and worn. Bea concluded that he'd probably never recovered from his mother's early death.

"Yall sho's a sight for these here ol red eyes," Willie Ray said. "It's been a long time."

"Where's Lilly Pearl?" Neallie was calling from her bedroom. "Hey, out there! Can yall hear me?" Drowned by an ocean of sounds that flooded the Ealy home, her voice could not be heard. She slowly made her way to the front door. "Hey, yall! I said, where's Pearl?"

Suddenly there was quiet.

"Hello Momma!" Lilly Pearl had entered the crowded yard, speaking to her relatives and old acquaintances as she walked towards the porch where her mother waited. "Momma, I love you. I love you, Momma." Lilly Pearl's warm tears united with Neallie' as they embraced.

"Come on in, child. I been waitin for ya. Elton's gone, Pearl. He done gone an left me. I can't hardly stand this here pain."

"You'll be fine, Momma." Lilly Pearl said. "You're going to be just fine. I'll stay here and take care of you. You'll see. Why, you're trembling all over! Let me help you to your room, Momma."

With arms interlocked, they walked slowly to Neallie's bedroom. Lilly Pearl eased her mother into her rocker. Then Neallie placed her hand on the back of Elton's chair beside her. "You sit down, Pearl. Sit in your Papa's seat."

"I'm really not very tired, Momma."

"That's all right, child. Sit down an rest yourself."

Lilly Pearl settled herself reluctantly in Elton Ealy's creaky old rocking chair, the one he'd made with his own hands long before she was born.

"I know you ain't feelin too good bout movin back to Pearl City, child. It ain't gonna be easy for ya. But, with God to help, it won't be like a burden you can't bear."

"I know, Momma. We'll be just fine."

"Pearl, this here's a big ol house, full of my chillun and my chillun's chillun. It ain't right for just one child to carry three generations on her back. But there ain't nobody under this here roof can take over and run this house like Elton did. Me an your Papa knowed that all the time, even when you was little.

"When I had to let you go, I didn't have no words to give ya. Cause me an your papa had already put em inside ya--in your mind, in your heart. But when I seen ya git on that bus, goin up yonder, my heart felt like it had done swelled up in my bosom an was tryin to go wit ya. When you left, Pearl, you took a big chunk of my heart on that bus to Milwaukee.

"Elton used to say, we human bein animals is the only kinda animals that don't know when it be time to let our chilluns go. We's the only mommas who ain't told by nature when the time is come to push our babies outta the nest."

Lilly Pearl smiled. Her mother had broken into the singsong of family admonishment she remembered so well from happier days.

"Did you know that an ol eagle bird builds her nest in a certain kinda way, with thorns turned-down, to hold it together? Them thorns help to hold that nest together while she be hatchin babies. But she's told by nature when it's time for them to fly. Then, that ol eagle bird momma stirs her nest. She turns them thorns up so them little eagle birds can't be at peace sittin in that nest. They got to fly, cause she ain't gonna keep bringin em food."

"We human mommas keeps our chillun way past time to fly. We hold on--don't wanna let go. Don't wanna see they done changed from a child to a woman or man. Cause when they done changed, we know time done changed us too. Time and change sometimes be our friend. But we scared change gonna be our enemy. Cause sometimes the enemy-side of change comes walkin arm-in-arm with death. That, we can't hide from. We know change sometimes brings the good. And we know for sho it be finally bringin the end.

"Holdin on to ya chillun don't do nothin but stunt their growth, cept for that one twig what always breaks away an goes its own direction--be it good or bad. Every family's got one. You was our special little twig what took your own direction. You growed strong in your own way, so different from the rest that's still under this roof. They's long past growin."

Tears rolled down Lilly Pearl's cheeks. She was afraid

that she'd start crying uncontrollably. She was thinking, *What would Momma say if she knew I'd passed for white the whole time I lived in Chicago? What would she say? Oh, dear God, what would Jimmy Lee say? Papa would've been ashamed of me for sure. No one must ever know. They wouldn't believe me if I told them I never planned it that way.*

They were silent for awhile. "Pearl, honey, I know you's feelin tired, but Brown's waitin for somebody to come up there and make ever thing final for the funeral tomorrow."

"I'll take care of it, Momma. I'll have Jimmy Lee take me. You just relax."

Neallie visibly experienced a stronger sense of well being knowing that Lilly Pearl was there. "Oh, Pearl, take this here quilt. Tell Brown to be sho an put it on Elton. He likes a lotta cover at night. Take his pillow, too. He never could sleep without no pillow. And tell em to brush his hair to the right. He always wears it like that. Tell em to button his suit coat all the way down. And don't lace his shoes too tight. He don't like that. And tell em. . ."

"Momma." Trying to conceal the tears that had begun to rise again, Lilly Pearl responded in a low, trembling voice. "They have plenty of cover and pillows at Brown's. I'll tell them everything you said. I'll take care of everything. Papa will be just fine."

Her mother leaned back in her rocker that Elton had made. She glanced at his chair beside her. "You have to watch ol Brown, honey. I hear tell he takes things. He done been caught sellin good watches an rings belongin to peoples' dead kin-folks."

"Momma, I'd better go see about Papa now. I'll get

Jimmy Lee."

When she was alone, Neallie gazed at Elton's picture on the dresser next to hers. And, quite out of touch with reality, she stared at those two very young faces. Her wrinkles, those golden rings of experience that Elton had often said he admired, faded. She became the young woman in the picture, and Elton followed Neallie into her fantasy. He sat in his big old rocking chair beside her.

"Seems like time ain't touched you at all, kitten. You looks pretty as that there picture. You's my bride, my young beautiful bride. I'm still lovin ya more than when I first seen ya."

He placed his large warm hands on her beckoning breasts and squeezed them. She moaned with pleasure. Then his strong arms were under her, lifting her to bed. His hands searched her silky gown and instantly filled her with hot passion. His lips covered her anxious panting.

"Love me, Elton!" She pleaded. "Hold me!"

Like a vapor that rises from dew-covered grass, Neallie floated with the warmth of Elton's love. He was the sun that she rose to.

"The first time I seen you, I knowed you was mine."

He moved into her body like a fragrance, penetrating her senses. They were like a rainbow, visible only by the reflection of their love. Elton and Neallie floated like soft music to the height of climatic glory. Then he was gone.

Reality enveloped Neallie again. But now she did not feel alone. She smiled peacefully as she remembered the words that were song on her wedding day:

> *If you love me and do what I say,*
> *I'll make you happy. I'll never go away.*

My love will comfort you, now and eternally.
If you love me, I'll stay.

If you love me, you'll never be alone.
Soul-in-soul, just us, completely satisfied as one.
Don't let anyone else make this choice for you.
They don't know me the way that you do.

If you love me, and do what I say,
I'll make you happy. I'll stay.

If you love me, you won't have to be alone.
Cause I'll be with you now, and from now on.
Living in my heart always, you'll see.
If you love me, I'll stay.

If you love me, you won't have to be alone.
I'll make you happy. I'll stay.

The words and melody of the song faded as Neallie gave way to sleep.

- *24* -

Soldier Boy

When Antredious Bailey reached Gitter Bug's tavern, the juke box was blasting B.B. King's *Every Day I Have The Blues*. Nothing about the barn-like building had changed except for its surrender to the ravages of time. Even its raw-pine floor had sagged to the underlying soil.

Gitter Bug's was one of the two black taverns in Pearl City. Evelyn Hopgood, a middle-aged prostitute, owned the other one.

Evelyn catered to the more respectable black people of Pearl City and the surrounding area. Her clientel consisted of barbers, beauticians, school teachers, and a few brave church folks. She served noonday meals for workers and rented her banquet hall to certain groups for social events. Evelyn's prices were designed to keep out the riff-raff. But Gitter Bug's tavern was more popular than Evelyn's. He did not discriminate.

Along the left wall of Gitter Bug's Tavern, there were sets of splintered, wooden booths that faced each other, with narrow, table-like stands between them. The walls were decorated with dusty, outdated whisky and beer signs that looked dim and greasy. An antiquated juke box in the left corner, at the front door, carried a long list of old blues songs. At night the music could be heard more than a block away.

Near the juke box was an area for dancing. But when the place was filled to capacity, the dancers occupied whatever space they could find. When the dance floor was filled, they would dance between the customers who sat at old, square wooden tables that were randomly set about near the kitchen. Gitter Bug would insist only that the dancers leave a narrow walk for wedging one's way to the long bar that extended the full length of the building on the right side. When the room was filled, those who sat on shaky stools at the bar were often bothered by patrons crowding in behind them, eagerly shouting orders for liquor over their shoulders.

Gitter Bug's fry-kitchen was in back. He sold fried fish, fried chicken, hamburgers, and the pickled pig feet he kept in a huge jar behind the bar. From two blocks away, one could smell the greasy foods that Mayetta Moore fried in the tiny kitchen. She served orders on paper plates through an open hatch.

At night, the interior of Gitter Bug's tavern was bathed in a mysterious red glow, mixed with the heavy smoke from cigarettes and Mayetta's cooking. The smokey aura of the room served to disguise the ugliness of the expanse of grimy walls.

The exterior looked old, gray and decrepit at night, as it did during the day. The huge, clear, naked light bulbs, suspended one at each corner of the building and one over the entrance, exposed the effects of time on un-painted wood. The lights drew a continuous swarm of gnats, flies, and creepy bugs. But Gitter Bug's clientel had never been interested in such matters as atmosphere.

Fats McAfee was the first person to recognize Antredious when he entered the tavern. Fats was already filled with moonshine and catfish. He wiped his mouth on his shirt and called out to Antredious. "When the hell did you get here, Uncle Sam?"

"Who the hell is you talkin to, country boy?" Antredious responded as he walked towards the bar.

"Is Joe comin down for the funeral, man?"

"The answer to your first question: I got here last night--late last night. Now what was your second question?"

"Is Joe comin?"

Antredious was anxious to find Gitter Bug. He'd become irritated with Fats McAfee for delaying him. He answered Fat's question without looking at him. "Hell, I donno, man. If he's got any sense, he won't bring his ass in five-hundred miles of Pearl City, Mississippi. If he do come, an whitey gets wind of his being here, we might have two funerals. Cause they'd hang that sucker. If Joe's got any sense at all, he'd best drop Bea off in Memphis. But ain't no tellin bout Joe. Everybody knowed him for a crazy nigger when he hit that white man. These folks don't never forget stuff like that."

Fats stood up, holding a piece of fried fish in his greasy hands, waving it in the air and shouting loudly, "Man, Joe Stubblefield ain't scared of these damn red-necks down here!"

"No?" Antredious laughed. "He ain't scared long as he's up yonder in Milwaukee."

Fats didn't pursue the matter further. He knew that it was useless to argue with Antredious. "Uncle Sam, you better come over here an get yo self some of this good ol catfish." Fats called to Antredious.

"I gotta see Gitt."

"Oh, come on over here, asshole. I know you's hungry. You look hungry--skinny ol goat." Fats laughed at him. "You must got on somebody else's uniform."

"I ain't got no time for you, Fats. I got to see Gitt," Antredious told him.

Fats sat still holding the fish. "Well, go on, Uncle Sam. I ain't gonna beg you and feed you too. You crazy cocksucker."

"Well, if I'm a crazy cocksucker, tell yo momma to keep her ass clean. Cause she's the only bitch I'm gonna be suckin."

After taking a huge bite, Fats dropped his fish, shook his fist at Antredious and began talking with a full mouth. "Just for that, weasel face, I hope you go home an find a big ol black bear fuckin yo momma!"

Antredious looked at Fats in disgust. "Man, you know my momma's been dead for years."

"Well, then, I hope you find a damn grizzly bear wit his dick jammed up yo papa's ass. And I hope a motherfuckin coon digs up yo momma an fucks her too!"

Before Antredious could think of a suitably, matching insult, Gitter Bug came up behind the bar. He recognized Antredious and spoke to him in a jovial tone. "Hey, soldier boy!"

"Gitt, where you git that boy shit from? You ain't never seen a boy with a dick big as mine."

They laughed and shook hands after Antredious set the fruit jar on the bar. "How you doin, Bailey?" Gitter Bug asked. "It sho is bad bout old man Elton, ain't it?"

Antredious pushed the fruit jar at him. "Yeah. But we all got to go sometime. It ain't like bein over yonder gittin yo balls shot off while you still a young man. Uncle Elton done used up his time an got started on mine. Hey, Gitt, put somethin in this jar. My throat's dry as an ol maid's pussy."

Gitter Bug took the jar, reached under the bar, and filled it with corn whisky. He wiped the rim of the jar with a dirty, wet towel he used for cleaning the bar. "That'll be two bucks, Bailey."

Antredious snatched his money off the bar. "Two dollars! Damn! That's all I've got. When'd this shit get so high?"

Gitter Bug grabbed the jar and pulled it back. "Hell, soldier boy, if you can't afford it, you oughta quit drinkin and become one of them jack-leg preachers like yo brother, John Henry."

"You take that back, Gitt!" Antredious had become extremely angry. "You take that back! My brother's one of the best preachers in this here state."

The tavern owner laughed and pushed the whisky-filled fruit jar in his direction. "Hell, man, can't you take a little joke? I know bout yo brother. I know he's one of the best preachers round these parts. I was wonderin what-in-the-hell happen to you. How come you so fucked up?"

Without answering, Antredious tossed the two dollars at Gitter Bug. When he took his first drink he trembled all over. With a facial grimace that implied pain, he shook his head and gritted his teeth. "Man, someday I'm gonna stop drinkin this shit. It ain't nothin but strained cow piss-- rotgut. This shit is bad enough to make a damn jackass tap dance."

"How is Camille takin it?" Gitter Bug inquired casually. "She's the youngest, you know. Probably takin it hard, ain't she?"

The initial impact of the moonshine had changed from a sharp bite to a soft, warm tingle. Antredious started to feel better. "That stuck-up bitch ain't takin nothin hard but a dick. It takes more'n Uncle Elton's bein dead to make that hussy act right--the slutty little yellow whore."

Fats McAfee spoke up. "Hey, fool! Bring yo stupid ass over here, soldier boy." He was aware of Gitter Bug's affection for Camille.

"I'll throw the son-of-a-bitch outta my place," Gitter Bug mumbled.

"Hey! What's going on here?" Antredious asked. "Why you lookin at me like that, Gitt?"

"Tell im Camille used to be yo woman, Gitt," Fats

called out. "Tell im, man."

"Shut up, Fats. Ain't none of his damn business."

Even though he was married, Gitter Bug loved Camille, who chose that very moment to walk through the door, holding the arm of Joe Stubblefield.

Gitter Bug gulped and started to perspire. Apparently Camille's arrival was causing him to feel somewhat warmer than the temperature dictated. He looked daggers at Antredious, who himself was feeling quite mellow.

When Fats McAfee saw his old friend Joe Stubblefield, he almost knocked his table over. "Is that you, old pardner?" he shouted.

The two men rushed at each other like two tenpoint bucks in heat. When they clashed, it was an embrace that would have injured the average man.

"Joe, you is a sight to behold! I been askin bout you. I knowed you was comin. Things done changed down here. Niggers ain't scared of these white folks no more. We even got us a colored deputy now. Things is changin, man. What you been doin all these years cept hidin from old man Pickins?" Fats laughed heartily. He slapped Joe's back, almost driving his feet through the floor.

Joe playfully grabbed him by the collar. "Fats, how come you didn let me know you was takin one of them fuckin watermelons outta Pickins' cooler? That drunk bastard wanted to kill me over that damn watermelon. Fats, I swore if I ever seen you again, I was gonna ram my foot up yo ass for leavin me in a fucked-up fix like that. I had to lay that mother-fucker out to keep im from killin me. You sho was one stealin son-of-a-bitch when you was young. You still steal?"

"Is the sky blue?" Fats asked jokingly.

"Well, it was the last time I looked up."

"If the sky is blue, I still steal." They laughed so hard that tears ran from their eyes as they leaned against each other, shoulder-to-shoulder, holding their stomachs.

Gitter Bug had watched Camille sitting at the far end of the bar, looking bored. He hustled down to her and asked if she wanted the usual. She shifted in her seat, looking uncomfortable with her heavy belly squeezed against the bar.

"I guess I could stand a drink. But I ain't got no money on me."

The tavern owner lifted the top of a long ice-box, pulled out a quart of beer and an orange soda, and set them before her. Then he supplied a large, clean glass. "Bein broke ain't never kept you from gittin what you want," he reminded her.

Camille slowly and methodically mixed the beer and orange soda. Then she called him back. "Didn't you forgit somethin?"

"What?"

"You know I don't drink nothin without a straw, Gitt."

"Oh! I'm sorry, honey. Want a fish sandwich?"

"I ain't hungry."

"Well, you know ol Gitt's gonna take care of you, even tho you don't care a bag of beans for me."

"Oh, I like you okay, sweet thing."

"So how come you wouldn't marry me when I begged you to?"

"I reckon I just wasn ready."

Gitter Bug leaned across the bar so that only Camille

could hear him. "I done built Flora a nice home down in Gulfport. That could'a been yo house. But yo head was too high. Now you ain't got nothin cept them babies, with another one on the way. It could'a been you down yonder in Gulfport, livin in that mansion."

"I don't wanna talk, Gitter Bug." She turned her back to the bar.

"Hey back there in the kitchen!" Fats called out. "We need some service out here for my old friend, Joe Stubblefield."

Mayetta appeared in the kitchen hatch and screamed back at Fats. "What did you say, fool?"

"Brang us some more fish--a whole lotta catfish and some buffalo, too."

"I didn brang the first fish you just ate, and I ain't gonna move my feet for you now. You know you gotta come back here an order. When it gits done, you gotta brang yo butt back here an pick it up, asshole."

"That's the problem with you black, nappy-headed, evil nigger women. Yall too mean to uncross yo legs to fuck. White women serves they men with a smile."

Mayetta came out of the kitchen and shook her finger in Fat's face. "Listen here, you rusty motherfucker, if you want service wit a smile, go up to Perkins wit the white folks. See how many smiles you'd get when you drag yo alligator-face uptown."

"Get on back in that kitchen, woman. You ain't sayin shit. I kin go in Perkins' anytime I gits ready."

Mayetta walked towards Camille. "Hi, girl. Pearl here yet?"

"Yeah, she's at the house."

"I ain't seen that gal since we was in school. Tell her to come by and see me."

"When you gonna get yo ass in that kitchen, woman?" Fats shouted.

Joe touched Fats on the arm. "That's okay. Leave her alone, McAfee. I'll get some fish tomorra. Fish is food for funerals."

- *25* -

Unveiling

Enroute to Brown's Funeral Home, they drove without conversation. Jimmy Lee was deeply saddened over Elton Ealy's death. But his grief was modified by the fact that his mother had insisted that he return the sporty, new, blue and white Cougar to J.D. Trodder, and resign the position that Trodder had so proudly given him. When they arrived at the funeral parlor, Lilly Pearl gave her son thirty dollars. "This is more than cab fare home," she said. "I demand that you return this car immediately. Jackie will meet me here. I'll have her drive me home. Oh," she reminded him, "don't forget to quit the job."

When Lilly Pearl entered the building, the Brown's recognized her instantly. Before leaving Chicago, she had tinted her blond hair copper--it's natural color.

"You're Ealy's girl from up North. Aren't you?" Mrs. Brown spoke.

She looked at the timeworn, wrinkled faces of Mr. and Mrs. Brown who had been the only black morticians in Pearl City as long as she could remember. "Yes. Yes, Mam. I'm Lilly Pearl, Mrs. Brown." They started walking toward the chapel where Elton's body lay in state. The solemn aura of the mortuary suddenly filled Lilly Pearl with a sense of great loss. "The services are tomorrow," Mr. Brown said. "Your folks told us you'd be in today."

"Are there any problems with his policies?" Lilly Pearl asked. "I sent two thousand dollars to cover any costs beyond his insurance. That should've been more than adequate," she said. "I'd like an itemized statement after the funeral, of course."

"Oh, no problem," Mrs. Brown told her. "Reverend Bailey brought the money by this morning. I think we have everything in order, but it was necessary to have a family member view the body for final approval."

When they had reached the chapel where Elton's body had been placed, the front door opened. It was Lilly Pearl's twenty-six year old cousin, Jackie. She hadn't seen Lilly Pearl since she last visited Mississippi, four years earlier. They embraced affectionately. Jackie cried for Elton. He was her mother's last sibling. The young lady also cried because she feared her mother would soon follow.

The room where Elton's body lay was located on the east side of the building. It was decorated in three shades of blue which seemed to calmly accept the steel-gray, chrome-trimmed coffin that held Elton. The dark-blue shade of his suit was accentuated by the delicate pale-blue crepe interior of the casket. Set at each end of the exquisite chest were arrangements of red and white carnations, behind which stood marble pedestals, on which were placed dimly lighted, large bronze lamps.

Jackie looked at the gold-mounted three-carat diamond ring on Elton's left hand. "Cousin Pearl, I know you ain't leaving all that expensive jewelry on Uncle Elton," she whispered. "That gold watch, them gold cuff links, and that there gold tie clamp ain't gonna make it to the grave with im. Ain't you heard about the Browns--how they be taking good stuff offa the dead?"

Lilly Pearl recalled how diligently she had searched to find the almost perfect one dollar gold pieces from which the cuff links and tie clamp were made. And she had sent him the ring for his eightieth birthday.

"I'll give it some thought," she said.

"Gee, Cousin Pearl, that's a lotta money to bury."

"Let's just say he'll wear it to the grave," Lilly Pearl told her. "Then I'll decide who gets it."

As Lilly Pearl stood looking down at Elton, he looked much smaller in death than he had in life. She thought of her own factuality. In deep concentration, she considerd her past, present, and her future. She felt extremely depressed. Death had invaded the world that existed in Chicago, thwarting her aspirations forever, denying her the ambiance of exclusive, eloquent living. Gloom hang over her like a stubborn black cloud that foreshadowed an oppressive existence, itensifying her emotions of fear, insecurity, and the uncertainty of being a Negro in Mississippi. Lurking within the nucleus of the swelling obscurity were acid tears that fell from her slanted gray eyes.

J.D. Trodder's limp was more pronounced now that grief, age, tobacco, and corn whisky had conspired revenge upon him. He laboriously dragged along on a knotted cane, up and down the rows of his two-hundred and fifty acre sweet potato farm. When Jimmy Lee parked at the antediluvian farmhouse that had once been a place of beauty, Trodder waved to him. The white paint on the abode had peeled and pickets around the yard were missing here and there. The barren persimmon trees, pecan trees, and peach trees no longer yielded their yearly viands. And Ophelia Trodder seemed not to care about her languid magnolias and yellow roses. They used to be her pride and joy. They had always won first prize at the yearly fair in Jackson. She hadn't worked her flower garden since Teddy Joe died. Her two daughters, May Helen and Dolly had tried to keep them flourishing before they left their father's incestous household a decade earlier. But J.D. cared only about his precious sweet potatoes.

On the porch, lying under the squeaky, dilapidated swing, Bird Dog, Teddy Joe's old canine, was asleep. His ears were laden with fat ticks that he had grown accustomed to. After Teddy Joe's accident, Bird Dog used to growl constantly, run around in circles and snap at his tail. J.D. took him to a tree stump and chopped it off with an axe. The potato farmer had said the grieving dog had worms, and that was the only cure. It did prove effective. Bird Dog no longer chased his severed tail.

"Why're you here today, boy?" Trodder asked Jimmy Lee. Then he spat a humongous squirt of tobacco juice against the rust-corroded, useless water pump. "Didn't ya pick up your Ma in Jackson this morning?" he asked.

"Yes, Sir," the heavy-hearted young man answered. "She's up yonder at Brown's."

"So you stopped by to chat?" the farmer asked him.

"Well, Sir, it ain't just your regular kinda chatting that I came for," Jimmy Lee told him.

"Then what's on your mind, son?" Most times he called him that.

Trodder sat on the edge of the porch and motioned to his employee to do the same.

"You see, Mr. J.D., it's my momma. She's powerfully mad cause you gave me the Cougar. I gotta give it back and quit my job."

"Now why do you think she'd make you do a fool thing like that?" he asked the embarrassed young man.

"She ain't gave no reason. It's just something she wants done right away. When I asked her why, the veins rose in her temples and pure fire showed in her eyes. Seems like she don't like the idea it came from you."

"Did your Ma ever tell you who your pa is?" Trodder wanted to know.

"My father is dead," Jimmy Lee told him. "His name was Jimmy Lee Blood--a soldier who was killed in boot camp. It happened before I was born."

"I'm afraid your ma didn't exactly tell you the truth, son," Trodder said. "That Blood boy was after Pearl, but he'd gone bout two months before you was ever thought of. Maybe she wished he'd been your daddy, but he never touched her. And that's a fact."

"How you know all this, Mr. J.D.?" the inquisitive son asked.

The overall wearing, tobacco chewer tapped the dirt off his old high top shoes with his self-made cane. "I know it all cause you's mine," the old man said with assurance. "Nobody touched her before me. It was my seed what gave you life." Jimmy Lee stared at him incredously, wanting to take the cane from him and club him until he admitted he'd lied.

As the crippled farmer told Jimmy Lee the entire story surrounding his conception, Ophelia Trodder's coughing ceased. She sat on the swing knitting. But as usual, nobody paid attention to whether she knitted in silence or coughed with every other loop. Like Bird Dog, Ophelia seldom raised her head or looked interested in whatever was said or done within her immediate environment. And, as far as she and J.D. were concerned, there was no world outside of the two hundred and fifty acres of dust and sweet potatoes. J.D. had deflated his wife's womanhood long before he'd chopped off Bird Dog's tail. She was as acquiescent as the abused, helpless, half-starved dog. J.D.'s papa used to warn him about kicking dogs and cats, getting them afraid of him. "Sometimes a cornered animal turns on ya," he'd say. Trodder spoke around his wife as if she were just another loose screw in the unpredictable, deteriorated swing.

"But, Mr. J.D., my momma would'a told me if you was my daddy."

"Boy, I know you're mine sure as I know them's my taters out yonder. That's why I'm training you to take over. All them taters," with a wave of his cane, "gonna be yours some day," his daddy told him. "Teddy Joe went and killed his fool self, and I ain't leaving them gals a dime--the no good sluts. Ophelia's gonna cough her damned lungs out right soon," he predicted. "You see, you're all I've got to carry on this here farm. Plus you're the spitting image of me--look like a real white man. Maybe in a few years, if them freedom folks keep'a pushing, you'll be a respected farmer like me," he said. "Why, the white folks round here might even forget you ain't all white. Can't never tell what the future might bring. Course, I'll be dead and won't give a damn." He leaned forward and emptied his mouth again. "Somebody's gotta stop this crazy shit one of these days, but after I'm dead, for sure." Jimmy Lee's father laughed. "What the fuck do I care what goes on after I'm worm food and fertilizer?" Trodder wiped the brown spit from the corners of his mouth on the back of his hand and playfully slapped his son on the back. "I done had life's cherry pie. It was sweet--mighty sweet," he said.

Jimmy Lee became extremely distraught over learning that J.D. Trodder was his father. He finally understood his mother's rage. The thought of this man, his father, taking his mother by force when she was an innocent girl made him hate Trodder. He also hated himself for being the result of such a brutal and disgraceful act.

Trodder spoke openly so that his son might know his

innermost thoughts and understand his past deeds.

"You see, I feel kinda cheated cause I didn't have a hand in shaping your character," the white man said. "Why, I'll bet you ain't had no pussy yet. Is ya, son?"

Jimmy Lee trembled uncontrollably as he sat frozen to the edge of the porch beside his father, staring at the ground with tears dripping off his chin. He felt as if someone had driven an iron fist into his stomach and dropped an anvil on his head. Appalled, Jimmy Lee tried to speak, to tell his father what he thought of him, but he found himself gasping for air. Then the pain within his stomach rose, causing him to heave bitter gall.

"You ain't a strong man yet, boy, but you stick with your ol man. I'll learn ya."

Trodder spoke to Ophelia for the first time that day. "Go fetch my jug. And bring a cold, wet towel."

Moving like a robot, she obeyed.

"Now, get a hold of yourself, boy. Take a swig. Put this here towel to ya face. You must've inherited your ma's weakness, but I'll make you strong before I die."

Jimmy Lee took the towel and buried his face in it but refused the jug.

"I see you ain't got a stomach for good moonshine like Teddy Joe," he said, after gulping greedily from the jug. "You gotta learn a boy early how to be a man," the seasoned guzzler told him.

"You take Teddy Joe for instance. That rascal could out drink me at twelve. And he was bustin them little black cherries left-an-right by thirteen."

J.D. took another long swallow from the brown jug. "But it was kinda unfortunate what happen to that there

Honeysucker gal. Why, I ain't never seen a gal put up such a bull-headed fight in all my born days. I declare, she was a strong one."

Sweet potato man tilted the booze again. "Me and Teddy Joe was just havin a little fun when she kicked my boy in the balls. You see, he got sorta pissed-off and shoved her kinda hard. Hell, he never meant to hurt her none. She sorta lost her balance and cracked her head against a big old pine."

Trodder took an enormous bite of tobacco. "You know, I never figured out why that gal acted so dang wild. She woulda been alive today--sorta went stone loco out yonder in them woods. Weren't nothin to be scared of. It's pretty in them woods off Pristine Pike."

Jimmy Lee's intellect failed him. His father's words echoed through his head and held him captured in a state of horror. Suddenly, his trembling hands accepted the brown jug that his dad held near his face. He lifted it and swallowed until he choked. The fire hit his stomach, sending a shocking sensation throughout his body. He lifted it a second time thinking he'd gain the courage necessary to kill J.D. But he remained glued to the spot where he sat.

"You'll be alright, son," the farmer told him. "You'll do better than Teddy Joe," he said. "You see, he never really got over that Jessie Mae Honeysucker. He claimed she haunted him at times. Hell, everybody knows when ya dead, you can't bother nobody." Bird Dog raised his head and growled for the first time in years. The crippled old man reached over and banged the dog across the nose with his cane. "Now what the hell got into that damned mutt?" the master said. Bird Dog let out a painful yelp, brushed past Ophelia's leg, and ran under the house. She never stopped knitting, nor did she show any visible emotions.

"Sometimes I think Teddy Joe got too attached to black pussy, seeing as how he was trained on it." Trodder pushed the *corn* towards Jimmy Lee again, but his son couldn't move.

"That Teddy Joe went and got stuck-on a young niggeress over yonder in West Memphis. She birthed im three youngsters. That fool boy though he was in love." He turned to Jimmy Lee. "Can you believe a white man in love with a colored gal?" he asked. Petrified, Jimmy Lee couldn't answer.

"Why, he even bought that old Honeysucker place, plannin on movin her and them pickaninnies closer to home." Jimmy Lee's father slid off the edge of the porch to massage his numb, crippled leg. "Teddy Joe came mighty close to treatin that black gal like a white woman." The potato farmer paced back and forth in front of Jimmy Lee. "Nope. I never looked favorably on that," he said. "Musta been too much of Ol Riley's rotgut what messed up his mind. Don't never drink nothing from Riley, son. He brews that shit with cow piss."

While her husband paced and philosophied, Ophelia's cough returned, more severely than usual. But he paid no mind. He'd heard her coughing fits for years.

She slowly gathered her yarn and raised her frail four foot-eleven frame from the swing. Seeing her dark brown eyes through the thick glasses she wore magnified them to look like wide, glossy, doe eyes. They dominated her thin, pale face. Ophelia's long white hair reached below her waist, in one long braid down her back. J.D. never noticed she had disappeared.

"You know, I can see a white man trainin on black gals," he continued, "but it ain't wise treatin em like a real woman and havin babies by em. God ain't never meant no such thing like mating between the races--not on purpose."

"But what about me?" Jimmy Lee finally spoke. "When you took my momma, you weren't trying to make a baby. That means I wasn't on purpose."

"I'm trying to do right by ya, son. You look like me. I ain't ashamed of what I done, nor the outcome of it. Sometimes a man pays for his fun. You gonna get everything I got, but remember that old Honeysucker place goes to Teddy Joe's chullin. You see, it was they mammy what died with Teddy Joe."

"How many folks died because of you and Teddy Joe?" Jimmy Lee asked, feeling the effects of the liquor he'd drunk.

"We ain't never hurt nobody, boy. All the bad things were accidents. We never aimed at nothin but a little manly pleasure."

The generous father reached into his overall pocket, took out a dirty, worn handkerchief, in which was tied a roll of bills. He pushed six, one-hundred-dollar bills into his offspring's shirt pocket. "Now, go tell Pearl God's done parted my sins against her. I ain't takin back the Cougar. It's a father's rights to give his son a new car, if he's a mind to."

Hating himself for lacking the gallantry to avenge his

mother's rape, Jimmy Lee thought seriously of killing himself. As he drove away, the horror of J.D. Trodder's confession sent him on an insane escape, heading toward the highway, fleeting past huge trailers used for transporting sweet potatoes to market. He drove instinctively, half blinded by salty tears, driving until he came to a roadside tavern where he entered, laid a one-hundred-dollar bill on the bar, and ordered a bottle of whisky.

- *26* -

Confessions

He'd been missing for too many hours. His mother and grandmother had waited up for him. After most of the night had passed, Lilly Pearl told Neallie to rest for the funeral.

"That ain't like Jimmy Lee," Neallie said. "Lord, something bad's done happen. He don't never stay out past ten without callin. Wher'd he say he was goin when he left you at Brown's?" she asked. Before Lilly Pearl could answer, a hard knock came at the front door. "That's got to be him," Neallie said. "Get the door, honey."

Feeling slightly relieved, Lilly Pearl ran and opened it quickly. It was Sheriff Enus Handova and his black deputy, Froggy Fortune. They stepped into the house with drawn guns. "We're here to arrest Jimmy Lee Ealy for arson, the murder of J.D. Trodder, and the attempted murder of his wife, Ophelia," Handova told her.

"Murder! J.D. murdered?" *God, what have I done?* Lilly Pearl asked herself. "What makes you think my son murdered J.D. Trodder? Do you have evidence to prove your accusations?"

"His poor, half-dead wife's in Jefferson Davis Hospital, in a state of delirium, calling your boy's name over an over. That's evidence enough for me," the sheriff said. "Now, where's the boy?"

"But my son wouldn't hurt anyone," Lilly Pearl told the sheriff.

"Well, you go tell that lie to J.D.'s ashes and his dying wife," he retorted.

"Where's the boy?" he asked again as he looked over her shoulder suspiciously.

"He's not here," she said, trying to conceal her anxiety.

Openly, Lilly Pearl denied her son's guilt. Yet, within her soul, she felt that poetic justice had been served. Palpitating violently, she imagined her heart ripping through her chest and dropping at her feet. Then Enus and Froggy would see J.D.'s name stamped on it, underlined with hate, or her head might become transparent revealing her harbored secrets and quaking fears.

The two men pushed past Lilly Pearl and conducted a thorough search of the house, looking under beds, in closets, behind doors, and in the crawl space above the ceiling. Then they ransacked the entire house as if they had expected to find the six-foot-three young man in unpredictable places such as drawers, hat boxes and suitcases.

The entire family, excluding Antredious B. Bailey, had been aroused from bed. They gathered in Neallie's room, overwhelmed by the white sheriff and his black deputy rambling through the house with pistols in hand.

Neallie's grandchildren rubbed their eyes and yawned lethargically--dizzy, still half asleep.

The Ealys, Serpentines, Gatsons, and Poes mumbled among themselves wondering why their home was being invaded. Antredious, in full Army uniform, lay in a stupefied sleep on a pallet in the family room. Theodis Serpentine tried, unsuccessfully, to question Froggy concerning what black man J.D. had most recently fought with. Theodis' wife, Eula, and her sister, Azell, wept quietly and gathered their children under their wings like mother hens.

Chewing a half-plug of tobacco with a lip full of Garrett snuff, Satie Mae stood by her mother, wearing an un-wavering autistic smile that made Enus Handova suspi-cious. Camille sat in Elton's large rocker, totally disin-terested, holding her swollen stomach, feeling her unborn baby stretch and kick. Willie Ray stood directly behind Neallie's chair trying to comfort his aunt.

Upon seeing the sheriff and his deputy, Joe Stubblefield thought that Jim Bob Pickins had sent them to arrest him. He'd heard that Jim Bob had thrived twenty-eight years on the assumption that someday Enus would bring Joe to his front porch. Then he'd fill Joe's stomach with buckshot from his double-barrelled, sawed-off shotgun that he kept in a large leather holster, attached to the side of his wheelchair. Joe stood unobserved in a corner wearing his wife's reading glasses, with his head bowed, as if in prayer.

"He ain't here," Enus Handova finally concluded. Neallie reached past Lilly Pearl with her cane and touched Enus in the side. He whirled impulsively with his gun pointing in her direction. "What's on your mind, Antie?" he asked.

"Mister," she said, trembling and teary, "yall please don't hurt my grandson. He's innocent. Everybody knows he ain't got a violent bone in his body."

Enus and Froggy holstered their guns and walked towards the front door. "If you hear from that boy, tell im he'll make it easy on his self if I don't have to find him," the sheriff told them.

As the dawn of Elton Ealy's funeral approached, Lilly Pearl sat in her mother's bedroom, gazing out the window, while her head ached with conjectures relative to the safety of her son and his whereabouts. Neallie Ealy prayed and rocked worriedly. "Why would he go by J.D.'s farm? He didn't have to work." She pleaded with her daughter to help her understand why Jimmy Lee might have killed his employer. She spoke of the farmer's reputation, how he enjoyed confrontations between himself and young black men. But she had noticed his special interest in Lilly Pearl's son. "If he committed this ungodly act, what did Trodder do to provoke him?" Neallie wanted to know.

Lilly Pearl tried to remain silent, but the inflammatory past, regarding her relationship with the sweet potato farmer, elicited from her an uncontrollable, almost shouting response. "To avenge my rape, Momma!" Because of the deeply rooted hurt that grew and festered within her for so many years, she was unable to restrain her anger. "Jimmy Lee killed his daddy and I'm glad he's dead!"

"What's this madness, child? What ya saying?" Neallie leaned forward in her chair. "You told us that Blood boy got you in the family way. Why'd ya lie?" She knelt in front of her mother, crying. "Momma, I was afraid Papa would've killed J.D. They would've lynched Papa. And you would probably have died of grief. Too many tragic things would've happened. Don't you see?"

Neallie cupped her daughter's wet face. "Yes. I see. But when did ya tell the boy?"

"I never told him, Momma. When I learned who gave him the new car, I knew J.D. had figured it out. So, I made him take it back. That old crippled bastard told him."

During Lilly Pearl's moments of confession, Neallie's eyes were also filled with tears. She stroked her daughter's hair gently. "Now the time's come for you to know the truth bout your real father." Lilly Pearl looked into her mother's eyes and a frightening chill shook her body. "Momma, what do you mean--my *real* father?" she asked. Her mother told her how they had worked as sharecroppers on Zack Gilmore's plantation, saving to someday buy their own land. Gilmore insisted that Neallie work weekends in the company store where she was coerced into fulfilling his sexual desires. "He made it quite clear that he'd fire me if I refused him, and I was afraid to quit. Whatever the reason for leaving, telling Elton the truth woulda sent him after Gilmore. That crazy Gilmore woulda killed Elton, leaving me at the mercy of his own desires.

"When you was born, Elton knowed you had too much white blood runnin through your veins. We's a high yellow family, but we ain't white. Elton kept waitin for your color to change. So, I had to tell im what went on with me and Gilmore. Elton ain't said a word. He just got Ol Simon and his shotgun--went to kill Gilmore. They said when he stepped inside the company store, Zack Gilmore was behind the counter. Elton still ain't said a word, raised his gun and shot-im--straight forwards. He thought he'd got im in the heart, but the bullet struck his shoulder. Elton turned to walk out. Zack reached under the counter, got his gun and shot Elton in the back. Ol Simon moaned like he'd been hit. Seein all that blood comin outta Elton's back, he laid his big, saggy face on the wound. Doc Word said that old hound slowed the bleedin--saved my Elton's life. But the bullet was too close to his spine. Doc Word had to leave it there.

"Elton stayed up yonder in state prison three years, all crippled-up like that. Folks said he was lucky. You don't shoot a white man and live."

Still on her knees crying, with her head resting on Neallie's lap, Lilly Pearl wanted to know, "Why didn't you tell me this before now, Momma? It isn't fair, you and Papa keeping this all these years."

Neallie embraced her daughter while they both cried. Then she spoke softly. "Knowin the truth woulda hurt ya, like it's hurtin ya now. The sin wasn yours. No need to put the pain in your heart, child. I reckon you understands that now."

Lilly Pearl understood her mother's dilemma and prayed that her last secret would never be known.

- *27* -

My Boyhood Days

"I didn't know the deceased very well, but it doesn't matter now," the Reverend Le Felton McLaurin said in a loud pompous voice. "Whatever is between this man and his God has already been decided. So, let us pray for ourselves and this large caring family today, whose fate is yet unknown. If we keep our eyes on the Master, our lives will have meaning and order," he said. "Let's keep our priorities straight, sisters and brothers. Choose love over hate; right over wrong; peace over war. Amen."

With heads bowed, a host of relatives and friends stood

solemnly on the porch and lawn of Elton Ealy's home, in observance of his pre-funeral ceremony. Parked on the dusty road out front was a parade of cars headed by a long black hearse that bore Elton's body. Neallie, shaken by grief and age, prayed:

> My Lord, my loving God,
> I know Thou art near.
> I call when I feel lonely,
> Lord, I know You hear.
>
> I trust You so,
> Cause You're by my side.
> You love me, Lord--
> My Father, my Guide.
>
> Lord, while I live,
> You'll be my Shining Star.
> I'll follow you,
> Matters not how near or far.
>
> Oh, my Guide, through darkness unto light.
> You hold my hand in daylight and the night.
> I trust You so, my God. I trust You so.
> Please take my soul when it's time for
> Me to go. Amen.

Earlier that morning, Lilly Pearl had edited a poem that Elton wrote when he was in prison. John Henry Bailey stood at the top of the old wooden steps holding the paper that had yellowed and cracked with age. It quivered in the breeze that blew gently across the yard. He cleared his throat and read:

We had no house to call our own.
Many times we moved from place to place,
To find somewhere to lay our heads.
But me, I never worried, nor did I fret.
For that was back in my boyhood days.

Often as a lad, I stood on the back porch
And watched the clouds forming,
                    in such glorious ways.
It was there I caught the first glimpse
                    of an eternal power,
In my boyhood days.

I noticed how the seasons changed,
And knew not why the summer sun
                    never held its rays.
I learned so much about nature.
But knowledge never stole the thrill
                    of my boyhood days.

Our old weatherbeaten shacks were inadequate.
The oil lamps were dim.
Our parents struggled hard in many ways.
But it was just my destiny,
                    that God was shaping me,
In my boyhood days.

At night we strolled up and down the old dirt road
Watching the moon, the Milky Way, and a million stars
                    twinkling in their majestic ways.
With all the disadvantages we had,

It gave me a deep sense of gratitude,

        to behold such glorious creations,

In my boyhood days.

The daytime was long and dreadful.

I never had the freedom of a child who runs and plays.

Now I'm a man and it seems like a dream,

        when I recall my boyhood days.

I remember my school days--

How we gathered around the fireplace,

        trying to learn life and its ways.

It was a long and tedious struggle,

        I shall never forget,

That began in my boyhood days.

Many times to eat breakfast, Momma would say,

        "Wait til the hen lays."

But, to tell you this doesn't make me ashamed

        of my boyhood days.

Often we went hunting to make the pot boil strong.

It is a little regretful to know those days are gone.

For, Bill, Jim, Walter and I had fun in many ways.

You see, my brothers and I enjoyed our boyhood days.

Many times we had less,

But God gave us peace, joy, and happiness,

In my boyhood days.

    Lilly Pearl dried the tears that streaked her mother's

cheeks. Then suddenly, in a cloud of dust, a tall stocky man wearing a white suit and a straw hat parked on the opposite side of the road, adjacent to the hearse. He pulled out a large white handkerchief, blew his nose and placed it back in his pocket. Lilly Pearl gazed at him in silence, and everyone in the yard did the same. With much effort, he squeezed from behind the wheel of the long convertible Cadillac he drove. For a moment, Lilly Pearl prayed that this man had come with news of her son. But as he approached the gate, he paid little attention to Sheriff Enus and Froggy who stood watch, in hopes of catching Jimmy Lee.

The man made his way through the crowd and stopped when he reached Lilly Pearl. "Might you be the Ealy gal who's come home to run this place?"

She looked at him with contempt as they stood face-to-face. "I'm Lilly Pearl Lewis," she said. "Who are you? What is your business here?"

"Well, Lilly Pearl," he spoke in a cocky manner, "I'm Mr. Gilmore--Mr. Zack Gilmore, Junior."

Standing closely at her side, Lilly Pearl felt her mother's body grow tense. Then she knew he was the eldest of her father's two sons.

Being cognizant of the pain Zack Gilmore, Sr. had caused her mother and Elton Ealy, his arrogance weighed heavily on her shoulders.

"Are you the gal who's stepping into old Elton's shoes?" he asked.

She felt anger and rage rise inside her bosom. "What is your purpose for being here, Zack?"

Shocked by her tone of despisal, Zack Gilmore, Jr. bit

angrily into the ragged cigar in his mouth and spat at her feet. "I think you've been up North too long, gal," he said. "They call me Mr. Gilmore."

"And they call me Mrs. Lewis, Zack," she told him.

His stare was piercing and intimidating. He looked immediately into her eyes. "I'm here representing the Perry Drilling Company. I'd like to discuss an oil lease," he said.

With Elton dead, Gilmore had more faith in his persuasive abilities. The North/East section of Ealy's land had been sighted as the most likely area to produce oil.

"We have no business to discuss today or ever," Lilly Pearl told him. "Maybe you haven't noticed, we're going to a funeral."

"Well, you see, old Elton was a stubborn ol cuss. I reckon he ain't in no big hurry to go where he's going. They tell me it's pretty hot in hell." Laughing at his own joke, Zack Junior held his cigar while his round protruding stomach shook like jelly.

Impulsively, with all of the force she could muster, Lilly Pearl slapped Zack Gilmore Junior--her white brother. A muffled roar emitted from the crowd. Fright possessed them. With an incredulous expression on his face, Zack Gilmore Junior turned and looked at the people who filled the yard. He looked at Sheriff Enus Handova and Deputy Froggy Fortune, but they were preoccupied with the cars and trucks that occasionally passed the house. Red-faced, Zack Junior walked to his car and drove speedily away.

The funeral procession left the house, moving slowly along the dusty road. Joe watched quietly at the window, afraid Enus or Froggy might recognize him. Antredious sat on the front porch crying for his Uncle Elton and craving more moonshine. Finally, the sheriff and his deputy followed the family to the church, expecting Jimmy Lee to show up for his grandfather's funeral.

- *28* -

The Hand of Fate

The sharp pain brought her back to consciousness. From the sounds she heard, Ophelia knew she was in a hospital. She lay still trying to remember what she was doing there. Suddenly it came to her. She remembered the fire and what she had done. All of the terror returned, shuddering through her body, engulfing her in a nameless, sickening panic.

In the past, Ophelia had been terribly afraid of her husband and was completely acquiescent to his every command. But something in her suddenly changed as she listened to his confessions to Jimmy Lee. She couldn't allow him to change his will. The imminent prospect of murder made her realize, for the first time, how much she really despised J.D. There was a fear in her that was like a growing cancer. He had mocked the sanctity of marriage and made her life a living hell.

Ophelia remembered how she had carefully emptied each capsule until her entire prescription of tranquilizers was dissolved in J.D.'s corn whisky. As usual, he'd empty the jug before retiring for the evening. About 2:00 A.M., he sat in his huge recliner unconscious. The petite little lady placed three large knitted spreads around his chair and soaked them with kerosene. Then she doused the entire house with the remaining liquid. Perspiration beaded on her forehead. She quivered with cold, clammy fear as she took the money from his pocket and threw the lighted match at his feet. As the gruesome fire leaped hungrily about him, he moaned and gasped for breath. But only the flames, bright orange and blue, entered his mouth and nostrils.

Possessed by curiosity, Bird Dog watched quietly with one ear raised. The glow of the fire made an eerie wavering pattern on the gray wall behind J.D. Ophelia and Bird Dog stood watching as the man of the house became unconscious, enclosed in a halo of light. They could hear J.D.'s flesh frying and the scent of it made Ophelia heave.

Seconds later, as the ravenous conflagration spread, the room became engulfed with stifling heat and smoke. Ophelia stood frozen, not aware that a tiny blaze had caught her dress. Bird Dog whined and tugged tenaciously at her skirt. He pulled her toward the front door as she glanced back over her shoulder at the merciless flames that consumed J.D. Trodder.

Standing in the yard with Bird Dog, Ophelia listened to the crackling fire as it spread throughout the building. Then suddenly she remembered her wedding picture and re-entered the burning house. A feeling of suffocation closed in on her, choking her, filling her with mindless panic. She crawled on the floor through burning debris and found the sizzling picture. With it clutched to her chest, she fainted--no longer aware of pain.

Yes. The nightmare had been real. She'd murdered her husband, J.D. Trodder. The pounding of her heart shook her body. Ophelia wondered if Pearl City knew she was a murderess.

From beside her hospital bed, Ophelia, the pitiful widow, heard a familiar voice. "You awake, Miss Ophelia?" he asked.

Her world was black because of the bandages that covered her eyes. A strange croak caught in her throat when she tried to speak.

"It's me, Miss Ophelia. Jay. I brong you to the hospital. Been here with ya all morning."

She managed to whisper his name.

"You're a lucky one," Jay said. "Betty Sue happen to be up nursing the baby. She spotted the fire. By the time I reached your place, I seen Bird Dog with his teeth clinched in your skirt, dragging you from the house. I'm mighty sorry, Miss Ophelia. I couldn't get your husband out. I feel awfully bad, he didn't make it." But he assured her: "We know who did it, Mam. Ol Enus and Froggy'll find that Ealy boy. He'll pay for the pain he's put you through. The sheriff's gonna find im for sure," he said.

"No," she spoke in a ragged whisper. "It was the hand of fate. Jimmy Lee ain't done no wrong. It was the mighty hand of fate what got J.D.," she said. "Tell Enus the boy is innocent."

- *29* -

Compassion

Ironically, at the same time that his father was being transformed into a pile of ashes, Jimmy Lee lay unconscious with a bloody gash in his head, sprawled in a wooden area near the tavern where he'd stopped to drown his frustrations. He had fallen prey to three men who'd sat at the bar and conspired to relieve him of the money Trodder had stuck in his shirt pocket. As the dawn brought light to the woods, two men on a rabbit hunt discovered Jimmy Lee. Unconscious, he was taken to a nearby hospital, but the robbers had left nothing by which to identify him.

When the family had arrived home from Elton's funeral, Joe informed Lilly Pearl that Jimmy Lee had been hospitalized in Bogalusa, Louisiana.

She ran to the phone and called the hospital, but failed to obtain information concerning Jimmy Lee. Lilly Pearl's imagination went wild--conjuring up an infinite number of tragedies that had befallen her son. The blood seemed to drain from her body, and her strength was consumed by the realization that he might be dying. *Dear, God, please don't take my son,* she prayed. *I need him more than ever before.* Lilly Pearl grabbed Theodis' car keys and sped away without a word. And, as she drove toward Louisiana, fear clutched her in a tighter and tighter vise.

Did he kill J.D., she wondered?

In less than three hours, Lilly Pearl had reached the hospital in Bogalusa. At first, she felt numb inside. Her eyes were red from tears and worry. Lilly Pearl kissed her son and cried until the knot inside her began to dissolve, and a feeling of thankfulness filled her. Jimmy Lee looked at his mother and smiled. Then slowly she sank into the chair beside his bed, and the tension drained out of her. "I must explain why I lied about your father, Jimmy Lee. Please forgive me. I did what I thought was best."

"No. Please, Ma. No need to bring the pain to mind," he said. "I understand some things might be better buried in the past. That's what Papa used to say. No need to cry over things you can't change. The sinful deed wasn't yours," he said. "Old man Trodder told me everything."

Jimmy Lee squeezed his mother's hand. "I wish I had

the power to erase the past, Ma--just for you. I'd wipe away every bad thing you've suffered."

"Did you and J.D. fight?" she asked.

"I wanted to hurt him for what he did to you, but something held me back. Maybe it was fear. Or maybe I just couldn spill my own father's blood," he said. "So, I ran off and got drunk. I guess I ain't a strong man, Ma. At least, that's what old J.D. said."

"Never mind what J.D. said, dear." She touched his cheek affectionately. "A man's true strength isn't measured by a violent nature," she said. "There's more strength in compassion."

After he explained what had happened, she knew he couldn't have been near Trodder's farm when the fire occurred. And when she called home, Neallie told her that Jimmy Lee was no longer a suspect. Feeling peaceful and tired, Lilly Pearl slept in the chair beside her son's bed.

- *30* -

Common Grounds

The following morning, the world looked so very beautiful to Lilly Pearl. The sun made the dew glitter like diamonds on the grass and leaves that rolled along the roadside, as she and Jimmy Lee headed for home. She felt that the time was right. So, she told her son that Trodder had died. "I don't want you to live with malice in your heart because of J.D.," she said. "He's gone now. Hate consumes the soul and clouds the mind until a part of you dies. I won't have that happen to you, Jimmy Lee. God knows, I've hated him enough for the two of us."

When Lilly Pearl and Jimmy Lee approached the Early home from the hospital, they saw a well dressed man standing in the yard talking with Willie Ray. *He looks familiar,* Lilly Pearl thought. She drove closer and parked near the gate. He turned around. Suddenly, there was a frightful feeling in the pit of her stomach. It grew and moved upward and choked in her throat. At that moment, she knew with a mind-smashing certainty who he was. He looked at her with a strange, puzzled expression on his face. He started to speak, but the sound that escaped was frightening. Lilly Pearl got out of the car. She stood rooted in cold silence, feeling as though she had been struck by the invisible forces of retribution. For an instant, she was tempted to run.

"Lilly!" He managed to call her name.

She opened her mouth to see what would come out. "Grant!" She swallowed. "How did you find me?" She wanted to run to him and kiss him long and hard. She wished that he would take her in his arms like so many times before. But she knew she'd never know his embrace again. She'd never feel him inside her, whispering sweet words in her ear.

"I didn't come because of you," he said. "I flew down to help my brother negotiate oil leases. He needs me now. You see. Our father is dying of cancer."

Lilly Pearl instructed Willie Ray to help Jimmy Lee into the house. He and Jimmy Lee walked up the steps muttering between themselves. Then she stood there in agony, looking at Grant. She fought the nausea that rose in her stomach. The last three years flooded through her memory, and the pain increased. Lilly Pearl's mind raced furiously. She racked her brain trying to think of a way to explain. Nothing she could think of made sense. So she decided to tell the truth. Lilly Pearl opened her mouth to speak then she stopped. She knew that what she was going to say was very important. They stared at each other for a moment. Then she spoke. "I would like to believe that you are the same intelligent man who loved me when I was white." She told him about her past and who her father really was. In the back of her mind was a sharp foreboding. She'd never know another man like Grant. Lilly Pearl well remembered how she had sublimated her sexual feelings before they had met. Her sexual desires had been deeply buried, and it had taken time before Grant could arouse and bring them to the surface again.

Grant's body tensed with fury. His eyes grew narrow. His lips were tight with anger. And when he spoke, his voice was filled with rage. "I gave myself wholeheartedly, and you deceived me! I am the son of the man you claim to be your father!" He did recall the rumors that had floated through his father's house when he was a child-- rumors that, in his mind, had killed his mother. The Grant that Lilly Pearl had known in Chicago had vanished forever, and in his place was a man filled with anger and confusion. He was Zack Gilmore, Sr.'s second son--the son who despised his father enough to leave home and assume his dead mother's maiden name.

Lilly Pearl and Grant Gilmore, a.k.a. Grant Gilley, stood there on the bare earth, momentarily transfixed. He believed that she was his sister, and they could never be lovers again.

Old man Gilmore, Lilly Pearl's natural father, lay on his deathbed under the illusion that he was at peace with God. Zack Gilmore, Senior had grown frail with age. He had become a pale carbon of what had once been a handsome, vital man. Gilmore's head was now bald, and his hands had become deformed with arthritis.

During a moment of vindictive anger towards his *wayward* son, Grant, he had changed his will. And, to atone for his sins against Neallie and Elton Early, he had remembered Lilly Pearl. His loyal son, Zack Junior, would inherit seventy-five percent of his wordly possessions, leaving Lilly Pearl and Grant a common share of the remaining twenty-five percent.

As he neared death's blessed slumber, the explosive secret of his will ticked louder and louder in his feverish head.

Zack Junior sat at the right of his father's deathbed in deep grief, while his old maid aunt, Augusta Elizabeth Gilmore, cried in silence.

Doctor Elmore Lee Cox, Zack Senior's friend and confidant, leaned over his old friend, listening with his stethoscope. A worried look crossed his brow. He raised himself to an erect position and shook his head from side to side. Then he walked to the window and looked at his gold pocket watch.

The Gilmore house was as quiet as death when Grant arrived home. Doctor Cox's dusty old 1942 vintage Packard was parked out front. Grant rushed through the front door of the well maintained, antebellum mansion and proceeded up the stairs to his father's bedroom. He flung the door open without any consciousness of what was actually taking place inside. Everyone, excluding his father, was startled by his abrupt entry. Grant beckoned to his brother. He had to tell Zack Junior about their sister. But, before Zack Junior could leave his father's bed, old man Gilmore yawned. With his dimming gray eyes fixed on Grant, he smiled. Finality possessed him.

Doctor Elmore Lee Cox's eyes were filled with tears. After Zack Junior and Augusta Elizabeth had left the room, like the concerned parent, he gently stroked the hair of his weeping, remorseful son, Grant. Looking down at his old friend's lifeless body, he said to Grant, "Now the time has come for you to know the truth about your *real* father. . . ."

THE END

Johnnie Mae Nolen-Foote was born in Pine Bluff, Arkansas. The University of Wisconsin-Milwaukee conferred upon her the degree of Master of Science-Educational Psychology.

Jim Edward Foote, Sr. was born in Braxton, Mississippi. The University of Wilsconsin-Milwaukee conferred upon him the degree of Master of Science-Social Work.

They live in southern California near Palm Springs.

Buy at your local bookstore or use this Order Blank

WHEN I WAS WHITE—$10.95 per copy

INDIVIDUAL ORDERS
BookMasters, Inc.,
638 Jefferson Street, P.O. Box 159
Ashland, Ohio 44805
1-800-247-6553 or 1-419-281-1802

BUSINESS ORDERS (Bookstores, Libraries, etc.)
56 Palms Publishing Co.
P.O. Box 31
Palm Springs, CA 92263
1-619-321-0083

Please send me _____copy/copies of *WHEN I WAS WHITE,* by J&J Foote. I am enclosing $_____ plus taxes where applicable.* Send money order, check, or order by major credit card--no cash or C.O.D.'s. Add $3.00 per copy to cover handling and postage (allow 4-6 weeks for delivery). For quick delivery add $5.50 for handling and postage.

ALL FOREIGN COUNTRY SALES AT COST.

NAME_____

Address_____CITY_____

STATE_____ZIP_____Country_____

*States that require taxes to be collected by Distributor: OHIO   PUBLISHER: CALIFORNIA

Buy at your local bookstore or use this Order Blank

WHEN I WAS WHITE—$10.95 per copy

INDIVIDUAL ORDERS
BookMasters, Inc.,
638 Jefferson Street, P.O. Box 159
Ashland, Ohio 44805
1-800-247-6553 or 1-419-281-1802

BUSINESS ORDERS (Bookstores, Libraries, etc.)
56 Palms Publishing Co.
P.O. Box 31
Palm Springs, CA 92263
1-619-321-0083

Please send me _____copy/copies of *WHEN I WAS WHITE,* by J&J Foote. I am enclosing $_____ plus taxes where applicable.* Send money order, check, or order by major credit card--no cash or C.O.D.'s. Add $3.00 per copy to cover handling and postage (allow 4-6 weeks for delivery). For quick delivery add $5.50 for handling and postage.

ALL FOREIGN COUNTRY SALES AT COST.

NAME_____

Address_____CITY_____

STATE_____ZIP_____Country_____

*States that require taxes to be collected by Distributor: OHIO   PUBLISHER: CALIFORNIA

Buy at your local bookstore or use this Order Blank

WHEN I WAS WHITE--$10.95 per copy

BookMasters, Inc.,
638 Jefferson Street, P.O. Box 159
Ashland, Ohio 44805

Please send me _____copy/copies of *WHEN I WAS WHITE,* by J&J Foote. I am enclosing $_____ plus taxes where applicable.* Send money order, check, or order by major credit card--no cash or C.O.D.'s. Add $3.00 per copy to cover handling and postage (allow 4-6 weeks for delivery). **For quick delivery add $5.50 for handling and postage.**

ALL FOREIGN COUNTRY SALES AT COST.

NAME_____

Address_____CITY_____

STATE_____ZIP_____ Country_____

*States that require taxes to be collected by Distributor: Ohio, (States where applicable).

Buy at your local bookstore or use this Order Blank

WHEN I WAS WHITE--$10.95 per copy

BookMasters, Inc.
638 Jefferson Street, P.O. Box 159
Ashland, Ohio 44805

Please send me _____copy/copies of *WHEN I WAS WHITE,* by J&J Foote. I am enclosing $_____ plus taxes where applicable.* Send money order, check, or order by major credit card--no cash or C.O.D.'s. Add $3.00 per copy to cover handling and postage (allow 4-6 weeks for delivery). **For quick delivery add $5.50 for handling and postage.**

ALL FOREIGN COUNTRY SALES AT COST.

NAME_____

Address_____CITY_____

STATE_____ZIP_____ Country_____

*States that require taxes to be collected by Distributor: Ohio,(States where applicable).

2944